Impeccable

Jameel Sandham

Impeccable

ISBN 978-1-9161769-0-4

Cover art by James Lacey

jameelsandham.com

for Mum

Acknowledgements

A special thank you to Lizzy. This book wouldn't have been finished without your support.

Tim Rhys, your guidance and tutoring at Cardiff University significantly impacted this work. Thank you.

Cally Worden, your editing was excellent. Thank you.

Everyone else who provided feedback, support, and encouragement. Thank you.

Mother, your strength inspires me.

5% of the profits of this book will be donated to the Open Medicine Foundation and other organisations helping people with ME/CFS and other chronic debilitating illnesses.

Part 1

Chapter 1

It's strange. When you're on a high, and it's too good to be true, deep down you know shit will hit the fan. You just carry on going as if it won't, but it always bloody does. And when it does, it all hits at once. Never splashes and spatters so you can dodge it and clean it up. No. A whole cesspit at once and there's nothing you can do about it. That's life. Shit. Shit. Shit! The question is, how do you handle it?

★★★

I've just left my student house on Woodville Road. I'm heading to uni and I'm on time for once. I've been off the rails a bit, and I'm trying to bring myself back. My mind is all over the place, I'm having a comedown. All my friends think I'm a lying twat, Isobel split up with me, and I can't shake the worry that there's more to come.

The pavement is peppered with pink and white petals. The tree ahead is in full blossom. Nice. The lamp posts are covered in stickers from underground brands. One says, 'Frenzy', in a bold white font, black background. That was my event. I smile every time I see it. The event went so well. Except now I feel sickly anxious because I let everything else slip, I feel like they're going to kick me out of uni, or somebody is about to die. Stop thinking like that, it's just the comedown. Everything will be okay.

There are students everywhere. There's something so charming about the student world, the carefree chit-chat, the bustle. A girl says, 'Oh my God, I can't believe how much I chundered before WePlay this weekend, how *revolting*.' She's young and pretty.

Chundered means puked. She drank too much. WePlay is a cheesy night out at the student union, every Saturday. I can tell she's proud of herself. I smile. The bustle.

People are looking at me, I wonder why. That guy in front just glanced, his smugness caught my eye before he looked away, said something to his mate, his mate looked back, caught my eye equally as smug – entitled, upper-middle-class smug – pretended he wasn't looking when he knew I knew he was. Why else would they be looking back this way, if not to smirk at me? There's nothing of note behind me, just a few small groups of people. Nothing worth staring at. They must have been looking at me.

My burner phone vibrates in my pocket, unusual for ten in the morning. Shitty brick Samsung that can't even internet. Unknown number.

'Hello,' I say.

'It's Connor, mate. No fucking about here, Arlo's been raided.'

Nausea. Everything goes horribly quiet, including Connor. Phone to ear, arm feels like lead. Legs unsteady, like I've been hit hard on the chin. Intense heartbeat.

'Jesus,' I say.

I feel the slightest sense of relief, it's strange; I knew this was coming, and now there's closure. And shock, and numbness. Fuck!

I should have this conversation in private, but I'm too desperate to hear what Connor's got to say. The sounds in my head are still murky. The news has cut me in half. I should have listened to my gut, just like Mum always says. Not that she knows about any of this. Normal sound returns, heartbeat still heavy.

'Din was there,' Connor says. 'They got the safe houses too.'

Waiting for the pedestrian signal to beep at the Cathays Terrace crossing. People standing next to me, none the wiser. Cars swooshing by. Looking down the road to my right to see more cars approaching, people walking, so much concrete, parked cars, house after house after house. Just a few trees. Never enough trees. People going in and out of Lidl. The café opposite has lively event posters on its wall. I bet they make more money from advertising than selling coffee. Giant colourful billboards across the road. The lights usually turn red fast once the button is pressed, but this feels like an eternity. Dull white sky. The sound of a train gathering speed.

Connor says, 'You gotta ditch everything. Get away, mate. Get away as fast as you can.' He's talking so quickly. Maybe he's high again. 'They got so much shit: the flake, mud, the cash, debt lists, phones, all that. Fucking hell it's so tits up I dunno what to do. Terry's probably heard already. He's gonna want his money.'

The Welsh accent grates on me when it's panicked. Cardiff has so many English you never really get used to hearing the Welsh accent. And when you do hear it, there's usually something attractive about it. Not Connor, not now.

Connor doesn't know that Terry is fond of me. Terry's the kingpin. He ticked Arlo and Din shitloads of cocaine every week. I worked for Arlo. Connor worked for Din. Now they've been arrested, the debts get passed on to us. This is bad, really fucking bad, but maybe I can find a way out of it.

I need to talk to Terry.

It's all over. The whole fucking thing. Just like that. Sight blurring like I'm lacking sugar. My legs take me across the road with the crowd but I can't hear the signals beeping. I'm going to faint. Grab on to bridge barrier.

I feel like that guy in *Lock, Stock* when he loses the poker game and everything gets woozy and surreal because he knows he owes a dangerous cunt five hundred grand or so. The cinematography is on point. It's like I'm going in and out of a nitrous oxide (NOS) balloon trip. Distortion of senses. Time moving strangely. Takes me a while to feel remotely normal.

Breathe. Sight slips back into focus. I'm getting some strange looks.

'You there, mate?' Connor says.

'I'm here,' I say.

'We're so fucked. Terry'll kill us, we'll get arrested. There's no way we're getting off light, you know that don't you?'

'Connor. Calm down. This panic isn't going to get you anywhere. Take some deep breaths. Seriously. Deep, aggressive breaths. Once you've got your head together you should think about disappearing, fast. Trust me. You'll be fine in that case.' I can barely breathe, but he sounds like he's on the verge of a heart attack. 'I'm not going to run. I'm sick of it. I'm sick of losing,' I say.

End call. Throw phone off bridge. More strange looks.

I walk on. Concrete wall to my right. Makes me think of prison. Turn into the university grounds, past the library. Thin trees towering above, so vigorous with thousands of little leaves.

It's probably best I don't go to the creative writing workshop now. I need to calm down. At least the university grounds feel safe. Academic. Not a place for gangsters.

Nowhere is safe any more.

Keep calm and carry on. I fucking hate that saying.

John Percival building. Congregation of people by the revolving door. Take side door. Shoot upstairs. Keep left. Why can't the fucking first years follow a simple instruction? Barge through two guys in my way. Keep left. They almost fall over. No time for idiots now. Corridor full of artificial light. Barrage of education-related posters pinned on walls.

I need to talk to Terry, but you can't simply ring Terry. It doesn't work like that.

First floor toilets are empty as usual. They smell weird. Run the cold tap. Splash water on face. Cold kick. Breath sucked out of me. The sensations draw me into the moment. Reality. No thoughts, just the feeling of crisp coldness on my skin, and for that moment everything is okay. It doesn't last long. Numbness resumes as water warms on my face.

Droplets tainted by dust trickle down the mirror. I look unhealthy. Pale. Skin a bit lifeless. Darkness around my eyes. They're not as blue as usual.

This is the turning point. I can feel it in my heart, and in the fire in my veins; it's the feeling of the subtle fabric of the universe. I am not going to fail! We stand to gain the most from our greatest adversities. I will no longer fear myself. I can face anything. I need to go home, fix this.

★★★

My room is a joke. Clothes all over the floor, boxing wraps tangled on the bed, skipping rope hanging off a chair, dusty surfaces, coffee circles on my desk, piles of paper – the remnants of an abandoned manuscript – and my expensive laptop.

There's not enough natural light. I like things bright and spacy, like the Bay House. Like the balcony of the

Whitehouse. Now Arlo's been done, I'll never set foot in the Whitehouse again. And the Bay House is not safe any more. It's all over.

The only thing I like about my room is the houseplants. They make the place feel real. My own little jungle. They remind me of Isobel. Our walks. The lake. It's all over.

The most aesthetically pleasing plant is the Wandering Jew. I got it when it was weak and frail, from Wilko, a big home-bargain store in the city centre, the upstairs of which has zero daylight. What a stupid place to sell plants. Isobel was with me. She was there when I got every single plant on separate occasions. It was our thing. The walks. The lake. The plants. Fuck. It's all over.

The Wandering Jew changes colour all the time, it is in a constant state of flux. It has grown three times as big since I put it in my room, much stronger and healthier. Today everything is pale. The purple underside of each leaf, the reddish-purple stems. The tops of the leaves have a green layer, then a silvery-green one and then another green one beneath that. Whitewashed pinks and purples find their way into the greens in places, subtly. It looks like it's from a fantasy world.

I'm lying on my bed. All those nerves have wiped me out. Isobel doesn't like this memory foam mattress much: too firm. White Egyptian cotton sheets and a brown duvet cover. I want to get under the covers but I fear I'll never muster the strength to get back out. Soft silk pillows, the perks of being a student entrepreneur.

A thousand thoughts flicker at once. Prison! Terry. I fear being stabbed by one of Terry's lot, maybe he wants to make an example of me. Maybe he'll let me off. He won't let Arlo off. I picture Arlo in a concrete box with cold metal bunks, tortured, killed, his dopey face covered in blood. I hate my imagination. Ugh. Din, hanging: cold, lifeless. Connor's body found by someone walking innocently in the woods.

No, it won't come to that. You have to fix it, Tommy. This is on you now.

I feel like ringing Mum. I want to cry, I want to tell her everything. She will know what to say, but I can't tell her, stress makes her illness ten times worse.

I did this all for Mum. She has a horrific disease called Myalgic Encephalomyelitis. ME. Some call it Chronic Fatigue Syndrome, but I don't like that name. Mere fatigue would be a blessing compared to how Mum feels. It destroyed her life, every single bit of it. Enough was enough, I had to do something to help her live again.

I remember when I'd just started uni, and I got the dreaded call. Mum didn't want to take me away from my new life, but there was nothing else she could do. There was no one else to help her, no sense of community anywhere any more.

When Mum had let me into the crooked little flat she used to live in, in Cornwall, she had looked haggard, but not strictly ill. What does ill really look like? You can't distinguish a cancer patient until their hair starts falling out, or their face pales and turns yellow from chemo.

We stood in the narrow hallway, cream walls, an ugly, industrial-brown carpet. There was no central heating, the windows were single glazed. It was cold. She lived on the top floor of a large, old house that had been converted into apartments.

Mum had thin, mid-length grey hair, puffy skin, and bags around her eyes. She was short of breath, even getting the door took it out of her. But although the illness had robbed her of everything, it couldn't take the colour from her eyes, still beautiful, blue, with a gentle silver wash.

We hugged. 'How are you?' I said. I held her tight.

She is about five feet six inches tall. She was always thin

until she got ill. Now she's obese. ME is a metabolic disease, managing weight is nearly impossible. She eats with more discipline than an Olympic athlete. And yet her weight is the least of her worries.

'Still shit,' she said, slouching over herself. Her posture had given up on her. I knew it wouldn't be long before her back was completely hunched. 'I feel like I've been kicked in by a rugby team.'

I hate it when she uses that line. Imagine your mum getting kicked in by a rugby team. And the doctors laughing and saying it's not real. And then the Tories sipping their champagne and telling her that she needs to get down to the Jobcentre, whether she's getting battered by a rugby team or not.

'I hope you feel better soon,' I said.

You say things like that even when there's no hope, even when you know it won't happen.

'Do you want a horsetail tea?'

'That would be lovely, thank you,' she said. We moved into the cramped, open-plan living room and kitchen. She lay on the tatty, navy blue sofa. I put the kettle on the hob and fired the luminous blue gas underneath it.

The kitchen floor slanted downwards to the living room floor, which was flat for a short distance and then slanted again to the walls. Dodgy landlord saving on costs, no doubt. When you're disabled, accommodation options are few and far between. Most landlords won't rent to benefits claimants. It doesn't matter to them whether the claimant is on Jobseeker's or Disability. Discrimination at its finest. But the Tories don't give a fuck, because every single fucking one of their friends is a landlord.

The place was messy, not quite chaotic, but almost. The kitchen was scattered with used cooking equipment, ingredients, a few used plates and bowls and cutlery waiting to be used again. Some of the plates had dried food residue on them. It smelt a little funky, but not savage.

Mum is too ill to keep up with it all, physically doesn't have the stamina. Her muscles are so deteriorated, her body so biologically dysfunctional, that what would be a normal person's mundane task is, for her, a marathon. Except normal people recover from marathons quicker than she recovers from everyday tasks. It's difficult to imagine, but that's how it is.

Mum said, 'So, how are you? Tell me about university. I so badly wish I could come see where you live, what's Cardiff like? I hope you're looking after yourself.'

'I like it, my housemates are nice. I'm only living in halls, so there's not much to see, the room is tiny. The social side of it is wicked though. Ryan stayed for a few nights in Freshers' when he drove me up, and we went out with all my housemates to some events at the students' union; everyone was really nice, we met loads of people and had lots of fun,' I said.

I put four heaped teaspoons of dried green horsetail herbs into a lemongrass-green teapot. 'Cardiff is a nice city, it has a lot of character, and it's not so big, so it's not so busy and everything feels quite easy to get to,' I said.

'I'm glad you like it,' she said. 'I hope you make lots of friends and have all the fun in the world. I'm so sorry for making you come back here.'

'Don't be sorry, it's a pleasure to see you. What have you been up to?'

It was a stupid question. I'm not even sure now why I asked it.

I poured the horsetail tea into two plain mugs, handed one to Mum. Horsetail tea is mild, slightly herby, slightly earthy. It tastes like it's got lots of nutrients in it.

'Nothing. I'm so bored I want to die.'

She was already dead inside. Humans can't live like she was having to. She went outside less than a well-kept dog, and most dogs do not endure as much pain and discomfort. But she doesn't believe in suicide, because of spiritual implications.

'I'm going to write loads of books this year and they'll make them into audiobooks for you to listen to so you'll never run out of entertainment. And I'll get them to make the books into films. And when we're rich, you can have a nice house with a garden, and a carer, and all the best doctors in the world,' I said.

I said it knowing full well it was never going to happen, but in situations as dark as those, all you can do is fantasise. Mum prefers audiobooks because she can lie down with her eyes closed, or sometimes films because they don't require a lot of brain power. Too much sensory overload, sometimes even just normal daylight, can make her more ill. Mum inspired me to be a writer, yet because of her cognitive dysfunction she cannot read or write for more than a few minutes at a time. Life is full of ironies.

She said, 'That would be perfect, what are you going to write?'

'I'm not sure yet, maybe a crime thriller set in Cardiff,' I said. 'Maybe an epic fantasy. Which would you prefer?'

'Both,' she said, 'I can't wait.'

'You should drink your tea in bed,' I said. She looked uncomfortable on the sofa.

I helped Mum up, and I followed her to her room. She slumped into her scruffy little bed, where she spent most of her life, year, after year, after year.

A nice view was Mum's salvation. From her bedroom, in that bed where she spent her life, she could see coastal cliffs overgrown with greenery of all tones and textures that had flourished in the summer, and beyond that, the ever-changing Atlantic expanse. Mum hated summer because she had to witness it from behind glass and concrete, like a zoo animal.

That day, the sky was grey. Wind tapped its fingers against the window. Summer was dwindling into darkness. The surging ocean shoulder-barged the beach. I love it when it's like that, when it's raw, natural, real. Life isn't like the adverts.

As I looked out over the Atlantic, I thought about how publishing a book takes years, and how Mum had suffered long enough. 'Are you hungry?' I said.

'Bloody starving. I've been so ill I couldn't make anything good to eat, and you know how those supermarket ready meals kill me, it's been a nightmare.'

'I'll make some food,' I said.

At least zoo animals don't struggle for food, they have it handed to them on a plate. When Mum got ill, we had to do a lot of our own research. Most of the NHS doctors admitted they knew absolutely nothing about her illness at all. And they were clueless about nutrition. Research suggests people with ME have a different gut microbiome to healthy people. But we tried talking to NHS doctors about gut microbiome and the link between digestion, nutrition, and metabolic function, and they didn't have a fucking clue. It was a shock.

In the early days of her illness, I found looking after Mum a chore. Why do I have to have an ill mum? What did I do to deserve that? Later, I tended towards the idea everything happens for a reason. I'm not completely convinced by it, but I feel there are intrinsic links between seemingly unrelated events in life. I like to think of these links as the subtle fabric of the universe, an infinitely complex weave that we could never hope to understand. Not with the way we currently approach things, anyway.

If Mum hadn't got ill, we wouldn't have learned so much

about health. Knowing about health is a blessing. We sat at the dinner table. Organic chicken with mixed herbs, asafoetida, salt and rich red paprika, smelling fucking banging. Good salt, of course. None of that table salt with added shit in it. Just pure Himalayan salt. Steamed greens glazed with real, raw butter. They told us the saturated fat in butter was bad for us. That we should eat margarine, and other lighter, artificial products high in polyunsaturated fatty acids. They were wrong, or they were lying. The realisation of that was a shock too.

It was difficult being around Mum. The mood was often sombre because her life was so mundane. She had nothing to be cheery about. I said, 'My God, I love chicken wings,' because I didn't know what else to say.

I'd wanted to say something interesting, exciting, stimulating. She never got to talk to people, she lived in unbearable isolation. Society isn't designed for the unwell, for those who can't go to the pub or yoga class after working a shitty repetitive job.

Having no friends is one of my biggest fears. I remember when I was about eight, Mum asked me what my greatest fear was. I was young, my greatest fear was probably never getting a chance to play football for Manchester United. I can't remember my answer. Hers was that she worried people didn't want her there. I couldn't really comprehend, I was too young. Now I take that to mean she worried she wouldn't fit in, or that she felt helplessly lonely, uncomfortable in her own skin. It's strange that her fear came true. Life makes you deal with yourself, eventually, whether you like it or not.

'This is delicious, thank you, my angel,' she said.

'My pleasure,' I said. There was nothing pleasurable about that dimly lit room, and my morbid mother. After dinner, she went to bed.

I slept restlessly on the sofa. My only solace, the sound of the ocean. I wondered how many of my uni friends slept on the sofa when they went to visit their parents. Probably none, but we hadn't got to talking about our home lives yet.

The next morning, Mum sat at the dining table, opening her post while I cooked her breakfast. 'Oh God,' she said, distraught. 'They're taking my PIP away from me.'

PIP is Personal Independence Payment, a welfare benefit that's supposed to help with the extra costs of having to live with a long-term illness or disability.

'What the fuck? Nothing's changed, how can they do that?' I said.

The bitch who came to do Mum's assessment seemed so nice and understanding. How sly she was. They do the dirty work of the Tories, they get rewarded for cutting people's support, whether those people need the help or not. Cut, cut, cut.

'If anything, I'm worse than before. What the fuck am I going to do? I'm in so much debt already,' Mum said. She dropped, and as her head hit the table, something grabbed my heart and yanked it. In that moment, my fire was well and truly lit. I was no longer going to respect their rules. Respect must be mutual.

I wondered how much money that bitch got for slitting Mum's throat. I bet she was never disciplined or penalised for fucking the assessment up. Funny, that.

I hugged my crying mother, and I decided enough was enough. I said, 'Don't worry, I'll help you with your appeal, and in the meantime, I'll get work in Cardiff.'

★★★

I'm lying on my bed, the memory fades but the hard feeling

in my heart lingers. I phone Mum from my personal phone. I need to hear her voice.

'Hello, son,' she says.

'Hello,' I say. 'I thought I'd see how you were.'

'I'm okay, thanks. I just did some gardening, that was bloody lovely. Now I'm a bit dead. And how are you?'

'Yeah, I'm fine,' I say. 'Busy, but everything is going well.' I picture Mum happy in her garden and I smile.

'I hope you're not burning yourself out, what have you been doing? How is your business going?'

'The business is fine,' I say. I fight the urge to tell her what a mess I'm in.

'You don't sound too good, you bloody are burning yourself out, aren't you!'

'I haven't been sleeping well, I think it's all catching up on me. I'll be okay though. I just need to focus.'

'Yes, you do. Try to stop biting off more than you can chew, you've got to do everything one step at a time. You've done so well already, you should be proud of yourself.'

'You're right,' I say. 'I'm sorry I haven't spoken to you in a while, I've put some structure in place to make sure the business can run without me. I'll come see you soon.'

'It's okay, my angel, I know you've been busy, don't worry. It will be lovely to see you.'

'Yes, it's been too long,' I say. 'Anyway, sorry, I'd better go, I want to meditate, and I have a lot to do. I hope you feel well later.'

Mum likes it when I meditate. She likes it when I look after myself. I have a feeling she fears I'll end up like her. There wouldn't be much worse than ending up like her.

'Goodbye, my angel, I love you,' she says.

'Love you too,' I say.

I lie there, anxious, my thoughts swirling into headache.

I need to talk to Terry, but you can't simply demand to see Terry. It doesn't work like that.

Trying to meditate. The first step is to find some calm. Focussing on breathing is a good way to go about it. I bring my attention to a small area on my nostril and try to feel the sensations there. No thinking, just experiencing the sensations, mainly the feel of the breath going in and out. In, and out.

You should have ditched Arlo! You always knew this was going to happen. Should have taken Terry up on his offer. No, respecting Arlo was the right thing to do. Integrity. Wait. How could it be? Arlo fucked it. But respect is respect. A deal is a deal.

You've lost your focus.

Meditation is not easy when you're anxious. When you lose your focus, gently bring it back. Don't control your breath, just let it occur naturally. My breath is heavy, laboured. Breath goes in. Breath goes out. I can feel the difference between the in-breath and the out-breath on the end of my nostril and even though I know I'm not supposed to think about it or analyse it, it's clear that in-breaths are cooler and crisper and out-breaths are warmer, moister. In-breath, out-breath, in-breath.

How am I going to fix this? Don't let it ruin everything. Find a way. Make sure you stay focussed, don't wallow. Mum wouldn't want you wallowing. It's a challenge. Everything is a challenge to a warrior, I remember her saying.

Get back into the moment. In-breath. Out-breath. In-breath. Out-breath.

A call on my personal phone, unknown number. I answer hesitantly. A deep voice says, 'Get in the car outside,' and hangs up. Only one person summons you like that: Terry.

I get into the back seat of the black Mercedes with tinted

windows outside my student house, hoping none of my student friends have seen me. The driver takes no notice of me, the car pulls off. Next to me is a man known as The Messenger. I've only ever met him once. He's thin, hard-faced, wearing a cream tweed suit.

The car stops several doors down from the entrance to Terry's club. The Messenger opens his door, signals for me to get out. He unlocks a gate and escorts me through an alleyway, which must be the back entrance to Terry's club. I fear nobody has seen me enter. They could do anything to me.

***

I'm in Terry's office. The Messenger has left us alone. Terry is sitting at his desk. There is just one burnt-orange light on. The curtains are closed. The room appears singed and shadowed. Terry gestures for me to sit on the chair opposite him.

Terry is only capable of two emotions: dissatisfied, and when he is more positive, slightly less dissatisfied. Right now, he's dissatisfied. He is always alert, sharp. The wear and tear on his face isn't immediately apparent; you're drawn first to his glaring platinum-blue eyes, his meticulously combed, white hair.

I wonder if he thinks I'm here to grovel, to beg for forgiveness, for him to spare my life, like he is the gamekeeper or something. That's not going to happen. I'm not going to let him get the better of me.

Terry is so far up the ladder it appears all this is a game to him, a game in which you can play well and prosper, or make mistakes and lose. A game like chess. But I'm not playing the game any more. In his game, like any other game, there are measured sequences and outcomes, and rules that govern these moves. What Terry forgets, I think, is that life is dynamic, the rules flux. I feel I'm about to change the rules, I just don't yet know how.

I look about as I wait for Terry to talk. He's shuffling a few papers around on his desk. There are piles of books, papers, files, everywhere. It all looks quite chaotic in ways, but I know there's a strict order to it all. Not a computer in sight, it's like the nineties. The bookshelf on the left is full of fiction and non-fiction, it covers a whole wall. Martin Amis's *Money* stands out.

'We've got a mess here, haven't we, Tommy,' Terry's voice is strong, but husky with age. 'What did I tell you the first time we met? Be very smart about who you work with. I said it once and I'll say it again. You could have had it all but you stuck with Arlo. What do you think he would have done in your shoes, Tommy? He'd have ditched you quicker than you could say come back. This game's all about the money, Tommy. Weighted risk, calculated reward. There are no friends here. The way I see it, Arlo has really fucked you. His idiocy got your pants down and you've been absolutely shit-tered. You saw it coming. We all did. I'm not the one with ties to him, Tommy. I haven't even met the man. There'll be no police knocking on my door.'

I'm struggling to maintain my focus on Terry's words. I want to say, Shut up and get to the point. I remain silent, sitting as calmly as possible. I will not let Terry intimidate me.

Terry says, 'Listen. You're like a son to me, truly. But you know that already. Arlo owes me seventy-five grand. Din owes me a hundred. They're both going down for a long, long time; the idiots got caught at Arlo's place with enough evidence to put them away for a long, long time. What the fuck do they think safe houses are for? We're talking ten years each, ten years if they're lucky. Unless they talk. Now, if they talk, that would be inconvenient.'

I dread to think about what Terry does to snitches. He couldn't have gotten to where he is without setting examples so severe these things never happen again.

'So where does that leave me and my money? No-fucking-where. I should have them killed in prison, and any other fucker who was associated with them, including you. How many fathers do you know would let their sons off a debt that big? Not a damn one, Tommy. Not a single soul.'

'You want your money. I think you should give them a chance,' I say.

'Don't be so bloody stupid. What do you think will happen if I give every fucker that lets me down another chance? Tell you what, I could halve their debts just to make it easier for them, or take instalments, like a DFS half-price sale. Four years of interest free credit. Is that what you think I am? DFS, Argos, a NatWest personal loan? Fucking 'ell, Tommy, you think I got here picking up after other people's mess? You really are, for want of better words, one of a kind.'

This is how I know I'm not cut out for this business. I could never be as unforgiving as Terry is.

Terry says, 'Look, Tommy, you know I'm going to give you a chance, you always knew that or you wouldn't be here. A challenge. And if you succeed, I'll forget this whole thing happened. I'll consider it a minor inconvenience, nothing more. You do whatever it takes to get me that seventy-five grand, and if you do, you win. Understand? I'll take you under my wing, just like I've always wanted. We'll run things like a family, now that Arlo has lost his right to your loyalty. How does that sound?'

'I'd like that,' I say. 'I need some guidance. I was so close to being sorted.' I suck it up and say these words like I mean them with all my heart. Do I fuck. I'll get him to drop his guard, and then he'll be mine for the taking. 'But if I win, no one gets hurt. Nobody. All of Din's lot get a chance to pay you back too.'

He deliberates. Clears his throat. Says, 'Fine. Their fate is in your hands. Why not. Here's the deal. You've three weeks – that's twenty-one days to be exact – starting from this very minute of this very hour,' he looks at his watch. Hublot. Big. Hideous, but worth a fortune. 'Twenty-one days from today, I want seventy-five grand, cash, in person, right here. This very office. And if you don't make it, well, I'm sorry to say, Tommy, lessons have got to be learned. Points have got to be made. My apologies, I'm truly sorry. That is the nature of the beast, Tommy.'

Chapter 2

As well as working for Arlo, I have other income streams. Moose, Anthony, and I sell drugs to students. We also run a fashion business called Vintage and Vinyl, to wash the cash. And then there was the event I put on, which helped facilitate both. I'll never forget the event. It was an incredible party. A dream come true. I can't wait to do another. The music, the smiles, the energy; it was all so fulfilling to make that happen.

Moose's house is our safe house. All sensible dealers have a safe house. It is somewhere not related to the dealer in any traceable way. If Anthony was caught dealing, the police would never know to raid Moose's place. If someone wanted to rob Anthony for cash and drugs, they wouldn't know where the bulk of the stash was kept. For all you know, your neighbours could be fronting a safe house right now. You'd never know, unless their door was bashed in by police in the early hours of the morning, or the house was ransacked by yobs.

I let myself into Moose's house, and I say, 'Hello?' wondering whether Moose is at work or not. He is stretched to the max in the NHS. Fucking Tories.

The hallway walls are dull white, there are cracks in the paint in places near the roof. The carpet is thin, and navy blue.

The stairs ahead are wooden, painted white.

I feel awkward because Moose and I have fallen out. I have been keeping secrets from him, about Arlo and other things.

Moose grunts from his bedroom. 'I'm sleeping, got nights, fuck off.' South East London accent.

'I've got to tell you something so important I don't feel bad for waking you up, not one bit,' I say.

'Better be, then,' he says.

I take a seat at the table in the living room. Moose's living room is small and has lots of character. The curtains are closed, the lighting dim, it smells of weed, there are pictures of elephants, and patterned fabric wall hangings. The sofa is draped with a silky, light-brown cloth with darker brown squares edged with gold.

Moose appears in grey jogging bottoms, topless. He has broad shoulders, is muscular and lean, and has distinctly strong facial features and a big head, a bit like a moose. White skin, lightly freckled. Dark brown eyes.

'Arlo's been raided,' I say.

'Fuckin 'ell,' he says. 'Told you some shit like this would happen, what's going on then?'

'Connor called me this morning. Din was with Arlo, the police got cash, drugs, debt lists, their safe houses. Arlo owes Terry a lot of money. I went to see Terry, we made a deal. If I settle Arlo's debt, Terry'll give everyone – including Din and all that lot – a chance, nobody gets hurt. Terry's a psycho, but he's a man of his word, you don't get to be where he is without that. So now I've got to get seventy-five grand in three weeks and most of my money is tied up in the business, and in that house I bought Mum. I'm fucked.'

'Proper fucked,' Moose says. 'We ain't got a lot left here either. Anthony's been smashing sales. There's got to be a decent bit of cash in the business now. You reckon Arlo's gonna talk or anything dodgy?'

'I'm not sure what he'll do, but I doubt he would wrong me in any way.'

'Fuck that, Tommy, this game changes everyone, you can't trust anyone. You're lucky they got Arlo and not you, they're gonna want the higher-ups, not Arlo's bitch. He's not gonna get far if you're all he's got to rat about … And he's gonna be worried about you snitching on him. I bet he's gonna come for you like a cornered animal.'

'I hope you're wrong,' I say.

'Arlo would have got one phone call, did he ring you? Well then.' He pauses, 'I'm going to make coffee, and I'll ring Anthony.'

Moose is right. I was Arlo's bitch. I feel sick getting rid of an image of a man covered in blood trying to protect his face. It wasn't supposed to be that way. I let myself down. I let everyone down. That's not going to happen any more. I'm better than that.

The sound of coffee beans being ground in a machine. The trickling of water. Steam.

I don't think Moose has changed; he is still honest, still grounded, and not greedy, he was only doing it to get onto the property ladder. That's where I went wrong, I got too greedy. A couple of grand a month wasn't good enough, I wanted it all.

Moose rushes in looking serious, says, 'I swear someone was just nosing over the back gate.'

Rustling outside the living room window. Moose dives into the corner. I slip off my chair to conceal myself by the sofa. The thin strip of sunlight where the two curtains don't quite meet is shaded. Someone, or something, is close to the window. It lingers for a moment, moves across the window. Indistinct sounds outside. Silence.

Excruciating silence, for what feels like forever. Perhaps just a few minutes pass.

Moose whispers, 'Don't tell me you let someone follow you here.'

I say, 'I checked loads of times, and I got a taxi to a few roads off then walked, no one followed me.'

The aroma of coffee comes from the kitchen, it is slightly earthy, slightly nutty, and intensely rich. I love that smell.

Moose and I wait for a while. Nothing happens. There are no more noises outside.

'We won't get anywhere being that jumpy,' Moose says. 'Fuck it, if anyone wants to cause trouble here, it's their funeral.' He goes to the kitchen, comes back with two mugs of coffee.

The warmth of the mug comforts me.

Moose says, 'Come on then, what you gonna do?'

I say, 'I'm going to take the stash we've got here and sell it all, and then I'm going to figure out a way to get the rest of the debt for Terry. You lot don't deserve to be caught up in this, that's why I did everything the way I did; that's why you couldn't know about Leon.'

When I started working for Arlo, I created an alter ego called Leon. None of my friends or family were associated with Leon in any way. Leon lived a separate life to Tommy: he had an apartment on Cardiff Bay, he wore his hair differently, he never crossed paths with Tommy. That meant if anything went wrong, no one who knew Tommy would be implicated in any way. Until recently, none of my friends even knew Leon existed.

'You were a fucking retard to think we would just leave you to pick up the mess if the shit hit the fan though. This second life stuff is all good in theory, but think about it: if you don't sort that debt in three weeks, you're fucked, and that means we lose Tommy, not Leon.'

'It's not going to come to that,' I say. 'I'm going to figure it out.'

'Oh, fuck off, Tommy, you'll be dead if you try to magic seventy-five grand out of fucking nowhere. Take all the help you can get. I'm gonna get the stash from upstairs so we can see what we've got. You enjoy that coffee while it lasts, because things are about to get hectic, there's no question.'

I take a sip of the coffee. It is slightly nutty with a hint of creaminess, and the aftertaste is bitter. Brown residue remains on the outer rim of the mug, where my lips were.

Moose returns from his attic with a black holdall, unzips it. In the bag, there are several clear plastic freezer bags full of drugs.

The cocaine is unnaturally white. Whiter than snow. Snow is tainted by the ground beneath, footprints, earth, chemicals in the air, grass, whatever it touches. This white is in a world of its own. Ironic, considering how dirty cocaine is. It's so addictive and expensive that people kill each other over it.

Good cocaine goes by the name of flake. Cocaine has a thousand other names, like chop, charlie, coke, white stuff, powder, sniff, pub grub, primo, Mexican. This stuff is high-grade. It is slightly soft and oily, not powdery. It is clumpy, flaky. It has a distinct smell that is difficult to describe. Slightly chemically, not harsh. Perhaps like the faded scent of petrol. Everyone loves the smell of petrol.

The MDMA is formed of brownish-yellow crystal chunks. The main clump is one dense chunk of crystal, and the rest of it is formed of smaller shards. The chemical smell is much harsher, a bit like aniseed.

The pills are shaped like little gold ingots, about a centimetre long, half a centimetre wide, and half a centimetre high.

They're hefty. Edible gold glitter creates elaborate shining patterns within. They're called Gold Dust. Aside from the glitter, in them there is MDMA, caffeine, and an agent to hold the shape.

The ketamine is white, it is not as white as the cocaine. It is formed of fine, dry white crystals that do not clump together. It looks like a fine powder, but upon closer inspection, you can see slightly elongated shards. It is not moist or oily. It is reasonably easy to distinguish from cocaine. The scent is much less distinct to that of cocaine or MDMA.

Moose gets rough weights of the drugs by placing them on a digital scale. He says, 'About half a bar of flake, bar of mud, two Z's ket, and looks like about a couple of hundred pingers. What's that then? Summin like six for the flake, two for the mud, eight hundred for the ket, and five hundred for the pingers. Still sixty-odd grand to go then.'

He laughs, and I can't help but laugh too.

As the laughter dries up, I say, 'Well, we've got double that if I go out and sell it in grams like the good old days.'

Drugs are like any other commodity: the more you buy or sell in one go, the cheaper they get. The way to gain the highest revenue is to sell your drugs in grams, rather than ounces, bars or boxes. An ounce is usually rounded down to twenty-eight grams. Ounces are often called Z's. A bar is nine ounces, just over two hundred and fifty grams. A kilogram is also known as a box. When you sell in larger amounts, you gain much more revenue per sale, and you do much less work. There's nothing worse than running around delivering one gram at a time.

Moose says, 'There's not enough hours in a day, you'd be doing it for three weeks and still not have enough cash, mate.'

'You're right, but I haven't got any choice. I'll sell half of it in bulk, and half in grams. It'll stretch. I'll cut that flake fifty-

fifty, and bag everything in point-sixes, that's already shitloads more.'

The sound of a key in the front door makes me uneasy.

'That'll be Anthony,' Moose says.

Anthony comes in wearing medium-fit blue jeans, and a worn-out white T-shirt. He is medium build, has short, fair hair. His facial expression is always neutral. He doesn't conform to fashion convention. Everyone else, including Moose and me, wears skinny jeans, and has the back and sides of their hair faded very short, with length at top, pushed back. He places the retro beige holdall he is carrying on the table. 'Five grand. There's at least another five in the business account. Nothing suspicious outside.'

Anthony is reliable. He is the kind of guy that talks little, does lots.

'Thank you, Anthony,' I say. 'And how much stock have we got if we have a clearance sale?'

'Couple of grand I s'pose, more coming Friday. Another four or five grand if it all goes. I'll let the staff know it's a clearance sale. What's your plan with all this?' he points at the drugs. His eyes are a mixture of orange, yellow and brown.

I say, 'Don't worry about that, it's not your problem. Take some of that cash and get out of here for a while.'

He stands calmly, as if he's deep in thought. Says, 'I know, I've done my bit. You chose to do extra work with Arlo. That's not my business.' He takes two rolls of money from the holdall, shoves them in his left jean pocket. 'You've done your bit too,' he says to Moose. Anthony takes a phone and a folded piece of paper from his back pocket. He places them on the table. 'Ring my good phone if someone's about to die,' he says, before leaving.

The silence is empty, isolating.

The piece of paper Anthony left with us has phone numbers and names one side, and on the other, debt lists. I say, 'I'm going to text every one of our contacts to let them know we have discount gear, see who wants what.'

When selling drugs, texting is the stupidest thing you can do. It leaves clear evidence of intent to supply, conspiracy, and all that. I don't have time to ring each person on this list. And once I've sold this lot, I'm done for good. I'll get rid of this phone. In this case, the texting is a calculated risk.

'I'll get on with cutting and bagging this lot then,' says Moose. 'Where we gonna store it? It's all gotta be gone from here. When Daisy hears about Arlo she's going to tell me to pack it all in, she's already been on at me.'

'I've got an idea. We'll sort it once it's bagged.'

***

Moose and I are in his car. On my lap is a holdall full of drugs, which have been bagged in a variety of quantities. There are hundreds of bags of MDMA, pills, ketamine, and cocaine. The cocaine has been cut heavily with benzocaine. The larger bags hold quarter-ounces, half-ounces and ounces. The smaller bags hold roughly 0.6 grams, to be sold as full grams. The pills are bagged into three pills per bag. It's surprising how long it takes to weigh and bag things like this. We were sat there for fucking ages in Moose's living room, drugs, scales, scoops and bags all around us.

We're going to store half of what we have safely and take the other half out to sell. The stash we're going to sell later is in a holdall on the back seat.

Moose says, 'Where we going then? Fuck hanging round your Bay House, all of Arlo's lot know to find you there, and your student house is sketchy.'

'Hear me out first. We'll hide it at uni.'

'Uni? They've got CCTV everywhere, we might as well take it straight to the police. Why don't we bury it?'

'I thought about that, but we can't afford any room for error. I won't feel comfortable burying it, an animal can get to it. Where I'm thinking of will be safer than you can imagine, nobody would ever check there, and CCTV won't get looked at; they only look at CCTV when something bad happens, we won't leave a trace. The only tricky part is getting in there, but trust me, it'll work. I always think about things like this when I'm out and about, maybe it's time to start listening to those inklings.'

'What about putting it at Flash's or somewhere like that for a bit?'

'I'm not sure that's a good idea,' I say. 'I don't think Flash is the best of friends with me right now, and he got all his stuff from Arlo. He's probably as worried as all of us. And I don't want to drag anyone else into this.'

I feel sick about how I let Flash down, struggle to shake the image of Olivia's black lace and smooth tanned skin. And now I miss Isobel, great. Block it out. Now's not the time.

'Managed to piss Flash off as well did you? You really are a fucking nightmare,' Moose says.

Moose and I enter the John Percival building, Moose is carrying the holdall with half the stash in it. This building is where my lectures and seminars take place. I don't attend university much, I've been too busy.

We take the first flight of stairs. It's 3.30 pm, it's quiet, most people are in lectures. The hallways only get busy near the hour, when lectures start and finish. We walk down the corridor and back towards the front entrance again, approaching it from the other side. I get out my student card, and make sure I look a bit timid, nerdy even.

'Hi there,' I say.

'Hello,' security says.

'I've just been to my tutor's office, and he's not in. He said I could borrow a book of his. I was wondering if there was any chance you could let me in to get it? I've got an essay in soon and I really need that book. They don't have it in the library,' I say. 'Here's my student card.'

Security examines my student card. I worry he doesn't believe me. 'Come on then,' he sighs. Gets off his chair. 'Which room is it, who's ya tutor?'

'Tim Shackel, room one-point-zero-eight,' I say.

Security lets me into Tim's office. 'Don't take all day about it,' he says.

My heart is frantic, this is all so hectic. I go straight for the giant bookshelf, it's got hundreds of books crammed onto it, at all angles, I pretend I'm searching for it. The door clicks shut behind me. I keep looking for a little while. Pick up a copy of *The Long Firm* by Jake Arnott. On the way out, just as I open the door, I say, 'Got it, *The Long Firm*, good book,' and while I say this, I flick the latch up so it won't lock when it shuts. The click of the lock is drowned out by my voice.

'Right then, there we are,' security says.

'Thank you so much,' I say. 'Michael, we've still got to go to the undergrad office before the lecture at four, let's go now.'

'Okay, let's go,' Moose says.

'Thanks again,' I say to security. We all walk back down the corridor and as security departs down the stairs, we go up a flight. 'My tutor is away at a literary convention in America, all week,' I say. 'I left the latch open. Let's circle upstairs and come back down.'

'This is fucked,' Moose says. 'I haven't had a buzz like this in ages.'

We turn the corner to take the other stairs back to the first floor. Fuck. It's my tutor. Overwhelming anxiety. He's not supposed to be here! That feeling that nothing can ever go right. Don't listen to that feeling, things will go your way. Persevere.

Can't find words.

Tim Shackel has cold, hard, greyish-green eyes. He doesn't like me because I'm never around. He thinks I can't be bothered, but it's not like that. He reminds me of Professor Snape from Harry Potter, except Shackel's got short, wispy white hair, and he's lanky and bitter to the core. Snape was good in the end. I liked that.

Don't talk to me, please don't talk to me.

'Tommy,' he says, looks at the novel in my hand. 'Reading, for pleasure, are we?' Smirks. 'Reading, for once.' His lips quiver at his own joke.

'Uh, yeah.' There's hesitation in my voice. Stop being weak. 'Actually, I'm getting on with that essay,' I say, much more confident now. 'I thought you were away this week, otherwise I would have booked an office slot to talk to you about it.'

'That's an *interesting* text in context of modernism,' he says. 'Of all the texts one might choose.'

By interesting, he means stupid, irrelevant. I haven't even looked at the essay questions.

He says, 'Well, I shall be leaving later today, finally, the United States awaits. We were delayed, not that it's any of your business. I expect I'll see something of a draft when I get back.' *He's slow,* his icy eyes say, *I don't expect much.*

'Okay, I won't keep you, my apologies.' I look downwards, away from his eyes so that I appear nervous. Nobody expects the nervous, shy student to be doing what I'm doing. 'I'll do my best with the essay. Enjoy your week,' I say.

He walks off. I worry he's going to his office, that he'll notice the lock is open and the book is missing.

Moose looks at me all like, What the fuck?

'We have to follow him,' I whisper. 'Make sure he's actually gone.'

Moose and I linger at a distance watching where Tim goes. He gets in his car and drives off.

Unbelievably relieved, we go back to Tim's office. The door is still unlocked. It's rather gloomy in here. The shadow of the building opposite engulfs us. Tim's desk is messy with papers and books, an empty mug, and the computer on it is a chunky old Windows thing with a small flat-screen monitor, which is not actually that flat. There are three chairs, one swivel chair by the desk, and two square, metal-legged ones by a low table. Some filing cabinets along the walls, and the bookshelf.

'Right, we're going to hide it up there,' I say quietly, pointing to the ceiling.

'What if you don't get a chance to get back in here again?'

'You got any better ideas? We don't have time for anything else right now, I'll come and get it later when I've found somewhere else. At least it's safe in here.'

Moose puts his hands together and crouches. I put one foot on his hands, lock my leg, he lifts. There's a tile with a yellowing, damp stain on it, as if there was once water leaking around there. I shift the tile aside with ease. Moose lifts me a bit higher. It's pitch black up there. I feel around, there's no moisture. I put the holdall into the roof, ensuring it is supported by a wooden runner, and I shift the tile back into place.

'I can't tell whether you're a fucking genius, or whether this is like throwing the stash in the bin,' Moose whispers.

Footsteps outside. Voices by the door. Heart jumps about

in chest. We remain silent. What if Tim has come back, forgotten something? I hear the words, 'Students, great, engaged, rapport, teaching,' there's a lot of muffled sound in between. Must be tutors. They're just talking and talking, why won't they go away? Don't they have lectures to teach? Papers to write?

The noise goes away and we're left with peace and quiet. I still have that feeling of impending doom. I put my ear to the door, listen intently. No sound close by. We leave the office, leave the latch open, my tutor will be away for a week. I hope to have sold everything by then.

In Moose's car, we have half the drugs, and we have the debt list and the burner. It's ironic that all my moves in this business were designed to get me away from situations like this. I was smart, meticulous, and now look at me. Just a fucking yob punting grams and collecting small debts.

Moose says, 'Right, who's on the list? Start with the difficult ones, move onto the easy ones.'

Looking at the list, I say, 'Adey's owed two grand for four weeks now. Five hundred on top for interest. Easiest is probably Bento, he was always good for it. Rich parents. Cash on tap.'

A dealer is always owed, and always owes. His accounts are never settled. Usually it's fine because you have assets you can liquidate quite quickly, mainly drugs, but they got Arlo's safe house, so we have few assets to liquidate. Definitely not seventy-five grand's worth.

'Shady Adey it is then,' Moose says. 'That white Audi behind us, I swear it's following us.'

Behind us is a black taxi. Behind that, a white Audi.

'Great,' I say.

It's broad daylight, and we're in populated areas, we're okay for now, but we won't always be.

One of Adey's housemates answers the door. She's tall, in pyjamas. Short shorts and a cropped top. Students live in pyjamas. She says, 'Haven't seen you in a while; he's upstairs.'

I open Adey's door, he's about to hit a bong, his room is a mess. He panics, drops the bong, water spills on the dirty cream carpet. He springs to his feet. Moose pushes him back to the bed.

'We don't want to fuck about, Adey,' Moose says. 'We need that money *now*.'

'Tommy, Moose, I got the money, I got the money don't worry. I was going to give it to Anthony, he said I could have one more week.' Adey has one front tooth missing. He looks worn out. He says, 'I hide it under a tile in the back garden, come on, I'll get it.'

The kitchen is filthy. It's narrow, with cupboards to the right, and two sinks on the left. Two housemates sitting on the living room sofa avoid looking at us. In the poorly kept garden, Adey says, 'It's under there, where the scratch is. He points at a patio tile with a clear, small cross scratched into it. The edges are not sealed to the other tiles, there's a small black gap. 'I've gotta get the scraper to get that tile up, it's in the shed.'

The garden is fenced. There are flowerbeds lining the fence. The beds are scattered with weeds. Weeds also protrude from between some of the patio tiles.

Adey opens the door to the shed, about five metres from us in the back corner of the garden. Hops onto the roof, jumps into his neighbour's garden. Moose bolts for him. Adey's already vaulted over a second fence before Moose gets over the first fence.

I say, 'Leave him, Moose, he's got nothing.'

'Fucking weasel,' Moose says.

I get the thin metal scraper with a wooden handle from the

shed, and I use it to lift the tile. Under the tile is a plastic bag. Inside that plastic bag, another plastic bag, and another, and another, and finally, some cash. I count it. 'Only seven-fifty,' I say to Moose.

'Let's see what he's got in his room.'

As we walk through Adey's living room, Moose says, 'Tell Adey we're coming for that money next Monday or we'll burn this house down.'

Jesus.

Adey's housemates say nothing.

While we climb the dimly lit stairs, Moose says quietly, 'They'll club together and give us all they've got now. We can make sure Adey pays them back.'

Moose and I aren't bad guys.

We turn Adey's room upside down. Clutter becomes chaos. We find about an ounce of flake, half of bud, and some Valium.

'I thought I said no selling the white stuff to addicts,' I say.

Moose says, 'Anthony only sold him weed after you said that. Adey was getting that flake somewhere else, probably Flash or someone. We're not a rehab service, Tommy, not our problem if he's going somewhere else for it.'

The rest of the debt collection goes much more smoothly. Our final stop is Bento. Bento was my first ever bulk customer. He's your typical upper-class student dealer. The best type to sell to.

That Audi is still following us. 'Leave your car here. Bring everything into Bento's,' I say.

Bento opens the door. He's wearing blue chinos and a fitted white shirt. 'Tommy, Moose! Welcome. To what do I owe the pleasure?'

Rosie pops her head out of her bedroom door, the second door in the hallway. She's pretty, has strong eyes defined by naturally dark lashes. 'Tommy!' she screeches, comes to hug Moose and me, she is much shorter than us. 'Where've you been?' she says.

'That shop we got in town, been so busy it's killing me,' I say.

Oh, wow, how's that going? It's amazing what you've done with it, I go there all the time, look! She points at her jacket. It's vintage, denim.

I smile, 'You look good in it. Anyway, I'm sorry, we can't stay long, just need a chat with Bento.'

Bento has a good jawline, and healthy skin. His eyes are blue. His fair-blondish hair is short on the sides, and long at the top, pushed back.

Bento's room is tidy. On the white wall opposite his bed, above his desk, he has a poster of an attractive woman wearing almost nothing. He takes a seat at the pale wood-coloured workspace. 'What can I do for you?' he says.

'We need to settle our balances,' I say.

'Certainly,' he says. Takes cash out of the drawer under his desk, counts out one thousand, two hundred and fifty pounds, and hands it over to me without hesitation. He says, 'Why the urgency?'

I say, 'Long story. If you know anyone who wants bulk with big discount, let us know. By the way, we need to jump your back-garden fence. We can't use the front door.'

On Bento's desk, there is nothing but a cup with pencils and pens in it, a laptop, and a notepad with a pen next to it. The pen is neatly aligned, parallel to the vertical left-hand side of the notepad, with an aesthetically pleasing gap of about one and a half inches between the two.

'Be my guest,' he says, intrigued. Bento picks up the pen, rolls it in between his fingers.

'Give me a ring later to tell me how long it takes the white

Audi outside to leave. There's something in it for you.'

'It'll be my pleasure,' he says. You can see the excitement in his eyes. He thinks he's *involved* now, big time. I can only imagine the rumours that will ignite from this.

Moose and I climb over Bento's fence. There's an unavoidable bed of soil on the other side. We move quickly to the next fence so the next-door neighbour doesn't get worried. This time, we land in plants. The next fence, we struggle to avoid a tomato vine running up a lattice. One or two fences are nice and easy to jump, barely chest height. Now corrugated iron, the metal is rough and sharp underneath my hands. I worry someone is going to call the police. We'll be gone by the time they arrive, but I don't want to raise any suspicion around the area. After two more fences, we reach an alley that takes us to the road behind Bento's.

We go to Ashley's. Ashley is Harry's best mate. Harry is Moose's old housemate. A man I don't know answers the door. He looks at our trainers curiously. Our trainers are covered in dirt, along with the bottoms of our jeans. I say, 'Is Ash in?'

The man shouts, 'Ash, someone here for you.'

We enter the house. Dirty shoes on carpet. Ash comes downstairs. Ash is tall. He has slightly beige skin. We nip into his room and sell him half an ounce of cocaine. Few pleasantries are exchanged. Time is of the essence. We repeat this process at three more houses. Everywhere in Cardiff is close. It doesn't take long.

Only four people replied to my texts about discount gear. The rest of it must be sold in town, tonight. I fucking hate shifting gear in town.

We head back to my student house to prepare for the night ahead. It is impossible to open and close the front door of my student house quietly. Sammy shouts my name. I poke my head into the living room. It's dark. He's sitting on a sofa opposite the TV. The light flickering from the screen bathes his skin and glistens off his eyes. He's playing a football game on the Xbox. There's an empty sofa to the side.

He is a good-looking guy, his skin is smooth and pale, his beard shaved clean, his features symmetrical, healthy, if not a bit soft. His hair is short on the sides, mid-length pushed back on top, blondish, a bit browner in this light.

'How's it going?' I say.

'Good. You?' he says. He doesn't look at me. His hands are manipulating the controller. Sammy's build is healthy too, he's not thin, not too stocky, and his posture is well aligned. He says, 'D'you wanna come IFOR tonight?'

IFOR is a venue in town, usually has good underground music.

'I've got a few errands to run, but I'll see you there later if you like?'

'Same old,' he says. 'You should join us for predrinks.'

'I wish I could. I'm going to be a normal person again soon, just got a few ends to tie first,' I say.

Sammy knows I do illegal things, he simply has no clue about the extent of it. 'Whatever,' he says. He hates that I kept him out of it.

In my room, Moose and I tape the bottom of our boxers to our legs so nothing can fall out into our jeans. We're going to have to wear baggier jeans than usual. There's a system. Mud, front left. Pingers, front right. Ket, back right. Flake, back left. That's so when we sit, we don't crush the pingers and mud and the baggies don't rip. Ket and flake are soft enough, they'll be alright with a bit of pressure on them.

We're literally bulging with Class As and Bs. If we get patted-down on entry to any of the clubs, we'll get caught. But what choice do we have?

I write the phone number of our burner on loads of little pieces of paper to hand out. That isn't the best of ideas, because handwriting is identifiable. When you're in a rush, you need to make calculated decisions. We're quitting dealing as soon as this batch, and what's left in my tutor's office, is sold. I'll ditch the burner, there'll be no evidence. I'm fucking scared but savagely excited, I can tell Moose is too.

We're sitting on my bed, waiting for taxis to arrive. Awkward vibe.

'How we going about this then?' Moose says.

'I don't think we have a choice, it's got to be all guns blazing. Like a veg salesman at the market. Two punnets for a pound, shout it real loud, let the town know that for a couple nights only, we're in business.'

Moose laughs. 'This is going to be fucking loose, mate. You realise the chances of getting caught with all guns blazing is high? Really stupid high.'

'A story to tell the grandkids. We'll pull it off,' I say. I get the chills. Part of me wishes the taxi will never arrive.

★★★

Places like Lloyds, The Three Tipplers, Pryzm De La Shite, are always busy, so we head to Greyfriars Road. We get to the Park Place end, by the theatre. Moose opens the left side passenger door, half gets out, slides back in and slams the door shut. 'Hold about, driver, maybe a change of plan,' he says. 'I've just seen a guy I know, Deano, and a few lads get dropped off in that white Audi. He's dodgy. They must be after us. He's hard as well, nasty fucker. They're just down there,' he says. He points down the road, to our right, towards Pryzm De La Shite.

There are three men standing on the pavement, having a

good old look about. The road is relatively quiet, with only a few small groups of people walking the pavements. Sometimes the whole street is packed with drunken revellers.

'Deano's that bald one,' Moose says.

Fat bloke, this Deano, an ugly fucker, arms the size of my thighs, you wouldn't want him to get a hold of you. Dopey facial expression. Idiot written all over him. His jeans are baggy.

There are two other guys. One of them is tall, has a bony face, eye sockets protruding his beady, scrunched eyes. A black polo T-shirt that hangs short of his waist and tight on his arms.

The other is muscly, about six feet tall, looks like a hard bastard without a heart. He's wearing a grey vest. His arms are tattooed from his shoulders to his hands. His hair is spiked with wet-look gel.

These are not your average Greyfriars Road pub drinkers. They're looking for something, poised for violence. They head away from us, towards Tiger.

I say, 'We don't have a choice about this stuff. We've got to get rid of it. Just keep an eye out for those blokes.'

'Yeah, come on then, let's go,' Moose says. The taxi fare is seven quid. I give the man a twenty and tell him to keep the change, buy his kids something nice.

As we walk to Steinbeck the Straw, I glance back at the theatre with its red-brick walls, always said I'd go with Isobel, never went, never made the time. Chasing money sucks the character out of you.

I'm a bit nervous approaching security, two men with black trousers, white shirt collars above snug black jumpers, that Security Industry Authority badge on the arm, radios on the belt.

Please don't search us.

One checks our IDs, no pat-down. Banging.

Straight to the bar. Need as much Dutch courage as ever to pull this off. Not loving the cheesy R&B. The place looks and feels generic, wannabe-nice but the same old crap as every other bar geared towards the sheeple.

We get two Espresso Martinis each, down them. May as well do it in style. Make sure you don't get drunk, Tommy. You don't want to do anything stupid. Be brave, not stupid.

Couple of lads standing next to us at the bar. No time like the present, time to sell. Deep breath. Swallow. Hard lump in throat. It's been a long while since I sold to strangers. Even then, I never sold to strangers in public.

'Want any coke mate?' I say, close to the ear of the guy next to me.

He gives me a serious look. I wonder if I'm barking up the wrong tree. He says something to his mate.

'Proper flake or pub grub?' the first guy says.

'Proper,' I say. 'Tenner-a-point stuff, but I'll do it for eighty a G as I have a lot to shift, you wouldn't believe if I told you.'

The guys laugh.

'Fuck it, why not,' the other says.

'I'll do three for two-hundred if you want,' I say.

They're unsure, discuss the deal under low voices. They look like they're couple of years older than me. They're wearing jeans and tight T-shirts. Not a lot of character. Is that a hint of fake tan I see?

One of the most overplayed songs known to man, 'Mr. Brightside' by The Killers. A few pissheads singing along like it's the last song they'll ever sing. This, apparently, is culture.

'Trust me, mate, it's banging stuff,' Moose says, steps in next to me.

They talk more. 'Go on then,' the first guy says.

'Do it under the bar,' I say. 'Subtle.'

I feel a bit more comfortable knowing what Deano and those other two blokes look like, knowing if I see them coming at me I can do something about it instead of sitting there like a duck. But now I can't stop thinking about them, can't stop looking around and seeing their features among the people moving around in the dim bar lighting.

Moose and I go about asking anyone and everyone in the Straw who looks remotely game for some gear whether they want to buy some. After we've exhausted all options, we move on, thanking the bouncers on the way out.

Moose laughs as we walk down the street, 'Mate, so many people smashin' coke these days. I swear there are way more than when I was a student. Some of the girls in there, so tidy, too tidy to be smashin' it, but buying *loads*,' he says.

'I think it's always been like that, we just weren't so aware of it before. Nobody's too tidy these days, Moose. It's a fucking epidemic.'

We both laugh.

And I know what you're thinking, Barbs. You're thinking, surely, just surely! They can't waltz into any old pub and start selling drugs like that. You think I'm exaggerating. But I'm not. It's a fucking epidemic. The country is addicted to cocaine. It's on our banknotes. It's in our water supply. One day, we should really start asking why.

Barbara, or as I like to call her, Barbs, is a figment of my imagination. I had to develop her in a creative writing workshop, a character the complete antithesis of myself, and then learn to be empathetic towards her. The idea being that it would help me create believable characters with depth. The problem is that I haven't written in a long time, and Barbs is still stuck in my head.

Barbs is a bit bland, a bit stupid, a bit switched off. That Middle England sort who're turning the whole world to shit without even thinking about it. Mindlessly droning through life proud of her mortgage and her car on finance, and those two stunning sofas and a new, big TV from the Black Friday half-price sale.

Barbs condemns drug users and yet she drinks all the, 'Vino,' as she likes to call it – pronounced vine-oh because she's about as cultured as my left testicle – all the vine-oh she wants, because the government said so. Alcohol is fine, it's been around as long as man and time, just like, urm … murder? She's a bit of a monkey-see-monkey-do type.

I feel sorry for her and I desperately want her to be able to think for herself. Sometimes I feel genuine empathy towards that mind set. Sometimes I resent the lack of empathy that mind set is capable of. Empathy is supposed to be unconditional. I'm working on that.

The next bar is much busier. Still that same old shitty music, cheese-pop, tasteless. We're in there doing our thing and Moose pulls me to one side. 'Deano,' he says. We're concealed slightly, next to a table-booth. 'Over there.'

They're looking for us. There's a distinct moody seriousness on their faces, they're looking out of place amongst the lively revellers, eyes scanning with vicious intent. They think they're important. They know they're hard.

People are smiling, chatting, drinking and dancing around them. Deano and his two thugs are cold, quiet, stone and static.

'What do we do?' Moose says.

'No choice, just keep going, we'll go next door for now and just carry on to all the places down the road as fast as we can. Keep an eye out for them, don't let them see us before we see them.'

So we smash all the bars on Greyfriars Road and make a killing while we're at it. Not once are we searched on the way in to any place. Maybe it's coincidence, maybe it's luck, maybe fate or a mixture of all those things. Whatever it is, we can't complain.

After that it's Jive Lounge. Jive Lounge is an iconic cheese club in Cardiff known for its singalong pop music and outrageously cheap drinks. Nobody wants MD or ket in there, just good old-fashioned cocaine.

On to St Mary Street, where many large bars lie. From cocktail bars to big clubs to strip clubs. We scout them all. Who the fuck would pay sixty quid for a fifteen-minute dance and feel good about it?

The hours fly by. Dare I say, we're even having a bit of fun. Except for the thought of Deano and those blokes, or of getting caught by the police.

Moose and I are walking to IFOR. Town is busy now, people stumbling in and out of pubs, a few police about but fuck them, they're not after the nerdy student and his mate. When you've lost it all, it takes the pressure off, you just propel yourself in desperation, hoping for the best.

I say, 'What do you know about Deano then?'

'He thinks he's big time. Me an' Daisy met him at this house party once. He was telling us how he imports brown. He was fucked on speed though, so I reckon he was chatting shit, but he said he'd broke someone's legs for a hundred quid, stabbed a guy over a ten-bag. Fucking nutter, mate.'

Jesus.

IFOR for the final stint. This is more my thing. Reminds me of the night I met Isobel. No time to indulge in that memory now, stick to the mission. I'm loving the music. Nice deep house-beat with a lot of melody. Bam. But today is business, not pleasure.

Literally walking about saying, 'Anyone buying? Anyone buying? Anyone want any drugs?' I'll be branded as a knobend by some, and others will think it's some kind of cool. I never liked the loud and proud dealer, always thought he was a bit of a douche. I'm that douche now. Tommy the douche.

The sound system is punching heavy vibrations through me. Lovely. People are dancing everywhere. Smiles, and sweet, healthy movements. Smooth skin and gleaming eyes. Hips, the curve of the hip, of the back of a slim body. Flowing cloth, athletic legs. Bright trainers. The good old fashioned two-step.

Someone taps me on the shoulder. Bearded bloke wearing the latest Rhetorik T-shirt. His hair is black, his jaw is well defined, and he has nice eyes.

The Rhetorik T-shirt is black, it has a feather printed on it. Rhetorik is a clothing brand that Jimmy the boxing coach started up. Looks good, so easy to recognise. Sick geometric monochrome prints. Perfect for this scene. Why didn't I think of that?

'Got any ket, mate?' the bearded bloke says.

'Forty a gram. It's banging,' I say.

'They proper grams?'

'Definitely. I'll do two for sixty as well,' I say.

'Go on then,' he says. He two-steps while he talks.

Most people hate paying forty for a gram of ket; it's a bit of a price hike, but when you're in a club and fancy a tipple, what can you do?

I can't help but want that T-shirt. God damn. We stock Jimmy's brand at my shop. I think I'll get one.

A couple of girls come up to me right after. 'Got any pills?' the tall one says.

The other girl looks at me so wide-eyed, jaw rolling. She's flying. Time of her life. She's short, with chubby cheeks. She's wearing a crop top, nice flat stomach.

'Not for her,' I say. I'm desperate but I'm not a knobend,

right?

'Nah, mate, for me. She double dropped and I'm not feeling it.'

'How long ago?'

'Two hours now.'

'Go on then, three for twenty.'

'What are they?' she says.

'Gold Dust,' I say.

'Oh, nice one. I thought they'd dried up. I'll take nine coz my mates will want some when they get here.'

We do this deal subtly enough and while we're at it I get a thought: I'm too relaxed, not vigilant enough. I look about for Deano and his yobs, but all I see is people moving rhythmically with a lot of love and energy to the reliable four-four beat, giant smiles on their faces, loving life. Loving it! Attractive people. Dancey people. Cultured people. This is what it's all about.

Yet now I'm massively on edge, really expecting Deano. And when he comes, what do we do? I worry they'll find Moose on his own and do something nasty. Right, get on with it, be sharp. I have a good look around for Moose. Can't see him. Worrying more. Hurry.

And there it comes, like fate, some higher power telling me everything will be okay. The subtle fabric of the universe. I love that feeling, quite rare for me, but always powerful. When I'm there, really believing, everything will be okay. Weird how music can do that.

'Gammelan' by Lauer. Fucking banger. Those bass synths. That lighter one. Same tune that played when I met Isobel. My favourite track ever. And when he played it live at The Festival ... Good times. Perfect times. That is what it's all about.

I wade through the darkness and weave through the crowd

looking for Moose. My pockets and boxers are bulging with drugs and cash, mostly cash now. I look like I'm wearing a lumpy nappy. Amusing. How I haven't been caught yet, fuck knows. Where's Moose?

Moose is downstairs. It's much quieter here. Much smaller. He's chatting to a few mates of ours.

'Tommy! You made it. How's it going Tommy?' Rosie says. Excited, slightly husky voice. Nice green-and-silver glitter pattern on her face. I love glitter. Sexual attraction to Rosie. She's wearing white skinny jeans. A black crop top. Her skin is tanned and toned.

Focus on the matter at hand.

I want to tell her everything, but I refrain. 'You wouldn't believe,' I say. 'I've had a day stranger than Gold Dust.'

Everyone laughs. 'We just got some off Moose,' Rosie says.

'Tommy, we haven't seen you since that event you put on,' Laura says. Tall girl, mixed race. Big smile. Black meshed top with glittery sequins all over it. 'Sammy will be back soon, he's at the bar.'

The event I put on was a banger. It was the best night of my life. And the worst. Can't think about that now.

'I'm sorry I've been such a shit friend. I'm back in action now though, I'll catch up with you lot soon.'

'We have to,' Rosie says.

'I promise I'll make it happen. Got a few things on this month but as soon as its over I'm all there.'

'Happy days,' Moose says.

'Fuck me, you're actually here,' Sammy taps me on the shoulder. He's got a gleaming smile.

'Told you I'd make it,' I say. 'Let me buy you all a drink.'

'I've already got one,' Sammy says.

'I owe you one, have another.'

If this ordeal has taught me anything, it is to value friendships. I can't believe I ditched my friends for money. Fuck!

'Yeah, come on, let's go,' Rosie says. She grabs my arm and we all fly upstairs to the bar. I get a big round in. We say cheers and drink.

When people are high they get going much faster, everything happens in a rush. We get into the thick of the dance floor, dancing to the beat and smiling, everyone smiling, connected, synchronous, the whole group moving and smiling, especially Sammy. He's missed me. I feel terrible. I shouldn't have neglected our friendship.

Aside from the guilt of letting so many people down, I'm loving it. I love electronic music. I love the underground scene in Cardiff.

Moose pulls me close, 'Deano,' he says. Worried face. Tense. Rigid like stone. 'I saw him, think he saw me. Can't have him kicking off in front of this lot. We've gotta go.' Without a goodbye, we barge through the crowd, leave the club. Sorry Sammy.

'Keep your head down, I have a feeling this is going to get messy and you don't want your face all over CCTV,' I say. We leg it up the road, turn on to Queen Street. Walking now, merging into the nightlife, heads still down, there are a lot of people about, punters, promoters, the homeless. Fucking Tories.

We walk past a man lying still under a maroon blanket, I grab a wad of cash from my pocket and slip it under his cover.

'Fuck, they're still following us,' Moose says. 'Don't look back, they dunno I'm onto them, looking a bit lost.'

'Think they probably look lost on the best of days, Moose,' I say.

We pass Steinbeck the Straw, and the theatre, cross the road, pass the park and the museum. The lighting is poor. I glance back, no one is behind us. Grab Moose, pull him behind a small verge, where the bushes start. 'How handy you feeling?' I whisper.

'Fucking hell, not three big blokes handy,' he says. 'You saw the size of them.'

'I'll take two, you take the other,' I say.

His grin glows in the darkness.

The ground is earthy, covered in grass, twigs and leaves. It is cool and refreshing, perhaps the tiniest bit damp. I can smell nature, and I like it. It calms me a bit. The leaves surrounding us are small and plentiful, they're mostly shadowed, with a slight hint of dark green.

'Down there,' Moose says.

They're coming with strong strides. My adrenaline fires, body throbs. It's gloomy and they're quite far down the road, I can't see their facial features, can't tell how prepared they are. 'I'm going to lure them into these bushes,' I say.

'How the fuck you going to do that?'

I get out my personal phone, load a porn site. Click the first link. Silence media on phone. Forward video to the bit where the couple are having sex. Creep further into the bushes, Moose follows.

'You being serious?' Moose whispers.

'Trust me,' I say, grinning. 'Just take the one on the right.' The one on the right is the one with spiked wet-look hair, wearing a vest.

'You sure you want to do this?' Moose says.

'I'm sick of this shit, mate. I always showed everyone respect, time to get some respect in return,' I whisper. 'We're making a statement. We're saying, "Leave us alone or you'll regret it." No more fucking about. I want this settled now.'

'Yes, boss.'

The blokes are close. The road is quiet. The one in the

middle is the tall one with the pointy face and weird eye sockets. I hear him say, 'They can't be far now. Alright, when we get to them we deliver the message, bash them up a little and take their cash. No one gets killed.'

A car passes by.

I turn the sound on my phone up loud, rustle the bushes a little.

The blokes stop. 'Fucking 'ell can you hear that? There's a couple going for it,' Deano says, laughing.

'Come on, let's 'ave a look,' the one on the right says.

'No, let's find those lads and do the job,' the one in the middle says.

The woman's moaning and the man's groaning, they're really going for it. I turn the volume up.

'Fuck this,' Deano says. 'I'm 'avin a look.'

I jump out, crack Deano on the side of the head, hard. Sounds like he's been hit by a cricket bat. The other two appear dumbfounded. I uppercut the guy in the middle who was calling the shots. The porn couple are in full flow. Moose flies over and cracks the one on the right. It all happens in a flash, a split second.

All three of them are on the floor looking a bit sorry for themselves. I kick Deano in the head and he turns limp as a jellyfish. Three against two. They'd have done worse. But I still feel bad. You should never kick a man on the floor.

Moose is wrestling with his guy.

I pounce on the middle guy, get him in a rear chokehold. He's gasping. I know he'll be unconscious in a second, so I ease off ever so slightly. 'Stop moving or I'll give you brain damage,' I say. Surprisingly, he stops, he must know what a rear chokehold can do. 'You got something to say?' I say.

'You fucking idiots,' he whines. His face bulging with anguish, sockets barely containing the eyes, ugliness.

Moose is on top of his guy, battering him to a pulp.

The guy's squirming, 'Leave it, leave it.'

But Moose doesn't let off until there are no words left, just a gurgle. He jumps onto the guy I've got in a hold and whacks him in the face. Blood spatters on my jeans.

The guy laughs, 'Arlo says he better not have to cut off your tongue, Tommy.'

'Is that it?' I say. 'Give him another, Moose.'

Crack. I feel that one run through me.

'He wants you to set Terry up, he's looking at fifteen years if he can't get any dirt.'

'Are you fucking joking?' I say. 'Why would I do that for him? He's fucked this for all of us.'

Setting Terry up would be a death sentence. He'd have us all killed before we could stand in court.

The guy laughs like a madman. You've got to be a bit psycho to be in this game. He says, 'If you don't, Flash is gonna pay Isobel a visit, and he's gonna fuck every one of her tight little holes, then he's gonna slit her throat.'

I flip. Tighten my grip until I feel his neck throbbing, and then I nut him in the back of the head, over, and over, and over. He falls limp. His blood feels rancid on my face, my forehead is stinging. He's out cold. Blood pooling around his head, seeping into the dark, grassy earth.

'Fucking hell, Tommy, you've probably killed him,' Moose says. Moose puts his hand on the blood on the guy's head, takes a gloop of it and wipes it on the faces of the other two unconscious men.

That all-too-familiar sense of surreal sinks in, and everything is a bit of a blur as we leg it, taking an obscure route to mine around the back of the uni buildings. And I keep thinking, Fuck, what if he's actually dead?

'Get in the shower, Tommy, get that blood off you. Leave

me your clothes, I'll burn them,' Moose says.

The wet warmth in the shower closes over me and, amid the sound of rushing water, I feel strangely relaxed. Shock can have that effect. As my mind wanders, I remember back to when I first met Moose and Flash, at boxing.

I was horribly nervous when I arrived at the gym. There was nothing to be nervous about, I'd done it all hundreds of times, and yet still I doubted myself. I worried I wasn't good enough, or that I'd do something stupid.

There were a few people skipping, spaced around the room. The room had foam-matt flooring, some matts were pale red, some pale blue. The coach stood in the middle, he was medium height, with darkish skin and handsome blue eyes. He had a deep voice that commanded the room with ease. He said, 'Flat out, fifteen seconds,' and all the ropes around the room picked up speed.

I put my sports bag aside: ironically, a black holdall. I had a sip of water, found a space and started skipping. When you join a boxing club, nobody teaches you to skip. They throw a rope in your hands and leave you to it. Drug dealing is similar. Nobody gives you a how-to guide. They just put the drugs in your hands and leave you to it.

The university boxing gym was large. There was ample daylight coming through the windows. The bags hanging in the far right-hand side corner of the room looked new, clean, crisp. There was a nice, big, tidy ring in the left corner, beside the bags. The gym smelt pleasant, not like blood, sweat and tears.

This was not the boxing I was used to. Everyone wore overpriced, flashy sports gear. Leggings with super-glide technology, and climaflex fabric. Shorts with aeromax flaps and bright, look-at-me-I'm-sporty trainers with hyperflex mesh. Not the type of boxing that gets underprivileged kids off the streets.

A vibrant guy walked in, threw his bag down, looked like he owned the place. Blonde, meticulously groomed hair, pushed back with a decent hold of hairspray, short as it gets on the back and sides. The coach saw him and said, 'Yes, Flash, how's it going?'

'All good, Jimmy, geezer,' Flash said, as he took his red tracksuit jacket off. Through his white vest, you could tell he was highly athletic. His cheeky grin was infectious.

Jimmy went over to shake Flash's hand. They bumped fists, pressed their palms together and slid them backwards, finger to finger, in one swift move. A bit like a gang's signature handshake.

By the time training was in full flow, there were about twenty of us. You could tell the ones who'd been going for a while, they were all pally with Flash and Jimmy, and they were relaxed and confident. Jimmy paired the second and third years with us first years, for a bag-work drill.

I stood next to a long, heavy bag, with my hands wrapped and gloves on. Coach Jimmy sent a tall bloke with broad shoulders and a strong face to work with me.

He said, 'Hello, I'm Moose.'

'I'm Tommy, nice to meet you,' I said.

Jimmy addressed the whole class. 'Right, two to a bag. Give yourselves a number, one or two. Ones will hold the bag, twos flat out for thirty seconds. I'll say switch, you switch. And when I say flat out, I don't mean let your technique go to shit, I want to see fast explosive punches, fluid feet, good balance. Technique is everything.'

I appreciated that. Technique is, indeed, everything.

I wanted to make a good impression, so I dug those shots in like there was no tomorrow. I worked so hard I felt sick. Moose shouted, 'Come on, fucking 'ave it, everything you've got, dig, dig dig,' as he held the bag.

Jimmy shouted, 'Switch.'

I grabbed the bag and held it for Moose. I was too shy to motivate him. I could hear Flash digging into his bag from behind us. He had a thunderous punch, and he roared every time he fired. I longed for that kind of confidence.

When the drill ended, Moose said, 'You've got skills, Tommy, how long you been boxing for?'

'Since I was a kid,' I said.

'Banging,' he said. 'Always good to get more people in sparring.'

I got savagely nervous again. No one looked exceptional in the drills but you never know what someone's really made of until you step in the ring with them.

Moose and Marco got in the ring first.

Marco had a Spanish accent. He was a short, stocky man, arms the size of my legs.

I finished sipping my water and slipped on the first sparring glove. They belonged to the uni, I couldn't afford my own. With me, it was all idea, no gear.

The gloves were crisp and dry, and smelt of chemicals, not sweat. Too new, too fresh. Not enough thud. I slipped the other glove on. Relax, breathe, I told myself.

At most local clubs, funding is a real issue. The gloves are always half a decade old, damp, sweaty, rough, stinking. This was luxury boxing. I wondered if the sparring would be luxury sparring. Cushioned, for those accustomed to a softer, more comfortable lifestyle.

Coach Jimmy said, 'Right, Moose, don't take the piss. He's heavier than you but you've got the experience so just respect each other. Alright lads? Everyone watching these two, you'll have your turn in a bit. Go for it. Time.'

Marco came out gunning, swinging for Moose as if Moose

was an inanimate object, easy to hit. Moose used good footwork to stay out of range, and then hit Marco with a stiff jab on the nose. I liked Moose from then onwards.

Proper boxing requires timing, discipline, precision. Not swinging about like a twat. Blood gathered around Marco's nostrils. He wiped it with his glove. As he breathed heavily, more blood came. The red droplets glistened on the pale blue canvas.

While I watched, I shook my body out, bouncing on the spot, from foot to foot, gently, on the balls of my feet. This helped me relax, and it kept my body warm. I wanted to make a good impression.

Coach Jimmy said, 'What's your name?'

'Tommy,' I said.

'How much experience have you got?'

'Fifty bouts,' I said.

'Oi Oi,' Flash said. 'Let's have a go then.'

Coach Jimmy said, 'Go on then. Tommy and Flash, but take it easy, alright? Just a light move around so I can see what you're like.'

I was shit-scared. Flash was no doubt powerful, you could tell by the look of him. He had this confident tenacity about him that was sure to translate to success in boxing. Confidence is key. You have to believe in yourself.

Staying as relaxed as I could, I lingered outside Flash's range while he threw jabs and missed. Edged my way in, with small, measured steps. I needed to find a comfort zone just inches out of his range.

I slipped a few punches, and the moment he finished his flurry I swept in with a light overhand right. He walked onto it, and it knocked his head back, popped his nose. Blood trickled onto his lip. He grinned, stepped left, stepped right, threw his rear hand, hit me hard on the chin, and then his jab, bang on my eye socket.

The first hard punch you take in a session is always a bit of a shock. My head rang, I could hear my heartbeat, the adrenaline kicked in. I moved out of range.

'Stay sharp, you two, don't switch off like that,' Jimmy said.

Flash's personality is like his boxing. He's relentlessly determined, he will always get the upper hand. I'd hit him once, and he'd be so frustrated at himself he'd barge forward, punching and punching until he landed two. 'Persistence beats resistance,' he'd say.

Looking back, I was by far the best boxer there. I was more skilled than Flash, I just didn't have the same relentless confidence and determination. I didn't see it that way at the time, I thought I'd let myself down.

Everything in life is a matter of perspective, what we forget is that our perspective is constantly subject to change. If you'd tried to convince me that I was the best there on that first session, I would have told you to fuck off. Now, somehow, I look back and I see it all differently. It makes me think that we should try to be open to as many perspectives as possible. That's a difficult concept to truly grasp.

The water running off me in the shower is clear. There is no discolouration from blood or dirt. I feel only warmth and wetness. I don't want to move. Leaving the shower means exhaustion, headache, and fear. Leaving the shower means it's all real, and there's no going back. I want to stay here until everything is okay. But life doesn't work like that. You have to keep going. You can't give up.

Chapter 3

I'm at Isobel's front door, the wood has been painted navy blue, there's a distorted-glass pane in front of me. The doorbell doesn't work. Knock, knock, knock. Waiting. Horribly nerve-racking, all this waiting, like the first time I knocked here. Except, that time I was excited.

My forehead is uncomfortable, and there's a strange ache going right through my skull. In the mirror this morning I saw bruises and cuts from headbutting that guy last night, and my headache is no doubt accentuated by all the stress I'm under.

A figure approaches behind the glass. Please be Isobel. Can't handle her housemates right now. Door opens. It's her.

She's so fucking beautiful, no make-up, eyes big and blue against the soft pale skin of her face, cute cheeks, wavy blonde hair, bright, long, natural, so much depth, so many hues, there's something so vigorous about it. About her.

I say, 'I'm ready to tell you everything.'

She grunts.

Better than nothing, I guess.

Isobel runs upstairs into her bedroom. Bedroom door slams. I follow, slowly.

The hallway is littered with takeaway leaflets and junk mail. Her house is always warm. The stairs are poorly lit.

There are one or two indistinct items on the floor, socks maybe. Her bedroom door is heavy to open.

Isobel's room is clean and tidy, but not spotless. I can't stand spotless rooms. They're not compatible with real life. Real life is unpredictable, uncontrollable. I don't appreciate people who can't understand that. Isobel understands life in the way I do. We're so similar. In some ways, at least.

The room smells pleasant, although slightly artificial. The scent of a moisturiser with a blend of chemicals resembling a natural ingredient like cucumber. Stop letting your thoughts run away with you. That often happens when I'm nervous.

'Go on then,' she says. 'Don't waste my time just standing there.'

She always tells it how it is. It can be unpleasant sometimes, but I love her for it. She's on her double bed in the corner of the room. It's not a big room. I stand next to her wardrobe near the door. I don't deserve to move any closer.

I look around, avoiding having to say what I must. It's hard to get the words out. She's got posters and hangings on all the walls. One is a giant world map printed on fabric. The sea is dark blue, almost black. The continents are light brown, almost gold. She's coloured the places she's been to in red. USA stands out in red, and some Western European countries. We'd planned to go to the Philippines this summer.

She scowls at me.

I open my mouth, slowly, undecided what my first words should be. 'I made some really big mistakes this year, I'm sorry. I wish I'd told you everything, but I didn't want to expose you to it. I got involved in some horrible things with some horrible people,' I say.

And I tell her everything, about the dealing, my arrangement with Arlo, the Bay House, Terry, Terry's Club, all of it. The debt. The drugs in my tutor's office. Those guys last night. Flash.

She curls up into a ball under her covers and cries. The duvet cover is patterned with white, yellow, brown, blue and pink triangles in pastel shades; each triangle is about seven inches long.

'Can I hug you, please?' I say. I hate seeing her like this. She's too sweet to cry.

'Don't touch me,' she says.

She's already blocked me out. I don't blame her. I'm an idiot. Broken promises from a broken man. Why didn't you just sort yourself out? You stupid cunt. You had so many chances.

I stand motionless, wordless, like a stupid cunt. There's nothing I can say to make it better.

After the crying, she says, 'I don't judge you, everything you did was for your mum. I hate you for your lies.' She bursts into tears again, 'You really fucked it, you know.'

'I know,' I say.

Time passes. My mind is empty. Just a horrible knot in my stomach. And then I start thinking about what time really is. Is it an awareness of a series of instances and nothing more? If so, what makes it tangible, real? If nothing, then surely it doesn't exist? Maybe the concept of time is something that only exists in our minds. For fuck's sake, stop overthinking.

The sobbing stops. She emerges. Face reddened, especially her cheeks and nose. Eyes bloodshot. She says, 'I can't ever trust you, and if I can't trust you, there's no point in you being here. You are not the man I fell in love with. Just look at your face, you look like a thug.'

I don't know what to say, she's right, I do look like a thug.

She says, 'But I can't let you get into any more trouble, because then it was all for nothing, and I'm not going to let you throw everything we had away for nothing. I'm not going to let your mum suffer, just because you messed up. I've got savings, and I know some of your friends do. You should ask them to pitch together to help, you'll find a way to pay us back.'

'I can't, I've got to do this alone. I can't bring anyone else into it, it's my problem. I fucked it, and I'll fix it. I'm sick of backing down. None of this would have happened if I'd stayed true to myself, if I'd just had a bit of faith in myself instead of all that doubt, instead of being driven by fear all the time. I'm not having it any more. No more fear. I need to prove this to myself. The boxing, uni, the dealing, I threw it all away because I didn't believe I could do it.'

I close my eyes as the knot in my stomach tightens. Daylight causes a blanket of rich red through my eyelids. I say, 'And us. I threw that away too. All because deep down I felt like I didn't deserve you. I see that now, and I'm not going to repeat those shitty patterns.'

We're all creatures of habit. We repeat patterns, good and bad. Dealing with the bad ones and creating good ones is the only way to develop as a person. You can buy nicer cars, washing machines, TVs, whatever you want, but you won't be any happier unless you deal with what's going on inside.

'Stop being a fucking idiot, Tommy, there's no shame in accepting help, you know that.'

She's right, we can't get anywhere without support from others.

I say, 'My gut is telling me to do this one alone.'

'Fine. I don't care anyway. You can fuck off now.'

'I love you,' I say.

She laughs.

★★★

The night I met Isobel was undoubtedly one of the best times of my life. It was early in my first year. Sammy had made some second-year friends, and we were invited to predrinks at a house in Cathays. I was his plus-one. After the predrinks, we were going to an event that was supposed to be one of the best in Cardiff.

Sammy and I stood outside a house on Crwys Road, waiting for someone to answer the door. The door was light brown. House music boomed within. We were opposite some takeaway food places. It was the first time I'd ventured into Cathays. First years usually spend most of their time at their halls, at uni, and at cheesy clubs.

I was so excited, and I was anxious. I worried I would look stupid, or do something embarrassing. Doubt permeated everything I did.

Sammy knocked louder. The music was so loud, the door was unlikely to be heard. He was wearing black jeans and a white T-shirt. He told me he'd paid thirty quid for the white T-shirt. I couldn't help but think it was a waste of money for something so generic. I wondered if it was even ethically sourced.

Sammy was holding a pack of six Carlsberg. I was holding a plastic bottle filled with whisky and coke that I'd already mixed together at my flat. I took a sip so the alcohol would warm me. We'd decided not to bring jackets because the club would be hot, and we'd be drunk enough not to worry about the cold.

After more knocking, and me feeling that perhaps they didn't want us there, the door opened.

I was surprised to see Flash's big grin. 'Oi oi, Tommy boy, didn't expect to see you at a thing like this,' he said. He introduced himself to Sammy, they shook hands. Flash said, 'If you lot need anything, let me know.'

I wondered what he meant when he said he didn't expect to see me at a thing like this. It wasn't long before I understood. We followed Flash into the house, and past an open door to our left through which I caught a glimpse of someone who was sniffing drugs from the back of their phone. I wasn't quite sure I'd seen what I'd seen, it was slightly dark. I'd never seen someone sniffing drugs before, only in films. I felt uneasy.

A couple holding hands burst out of the dining room giggling. The girl wore a short, black playsuit, her body was fake-tanned. She had an amazing silver and white glitter pattern on the exposed part of her breast, swirling up to her neck, her face and around her eye. The guy wore black, super-skinny jeans and a white T-shirt, and his hair was incredibly sharp, short on the sides, long, pushed back on the top. He also seemed slightly tinged with tan. The couple skipped upstairs.

The dining room had been cleared of all furniture. Camouflage netting was draped from the roof. There was a DJ in the near left corner, and two big speakers next to him. He wore a black T-shirt with a big, white 'R' on it. The 'R' was filled with geometric patterns. A group of girls danced close to the DJ, fluidly, rhythmically, exaggerated smiles. Loving it.

The place was rammed with people, standing and chatting, dancing. Flash disappeared into the mix. The floor was plastic laminate, sticky from alcohol. Sammy knew people in there. He greeted them with pride, and introduced me without much enthusiasm. His shy, uncool, naïve housemate. I sipped my whisky and coke. Strong kick in the back of my throat. I passed the drink to Sammy, who gulped it.

'Let's get fucked,' he said, passing the drink back.

Through the dining room was the kitchen, equally as packed with people. Flash's voice, 'Look who I found earlier.'

He was speaking to Moose. Moose was leaning on the counter, which was matt blue. All around him, bottles, glasses, cups.

A strange intense whooshing sound came through the open window facing the back garden. I couldn't see what was out there, it was dark.

Moose said, 'Yes, Tommy! How's it going? Never thought I'd see you out of boxing, I thought you might live at that gym.'

Flash and Moose guffawed.

We exchanged pleasantries and I introduced Sammy. Another whooshing from beyond the window. I could only see the outline of darkened figures. I said, 'What's that noise?'

Flash said, 'Oi oi, Tommy boy, if you don't know, you're in for a few surprises tonight.'

Moose grinned. He said, 'Let's show him.'

The garden was large, there was no soil, no grass, just square tiles forming a patio. More people, standing, chatting. The smell of tobacco, maybe a hint of weed. The music was much quieter.

That was when I saw her. She was among a group of people, smiling, talking confidently. She wore a playsuit that had a mint-green pattern on one side, and solid black on the other, the two contrasting colours split down the vertical axis. Her hair glistened blonde, and her left eye had an elaborate pattern of gold, red, and chunky silver glitter on it. She was the most delightful person I'd ever seen. I forced myself to look away.

'Balloons,' Moose said.

That whooshing noise again. There was a guy in the corner inflating balloons with a metal device. I noticed the noise wasn't quite a whoosh, but something more like *tttttsssss-hoooowww.* The group of people around him tapped their inflated balloons together, leant back on the fence and started inhaling from and exhaling into their balloons. In seconds they'd all zoned out, their eyes glazed, wide, their puffing faces a little strange in the lack of light, their bodies rising and falling with each deep breath. Their skin turned pale, perhaps even slightly purple.

They all came out of it cackling, hard.

Moose said, 'It's good fun. You want one, Tommy? My treat.'

I said, 'I think I'll pass.'

'I'll have one,' Sammy said.

Sammy, Moose and Flash had a balloon. Sammy said, 'That was amazing, have one, Tommy.' His voice sounded slightly different.

Moose said, 'It's good but it's a bit short lived, and there's no studies on it yet. If you want a buzz have some MD, mate, it'll change your life.'

Flash said, 'He's right. Let us know if you want any, yeah?'

I said, 'I'll let you know.' I didn't even know what MD was.

Isobel was talking to a guy a bit taller than me, he had smooth body language.

I heard him say, 'Yeah, actually I'm DJ-ing tonight at the Rhetorik and Friends event. You lot all going, yeah?' He was tanned and good-looking.

Isobel said, 'Yeah, I know one of the guys that runs it.' Everything she did was composed, as if she was a celebrity who knew she was being watched. Even her facial expressions were calculated, collected. She said to the DJ, 'What's your name?'

He said, 'Alex.'

I forced myself to look away again. I didn't want them to catch me staring, or listening in on their conversation. Moose, Flash, Sammy and I stood in a close circle. Moose said, 'Time for a bump. Flash?'

Flash said, 'Oi oi! Get the key out.'

Moose took a key from one jeans pocket, and from another, a small plastic baggie. He opened the baggie, scooped out a small clump of white stuff onto the end of the key, and put it to Flash's nose.

Flash held one nostril, and sniffed with the other. The clump went up his nose quickly and smoothly. He said, 'Oi oiii.'

Moose said, 'Oi oiii,' then he keyed himself a bit of the white stuff and sniffed it.

I respected Moose and Flash, and I didn't look down on what they were doing, although it did make me a bit nervous. I was certainly curious. I was also amazed at how open they were about it. It was as if it wasn't illegal at all. I wasn't sure if it was the illegality or the bad stigma drugs had that made me feel nervous. I took a big gulp of whisky and coke.

I had never considered that Class A drugs could be associated with normal people in situations so common as predrinks. I had always thought of them as something devastating, only for junkies, like Mark Renton and Spud from *Trainspotting.*

Moose said, 'Sammy?'

Sammy felt pressured; I could see something in his tense, forced body language that said, 'If I don't do this, I'm not cool, am I?' He lowered his head awkwardly, sniffed the white clump off the key.

'Tommy's turn?' Flash said.

My heart raced. I didn't want to offend them by saying no, but there was no way I was going to take it there and then. 'I'm okay,' I said. 'I'll stick to this.' I sipped whisky and coke.

Moose said, 'Flake's a bit of a sketchy one anyway, so moreish, but there's a reason everyone loves it, no gurning, no wide eyes, no comedown, buzzing!'

Flash said, 'Tell you what, Tommy, take this bomb, put it somewhere safe like your sock. You'll have the time of your life later if you get on it. Here's one for you too, Sammy. It's MDMA.'

He gave me and Sammy a small plastic baggie each with a scrunched Rizla in it. I put mine straight in my sock.

Moose said, 'Do it as soon as you're in, or just before. It lasts a while and you don't want to be buzzing off your tits when the place shuts. And trust me, you're going to love it. MD is amazing, you'll be a different man, it makes you so confident and excited. Trust me! We'll all be on it later.'

After the predrinks, on our way to the venue, Moose, Sammy and Flash were chatting fast, loud and plentiful, like the conversation was their last, with over-exaggerated hand gestures and facial expressions. That was because of the flake.

A scruffy, skinny, ragged man approached us, 'You alright, lads? You couldn't spare me any change, please?' he said. He smelt of sweat and terribly cheap alcohol. His teeth were darkened, rotting.

'I've got nothing,' Sammy said.

'What's your name?' I said, as I got my wallet out, popped the change pocket and scooped all that was in it.

Seventy pence.

'Gary, bud. You alright?'

'I'm alright thank you, Gary. That's all I've got, sorry, mate. I'm Tommy, by the way.' I shook his hand. It was roughened and greasy. I felt bad, you can't buy anything with seventy pence.

'Thank you, Tommy. It's all good, bro.'

Moose and Flash gave him some change.

'Cheers, fellas, God bless you,' he said. One of his eyelids drooped and the outer skin was dark and rough. The other eye was intensely bloodshot.

I wondered if he even believed in God at all.

'I would have given him something if he didn't smell of

booze so bad, he's probably gonna spend it on crack,' Sammy said.

'I always think if you're desperate enough to ask, you deserve my money,' I said. 'Just imagine being so rock-bottom you have no choice but to ask strangers for change.'

'Even if you know he's going to spend it on drugs and alcohol?' Sammy said.

'Yes. What are you spending your money on tonight?'

'Yeah, but it's my money, I didn't beg for it,' he said.

'You didn't earn it, you asked the government for your student loan, and you asked your parents for your allowance. How's that any different to begging? Except for the fact you're not scraping yourself off the pavement every morning.'

'I suppose, I just think it's different. He's probably addicted, and he needs to get himself off the streets. He won't do that with more drugs.'

'Probably not, but he's not going to stop being addicted just because he can't get the money by begging, he'll turn to hard crime if he has to, mugging old ladies, shit like that. He needs support, a bit of love, a hand-up. The more you resent him the harder it is for him. Fair enough if you don't want to give him any money, that's your choice, but don't be judging him for buying and taking drugs when you're so happy to do the same. You're lucky enough to have the kind of life that you need to avoid addiction: family, support, love, all that, and enough cash from your mum and dad not to go bankrupt every time you want to get wasted. It's all the same though; a rich man getting wasted, a poor man getting wasted. I wonder what the common denominator is.'

I was a bit surprised by my outburst. I think it was my way of making sense of everything that had gone on so far. Flash and Moose had treated illegal drug taking as if it was as normal as drinking alcohol. Sammy had taken some of their coke.

Flash had even given me some MDMA for later. I didn't like the way Sammy seemed to think he was more justified in taking drugs and alcohol than the homeless person was. I thought about how helpless and isolated the homeless man must have felt to be so desperate to ask strangers for money. That put a heavy, uncomfortable feeling in my heart.

'Oi oi, getting deep there, Tommy boy,' Flash said.

Sammy stayed silent.

We arrived at the queue for the Rhetorik and Friends event. The event was held in a venue I'd never been to, Emporium Collective. People called it Emp Col for short. Emp Col looked the same as any other old building from the outside. White walls, two normal-sized, black wooden doors. No windows on the wall we queued against.

Everyone was colourful: girls in sequin tops, people with faces shimmering with glitter and vibrant paint. The energy was inviting. The contrast between all those colourful people and the city concrete was enthralling, a narrative of people finding ways to inject life into the dead, modern world.

I saw Isobel and two of her friends walk straight past the queue. They said hi to the bouncers and went straight in. I thought someone like her would never look twice at someone like me. I wanted to be the big deal, the queue-skipper, the guy that everyone reveres. I bet she'd like me then.

'You dropped that bomb yet, Tommy?' Sammy said.

'Not yet, I want to wait until we're in.' I was nervous, unsure I wanted to take the bomb at all. But I remembered Moose saying how amazing it was, and that it would make me confident. Part of me wanted to see what all the fuss was about.

Sammy said, 'Nah, mate, go for it now, we've all dropped. It'll kick in just after we go inside, you'll love it.'

It annoyed me how loud Sammy was being about it. He'd

gone from looking all nervous and scared of doing a key of coke at predrinks to acting as if he'd been doing drugs for years. Now, he thought drugs were cool.

Flash winked at me.

'I need to finish this before we go in,' Sammy passed me his can of beer. 'Wash it down with that.' He looked around conspicuously. He wanted people to know what we were doing.

I looked around more subtly, no security in sight, except at the front of the queue. A girl behind us smiled at me. Approval. Intrigue.

I thought about how this might be a good opportunity to try it, because Moose and Flash clearly knew what they were doing, and I liked them, yet I couldn't shake the anxiety. The conflict inside raged between yes and no, and my body autopiloted as I slipped the little baggie from my sock. I opened the fiddly plastic seal, and I took the Rizla from inside the baggie and swallowed it with a gulp of beer. The beer was warm and stale. The Rizla tasted of nothing.

'Oi oi,' Flash said.

'Welcome to the club,' Sammy said.

Moose patted me on the back.

I noticed Coach Jimmy at the entrance, talking to one of the bouncers, and thought, Oh shit, what if he saw me take that bomb? What if he sees me later when the drugs take hold? What's he doing here?

'What's he doing here?' I said.

Moose said, 'He owns Rhetorik, they're putting on this night. The man's got his fingers in many pies, they call him the Dark Horse. That's his girlfriend with him, Elizabeth, she does the drawings for the clothes.'

Elizabeth had long blonde hair with a peach tinge. Her movements were eccentric, her voice loud, confident. I couldn't hear exactly what she was saying.

Flash laughed. 'I've heard stories about the Dark Horse you wouldn't believe. This ain't the kinda place for that though.'

'Go on mate, you've got to tell us,' Moose said.

'Not here, too many people about,' Flash said.

I was intrigued. I made a mental note to ask Flash about it later.

A bit more queuing, into the venue, paid a tenner and walked up a narrow, poorly lit flight of stairs, which curved to the left. The stairs were metal, perhaps once a fire exit. Flash said, 'We're off for a piss, catch you in a bit.' He made a sniffing gesture with his finger to his nose as he left in haste with Moose.

You could hear the beat from the room we headed for, repetitive, heavy, inviting.

Sammy ahead of me, turned, said, 'This is gonna be banging.'

Through the second set of doors and into the room with the punchy beat. Funky techno, serious melodies, instant happiness, sound pulsed through the room, the people and me, indiscriminately.

Sammy and I lingered at the back of the rectangular room. At the far end opposite us there was a DJ on a stage. Elaborate lighting in white and green beamed, flashed and moved from the stage through a thin layer of smoke. A big light box glowed crisp white, displaying the word 'Rhetorik' in capital letters. People danced everywhere.

'His reasons for getting wasted are different from ours though,' Sammy shouted over the music.

'What?' I said.

'That tramp. He gets wasted because he's just escaping the truth that he's a tramp, and he's got nothing. Surely he has to face that, not ignore it.'

'Why do we get wasted?'

'Coz it's fun,' Sammy said.

'Maybe that tramp thinks it's fun too,' I said.

'Yeah, but you're not getting my point: it's different for us, we're not ignoring anything, we've got nothing to run away from.'

'Are you a hundred per cent certain of that?'

'Obviously!'

'I wouldn't be so sure,' I said.

He frowned at me. We bopped to the beat a little, looking around. I'd never seen so much energy and excitement in a club before. Everyone appreciated the music so much. They clapped and cheered when nice melodies sounded, and they gasped in awe when big beats dropped. I noticed I was feeling more excited than usual. The smiles around the room gave me such joy, I couldn't help but smile with them. The bomb must be taking effect, I thought.

A girl screeched, 'Sammy!' She dragged her tall friend towards us. He was wearing a crisp, light-blue shirt, dark-blue chinos, light-brown shoes. Such attire wasn't commonplace. Everyone else had on T-shirts and trainers.

The girl said, 'Hi, I'm Rosie, I'm on Sammy's course. And this is my housemate, Bento.'

I said, 'I'm Tommy, how's it going? You look nice.' She had three swirls of chunky rose glitter around her brown eyes.

Bento shook my hand, firm. Relaxed, upper-class smile, perfect teeth. Well-groomed fair hair. 'Pleasure to meet you,' he said.

Sammy said, 'You two on it tonight?'

Rosie, dancing, said, 'Course we are.' Oh, that smile!

We danced. It was dark. Above us, razor-sharp lasers in different colours, green then white then green then blue then white then green with the beat with the beat with the beat, beaming so intense like they were in high definition.

I marvelled, wondering whether my mind was playing tricks on me. Sounds distorted, wobbling through me, dancing around my ears, pulsing. Adrenaline and feel-good hormones flooded liquid bliss into my veins. Body throb, glee. Ecstasy.

'Holy fuck,' I said.

Sammy and I stared at each other, sharing something inexplicable. Oh, the smiles!

Rosie, dancing at Sammy's side, said, 'You're coming up hard. Banging!' White jeans, slim body. Bright blue trainers, moving to the beat, all sexy-athletic, sporty, slick. The smile.

'I can't stop my jaw moving,' I said.

'Third degree gurns,' Sammy said.

'*Mate!*' Moose arrived.

Flash bopping his head, hand on Moose's shoulder. The whole scene, incredible.

I threw my arms around them and we jumped, jumped, jumped, to the beat, the beat, the beat.

Light-headedness, deep breaths just to stay standing, closed eyes, vivid weirdness. Body getting rewired. Turbo boosted. Everything just so … brilliant. Fucking brilliant. Inside, outside, brilliant. Open eyes. Intense, too intense. Beauty in everyone, happiness, all the good. No thoughts, just feeling, awareness, perception. Internal rush!

'Mate, you loving it?' Sammy said.

'Loving it,' I said.

We danced wildly, that was the first time I'd ever really let go, just one hundred per cent enjoyment. All those melodies in the music, so exciting, so elating. Ecstasy!

Rosie said, 'I think I need some fresh air.'

We rushed to the smoking area outside.

I couldn't help but make eyes at everyone, loving the new

look about them, especially the glitter, and the energy in the eyes, and the female form, the skin. Everyone slim, athletic, good-looking. Healthy. Even the street-lighting was now beautiful, a warm glow over happy faces.

We chatted fast as fuck about fuck knows what. I made a million friends and I wondered whether I'd be friends with them in the morning. I wondered whether I would get addicted to the feeling. Wondered whether the confidence would stick.

But I felt restless too, like I shouldn't stay still. 'I've got to move,' I said.

'Me too,' Rosie said.

'I'll come in once I've finished this fag,' Moose said.

Flash was a few metres on from us, listing the prices of his drugs. Making a deal. Flash is a full-on fucking drug dealer. Jesus!

Sammy, Rosie and I held hands rushing back up the stairs, clammy but connected.

A lot happened, but I wasn't really paying attention to one specific thing, all of it merged into one big, beautiful moment with lights and the beat the beat the beat, harmonious electronic melodies and the smiles. Smiles all round.

Chatting to some random at the bar. Waiting for water. Thirsty. No alcohol needed. Felt too good. Big, deep breath. Air, filling me with lightness.

A girl said, 'You were at the house party.'

I knew that voice and I knew it was too good to be true. She'd noticed me. Me, that guy with scruffy hair, and old slim-fit jeans, not those super skinny ones you had to have to be cool. And ten quid trainers. And a plain blue T-shirt. Me.

'Yes. How's it going?' I said.

'Perfectly,' she said. 'I'm Isobel.' Her lips moved slowly, and her eyes – so blue. Light glistening off glitter. Smooth features in soft light.

'I'm Tommy,' I said, feeling instantly connected to her.

She said, 'Shall we dance?'

I followed her to a spot in the crowd. The room was packed, everyone faced the stage so they could experience the music with the DJ. It was all about the music. The people. The experience. Everyone was high, moving to the rhythmic beat.

Isobel danced in front of me. Mesmerising. Her skinny shoulders poised, her tight skin pale and smooth. Her playsuit clinging softly to her curves.

I stomped my feet awkwardly, trying to catch the beat. But the more I thought about the beat the harder it was to catch. I didn't want Isobel to think I couldn't dance, and the more I worried about it, the worse my dancing became.

She edged backwards, inch by inch. The hips the hips the hips. I wasn't sure if I was supposed to stay where I was, or to move towards her, or to give her space and move backwards. I stayed, like an awkward deer. Lights flickering all around us.

That guy from the party, Alex, was on the decks. He smiled humbly as he bopped and he mixed and he bopped. There was a crew of people behind him, dancing, enjoying the attention. They moved they clapped they cheered … the beat dropped and my God! Ecstasy.

The curve where her neck met her shoulders. Delightful floral scent. Her hair. The light touch of her arse on my jeans by my waist. Gently brushed my right hand against her hip. The soft texture of her playsuit. The curve of her neck, the curve of her breasts, the curve of her little stomach and the curve of her hips to her slim legs. Firm press. Deep breath. Her eyes and her smile.

A track unlike anything I'd ever heard. Such a perfect mixture of unusual, uplifting sounds.

Jesus.

Isobel said, 'This song, it's called "Gammelan".'

'It's incredible,' I said.

'It's by Lauer,' she said.

***

We got back to my bed in my halls room. I couldn't stop thinking about how lucky I was. I was nervous, but I told myself to get over it and I kissed her neck. She was soft, and she tasted fresh. She unzipped her playsuit. Toned muscle, taught, soft skin.

Buzzing, everything ten times more intense: the scent of her body and her perfume, the warmth of the duvet cover as I moved downwards, kissing her gently then firmly, gently then firmly, with the odd nibble with my teeth here and there.

She breathed heavily, thrust her hips, moaned as I slipped her playsuit down her legs, her knickers, mint, laced. Off. Kissing her clit, she moaned. I grabbed her arse cheeks, hard. Kissed harder. Her moans, louder and louder. I slowed my tongue on her, prolonged the moment.

'Come here,' she said. She pushed me onto my back, kissed me on my lips, my neck, my ear, circled her tongue on the lobe and outer, thrust into my head. Exquisite, seriously, exquisite. She rushed my top off, my jeans, my boxers. Slipped her mouth tightly around my cock, my leg twitched as she moved up and down, up and down as she played with my balls. Fucking delightful. Euphoria.

Tongue doing just the right thing, going all the right places. I worried I'd come too soon, but the MD kept things going. I pulled her waist towards me. Rubbed her clit slowly, firmly, as she sucked, sharing the same rhythm.

Breathing heavy, everything amplified. Harder, she

squealed. Slim, light body on top of me. Cock in, thrusting. My hands on her hips, rhythm, perfect waves, back and forth. Defined abs, rhythm. Intensity building with speed. Mouth filled deep with tongue. Closeness, wildness, heavy breaths. Too good to be true.

★★★

The next morning, Isobel and I had pancakes at a place called Café Sixty-Six. The pancakes were extra-thick, sumptuously fluffy. They had melted chocolate chips in them, and were served with vanilla ice cream and maple syrup.

I felt strangely emotional, as if the intensity of the night was about to equalise itself with sadness. I hadn't eaten out in longer than I could remember. Mum and I couldn't afford that kind of thing.

Isobel said, 'What's the matter?' You could tell she really cared.

I said, 'When I do nice things, I feel sorry for my mum. She's ill, she never gets to do anything.'

'That's sweet,' Isobel said. 'And sad, I suppose. I'm sorry.'

After pancakes, we wandered to Roath Park Lake. The sky was thick with whips of white and grey, and washes of deep pastel purples and reds. Yellow and orange leaves rustled on the trees, many had fallen to form a patchy blanket on the ground.

The vast silvery-grey surface of the lake reflected and distorted it all. The whole scene, so vivid and alive. I felt sad knowing this beautiful, surreal moment couldn't last forever. Knowing that Mum was in bed, eyepatch on, earplugs in, lonely as death.

Isobel slipped her hand into mine. She said, 'You're sad about your mum again, aren't you?'

I said, ‘Yes. Have you ever liked a song so much it makes you feel sad, even though it’s not a sad song at all?’

‘Yes,’ she said. ‘“Gammelan”.’

‘That’s how I feel now,’ I said. ‘This moment is so bitter-sweet.’

She squeezed my hand. I squeezed hers. The concrete path we walked was narrow. There was a scattering of tame geese, swans and ducks. Beside the path, grass, trees, and a road. A car engine broke the sound of the breeze and the birds as it droned past. Beyond the road, tall houses of various colours.

‘They’re so cute, aren’t they?’ Isobel said, about the ducks.

‘They are,’ I said. I kissed her softly on the soft curve of her cheek. She smiled.

A swan flapped its wings vigorously over the water, shooting forward with a heavy clapping sound, not much splash. You expect a swan using its wings to be elegant, but compared to birds like barn owls, they’re cumbersome, clumsy.

On the other side of the park, we found the conservatory. The conservatory was warm. Bulky tropical plants in all sorts of green grew everywhere, their forms much bolder than those of the plants outside. Water flowed down a bed of rock into a pond, making a nice, smooth, relaxing sound. Fish with metallic streaks in their scales darted through the water. The glass surrounding us blurred the real world outside.

The area exiting the conservatory had a small shop in it. There were several shelves with a selection of pot plants on them. I felt compelled to buy one, and I chose one with just a few small leaves, little, deep-green ovals.

Isobel said, ‘That’s a money plant.’

‘I wonder why it’s called a money plant?’ I said.

‘I’m not sure either,’ she said. ‘This has been lovely, can we do something this weekend?’

‘I would love to, but I have to go to my mother’s,’ I said.

Chapter 4

I've just left Isobel's and I'm feeling pretty shit, I'm not sure how to make it up to her. The road is quiet, lots of terraced houses, lots of parked cars. No people. Everyone is at work, at uni, at school, doing normal people things. I text Shady Adey, telling him to call me as soon as he gets the message, I have a way he can pay some of his debt.

'Tommy, I'll do anything,' he says.

'I'm going to text you Isobel's address. I want you to watch over her house and, when she leaves her house, watch over her wherever she goes. If there is any trouble, you call me, and you make sure nothing happens to her. Nobody at the address can know you're watching them, so be inconspicuous. This phone call never happened.'

I hang up, and I text Isobel's address to Adey.

At the crossroads where Cathays Terrace meets Crwys Road, a police car in garish blue and yellow cruises past. What if they're looking for me? Surely not.

Keep my head down. Keep walking. Dip into a coffee shop. Nice little place. An oil painting of a busy restaurant street somewhere in Europe catches my eye. Nice use of bold strokes. Red layered over white over yellow.

Taxi to a street near Moose's. Walk the last bit. Safer that way.

I let myself in. Moose is at the dining table. 'You alright?' he says.

I sit on the sofa. The cover draped over it is slightly cold, soft and smooth. The curtains are closed. 'Isobel still doesn't want to talk to me, and I've got a headache. Could be worse though. You?'

Moose says, 'More alright than you, that's for sure. Those cuts on your head look sketchy.'

'We were doing some extra sparring, our heads clashed,' I say.

'I got you,' Moose says. 'We made decent whack last night.'

'Good,' I say.

'You seen the news yet?'

I shake my head.

'You want coffee before I tell you?'

'Nah, tell me. It's going to be a rough few weeks, I'd better get used to all the setbacks.'

'A man was assaulted on Park Place last night, he's in a critical condition at an intensive care unit.'

'Jesus,' I say.

'Here's the good bit. Two men have been arrested, and I'm sure it's Deano and his mate. I reckon they legged it and got picked up later, all three of them were covered in each other's blood.'

'That is lucky. Putting his blood on them was ingenious, I owe you the world.'

'Oh, fuck all that. Just get back to being Tommy again and I'm all good, I'd never let a mate slip into the shit, you know that. We need the good times back, like the Frenzy night, that was banging.'

'Best night of my life, either that one or the Rhetorik and

Friends one where we all went out for the first time.'

'Hah, your first night on it, you loved it, that was banging too.'

'It was.' The memory puts a smile on my face. But the anxiety I'm feeling because the shit hit the fan makes me feel sick. 'Have you told Daisy about all this then?'

'Yeah. I told her Arlo got raided, and that I had some shit to help you out with, but when it's all sorted we're completely out of the game, no more. Nothing. She didn't take it too well but she'll be happy when it's all over, you know how it is. She was always well sketched-out having the stuff here.'

'I'm sorry we put that stress on her.'

'She was alright, the money was worth it.'

My personal phone rings, unknown number. Could be Adey reporting trouble.

'I don't mean to be rude,' I say.

'Take the call,' Moose says.

I answer.

'Tommy, it's Terry.'

'Terry,' I say. I hate the way he invades my personal life, knowing full well I made every effort to keep them separate.

'I'll keep it sweet, Tommy, there's a fight tonight and my guy has broken his wrist. If you jump in I'll cut five grand off your debt. If you win, make it seven.'

'What kind of fight?'

'Bare-knuckle.'

'Bare-knuckle. Jesus,' I say.

'I won't lie to you, Tommy, he's a hard bastard and he's had more bare-knuckle fights than you've had hot dinners, but he's got nothing on your skill. If you're clever about it, you'll do just fine.'

'I don't really have a choice, do I?'

'I appreciate it, son. I'll pick you up at seven.'

***

Terry and I are in his burgundy Range Rover. It's so slick, so clean it looks as if we're in a spaceship. Streetlight glows off its curves. I'm sitting in the back. The Messenger is in the front passenger seat. Terry is sitting next to me in the back. The driver is silent, almost robotic in his actions.

'You ready, champ?' Terry says.

'I'll do what I have to,' I say.

'Good.' He looks slightly less dissatisfied than usual. Terry's been in a fight or two, you can tell by the way he holds himself: confident, a man who's known victory in combat. I bet he's done some fucking nasty things.

'I put you on the card as Leon, by the way. I thought you'd prefer the anonymity, didn't think you'd want to tarnish your name in proper boxing.'

'I really don't care any more,' I say. 'All I'm thinking about is getting the job done.'

'Good boy,' Terry says. The engine purrs like an ultra-smooth, powerful cat. 'How are your mates doing in the nick then?'

'You probably know more than I do,' I say.

'Speaking of your mates, a birdy told me Din's little runt left Cardiff, he's staying in deep Wales. Lovely countryside out there, but not much chance of making cash. Are you going to tell him what a plonker he's being trying to hide out there, or shall I?'

I say, 'He's probably just having a few days to think. When I've paid my debt, he'll have the chance to pay his. Forget about him for now,' I say.

'I've always admired the way you talk to me, Tommy. You talk to me with the voice of a man with nothing to lose. I like that a lot. I'm going to keep a close eye on that little runt, don't you worry, son. Don't you worry at all. Yet one thing I still don't get, is why you're the one doing all the work, while Arlo, Din, Connor, and God knows who else, are getting all the slack. That's not kindness, not compassion. It's stupidity. Simply, they wouldn't do it for you, so you shouldn't bother for them.'

The wrinkles around Terry's eyes are more defined than usual. He looks aside for a moment of thought. Nods to himself. 'You know what, tell you what, I'll cut your debt in half this very second if you drop Din, Connor and all their mates from the deal. Thirty-seven and a half grand saves everyone close to you. That's your mum, Isobel, Ryan, Moose, Anthony, and even Arlo and everyone on Arlo's line, including Flash and all. All safe, untouched. I'll take care of the runt, and the pig, and you take care of your lot. How does that sound?'

'Sounds logical,' I say.

'So, it's a deal then.'

'No,' I say.

Terry is dissatisfied.

I say, clear and cold, 'I'm going to pay the whole debt, and you're going to leave every single person involved alone, just like we agreed.'

His expression changes again. He looks peculiarly *less* dissatisfied that usual. I'm surprised. I thought he'd get angry.

Lights shining at obscure angles on the slick paint of cars passing by, houses, warm yellow windows, walls of concrete, gates, pavements and people, shopfronts glowing as we drive through the city.

I close my eyes and visualise slick angled movements, fast, tenacious punches, precise, well-timed, knuckle bangs on the chin.

We arrive at a big, dilapidated barn. In the shadows, there

are some nice cars parked, and some bangers. We're somewhere rural, outside of Cardiff. A silhouetted house in the distance, no light coming from it. Fields edged by hedges add texture to the darkness.

At the entrance of the barn, there are two heavies. Both are wearing loose jeans, they are similar in height. One of them has pale white skin, the other, pale yellow. The pale white one is wearing a tatty blue denim jacket. The pale yellow one is wearing a green bomber jacket. There's a queue of people alongside the barn, waiting to go in. A shoddy light flickers above the entrance, so cliché.

The car door handle is luxuriously warm and smooth. My arms are trembling, my legs weak as I slide out onto a floor of stone and dirt, and some patches of short, dense grass. I take some deep breaths. Relax, Tommy. Can't fight when you're nervous.

Everyone knows who Terry is, you can tell by the way they look at us, look away, mutter under their breaths and cower in fear at his gaze.

Terry is wearing a charcoal suit, light grey shirt, no tie. He walks slowly, with a good, tall posture, but he's not very tall, probably an inch or two shorter than me. It is hard to tell because his brown brogues have a heel.

I'm wearing jogging bottoms, and underneath those, championship-red boxing shorts. I have a zip-up hoodie on over my T-shirt. There is a chill going right through to my bones. Nerves do that to you.

The heavies greet Terry as if they're enthusiastic to show they know him yet are trying to be casual about it, for the sake of appearing hard.

The barn smells of damp earth, alcohol, body odour and something a bit oily. The floor is dirty, solid concrete. There's a crowd gathered in the far-right corner, where the bar is.

They're chatting.

The mix of people is intriguing. Some are wearing cheap tatty clothes intended to look decent. Poorly cut jeans, shirts hanging too baggy or long or creased, big gold chains. They are shifty, voices too loud. Others are much better dressed. Fine suits, smooth shirts, neat shoes. Their speech is clearly articulated, their postures confident. The women scattered about are scantily clad, with heavy make-up. Everyone looks malnourished, no doubt heavy drinkers. I smell bud and cigarette smoke, hear sounds of cocaine-drip nostrils struggling to keep the leakage in. When it comes down to it, we are all the same. We are all excited by drugs, violence, sex.

A topless, barefooted man in denim shorts walks towards the congregation, clearly a fighter. The punters start firing up. The fighter is tall, muscular, looks like he could take a baseball bat to the head without flinching. Some of the punters are shouting abuse at him.

I am out of my depth, this isn't boxing, this is scummy scrapping. That bloke's twice the size of me, he would laugh me back to Cardiff.

Focus on the moment. Relax, breathe. Fighting is about skill, precision, speed, accuracy, timing, you've got all that.

'You're on sixth, what do you want to do until then?' Terry says.

'How much does my opponent weigh?' I say.

'We don't worry about weights here, Tommy.'

I picture a juggernaut, arms so big that my little fists can't get through to his face.

'I need a drink,' I say. 'Whisky, no ice.'

The bar is busy. Terry walks to one side, gets served immediately. He comes back to me, says, 'I thought you might like some good honey in your whisky. They're arranging it for you. Here's a straight one for now.'

It burns the back of my throat, warms my core. The alcohol should relax me a little, make me think less, help me trust my instincts.

Usually, I wouldn't watch the boxing matches before mine. Avoiding them helps me stay calm and focussed. This is different though, I need to be excited, firing on all cylinders. I need to turn the sickly feeling into pure determination, and rage. I can't talk myself into losing this one. Losing is not an option. I am a winner. I know what I have to do.

The crowd is getting loud, the first fight is about to start. I go over, Terry by my side. The crowd parts for him. A few people greet him as if they're unsure they have the requisite status to do so. Nobody addresses him as equal.

We get a good view at the front. There are no ropes, no barrier, no canvas. Just the mucky concrete floor. I rub my foot against it, it's not slippery, good, I can't win this without footwork. Footwork dissipates power, keeps your opponent out of range until you want to strike.

There's a man in the middle, a makeshift ref of some sort. He's actually dressed for the occasion, black jeans, white shirt.

The two fighters are opposite each other. They're both the same build, both big, athletic, muscular. The topless one I saw earlier has short black hair, a slightly receding hairline. His facial expression is calm, but I can see a nervous intensity in his brown eyes. His face is covered with scars, but beyond these his skin is healthy, almost vibrant. There's a massive scar across the top left of his chest, down to the bottom of his right rib, as if he was slashed by a sword or something. Jesus.

The other fighter is bald, his face is less scarred, except for a bust lip. Maybe he got that in training, it looks recent. His eyes are hazel, they're small compared to the size of his face. He's got big, bulbous cheeks and a rounded chin.

The ref stands aside, crowd roars, fighters tee off, determination in their faces. They don't look technically inadequate. Both have reasonably well balanced stances, hands high, guarding their faces.

Dark haired one throws the first punch, a big right-hand. Tremendous power. The other blocks it with his forearm. Crack! The sound, bone snapping on bone, and the high-pitched snap of a slap. Bald-head doesn't move his feet. Returns with a snappy jab, lands clean.

'Bald bloke, they call him the Hammerhand,' Terry says. 'I've got a lot of money on him. Just watch. The other guy, he's called The Stallion. He's no good against power, gets hit with unnecessary shots all the time. Good stamina though. Won't help him in this one.'

'Have you got money on me?' I say.

'Of course I have,' Terry says. 'But don't worry about that, that's my business.'

Dark hair is throwing loads of shots, Hammerhand taking most on his guard. Both have pretty poor footwork. There's not an awful lot of movement, and when there is, they're both miles out of range.

Hammerhand throws a double jab, and then there it is, the decisive blow. His right-hand swings big at a weird angle. Fast. Heavy. Clean on the cheek. Devastating as a sledgehammer. Force ripples through The Stallion's body. The Stallion hits the floor. Hollow thud.

Crowd so fired up now you'd think there were thousands of people here. There are just a couple of hundred. Get up you noncey cunt, they scream, come on, come on, get the fuck up. I expect the ref to get in there to start counting. Nothing.

Hammerhand kneels over his dazed victim, starts to hammer, hammer, hammer down with his giant fists. *Jesus.* Bash,

bash, bash. Ref looks at Terry, Terry looks at him, dissatisfied. Hammerhand's still bashing. The Stallion is completely unresponsive, slightly rigid, like you get sometimes when you're out for the count and your nervous system can't quite work out where it's at, body in a bit of a spasm. Blood gushing from his face, glooping around cuts, skin all crimson.

I feel sick. Hammer. Hammer. Hammer. I want to stop it. Crowd is wild, shouting, fucking have him, fucking kill him, Hammerhand, Hammerhand, Hammerhand.

Loose fleshy bits hanging from the guy's face. Ref looks at Terry again, Terry shakes his dissatisfied head.

My legs dart and, before I can think, I'm pushing Hammerhand off the guy. He's protesting, I read his lips saying, What the fuck? but I can't hear him, he's pushing my chest, I stumble backwards, I trip, hit the floor, he looks up, freezes, backs off. Terry is shaking his head at Hammerhand. The crowd boos and spits. I scowl at the ref and Hammerhand.

The Stallion is no longer recognisable. His body is limp, like there was never life in him to start with. No longer human. A fox torn apart by hounds.

Hammerhand raises both hands high above his head, roars. Victorious.

Chapter 5

'Easy money,' Terry says. 'You're lucky you're my fighter, Tommy, son. They'd have slaughtered you for getting involved.'

There was nothing easy about that. 'He was out cold, the fight was over,' I say.

'The fight's over when I say it is, alright?'

'Call me when I'm on,' I say, as I walk away from Terry.

We're two separate beasts, Terry and I, and he thinks I'm beneath him. That will be his downfall.

The light touch of the night's air welcomes me as I pass the two heavies on my way out. There's nobody else here.

There are breaks in the clouds in the dark sky, and in those gaps the stars are vivid and plentiful. I love the cosmos. It reminds me how insignificant we are, makes me feel there's so much more to everything than our stupid human brains can comprehend.

We look at life as we know it as the only possible life, this conscious material being is the epitome of success in an otherwise vacant universe. But the mathematical inevitability that there must be so much more happening out there, and so much more available to us down here, is clear. We're just too stupid to see it.

If I'd known things would turn out like this, I wonder whether I'd have started dealing in the first place. I believe things can't happen in any other way than they do. We make the decisions we do with all the resources available to us at that specific moment in time, so, what happens is somewhat inevitable, and there's no point in beating yourself up about it.

When someone like Barbs says, If I were Tommy, I wouldn't have done that, she doesn't realise that she absolutely would have, because she would be in my shoes, with my resources. To get into my shoes she would have had to endure my past. In my shoes, she would consist of my unique nature. She would be *me.* We are all equal in that way. And when Barbs says, as she often does, If I were homeless, I wouldn't beg, I'd get a shower and a job, she doesn't realise that she absolutely wouldn't get a shower and a job, she'd get a bag of spice and hit it, because she'd be in the exact shoes as the homeless, and her resources would be the same as the homeless person. The only reason she has the capacity to comprehend a different decision is because she simply isn't homeless, she simply has other resources, a different past, a different nature. You'll probably not grasp that one Barbs, but I tried. And it's not your fault. I hope we get to talk it through one day.

Dwelling on the past cannot help me now, not ever. But we're all creatures of habit, and we love dwelling on the past, as if the past means something. It doesn't, just look at the stars.

Where did it all start? Barbs would think, If he didn't start taking drugs in the first place, he'd never have gotten into this mess. But I don't think it started with the night I took MD. Plenty of people take drugs without ever selling them. I think it all started with Arlo.

***

I met Arlo at chess club at a community centre in town. The entrance was a spiked, red gate with a banner advertising a karate club tied to it. In the courtyard, there was a generic wooden bench on big grey paving slabs, and some outdoor plants along the wall. Even though there was no litter, it looked scruffy.

I entered the building, warily, shyly. It smelt a bit weird, like the essence of macaroni cheese.

There were too many laminate notices on the walls, why wasn't there any wall art? People of varying ages sat scattered about on cheap plastic seats, opposite each other at small tables with thin metal legs and tacky veneered surfaces, like the ones you get at schools.

Of course, a community centre would get little funding, because of the fucking Tories. Why fund poor communities when you can fuel projects closer to home? That's the true spirit of Tory community. 'Look after your mates' is the numero uno how-to-stay-rich rule.

Chess is the game of all games. You have to anticipate and adapt to every move, stay as many steps ahead of your opponent as you can. You can do that by reading their moves on the board, and you can also figure out their nonverbal presence, figure out the type of person they are, the type of move they are prone to making. Just like good boxing.

There was a bloke who looked a little older than me, sitting alone, waiting. The chessboard in front of him was set up and ready to go. He was pale, broad shouldered, slightly plump, with scruffy, medium length, curly hair, his face set in a slight frown. I felt nervous because I hadn't played in ages. Doubt permeated everything I did. I couldn't even go to chess club without feeling uncomfortable. That really annoyed me.

'Take a seat,' he said. 'I'm Arlo. You any good? I'm terrible, I just come here with my grandad, he loves it.'

Arlo pointed to an old man with thick grey hair who was sitting on the edge of his seat, leaning over the table so his face was close to the board. He was outplaying a much younger man who looked a little flustered, and had only a few pieces left.

Arlo said, 'His name's Patrick. Bloody genius that bloke.' Arlo's eyes were big and wild when he smiled, and his teeth were distinctly white and uniform.

Arlo really was terrible at chess. We played a few games each week, I'd play him and then move on to a more challenging opponent. It became a bit of a ritual. I wasn't great either, but I learned fast. Sometimes, I let Arlo win.

Our games weren't really about the chess. There was something comforting about our unusual setting, one that wasn't dominated by social games and superficial dramas, like who got the most wasted or who slept with who, or who was likely to get the best job and house and car on finance.

We talked about my mum often, he showed great concern for her, I appreciated that. Arlo came to chess club even when his grandad didn't, presumably to see me.

One day, we were alone, strolling, having just left chess club. Arlo said, 'Tommy, can I ask you a personal question?'

'Yes, I think so, go on,' I said.

'I've been thinking. You know your troubles with your mum? I know a guy who got fucking minted by selling drugs.'

'Right,' I said, caught a little off guard.

'He started a few businesses with the money and now he's seriously, seriously comfortable. I'm not saying you should go mental and become some sort of drug lord or anything, but when I was at uni so many students bought all kinds of things, the dealers didn't have to do much to earn good. I wish I'd done it, to be honest. I can take you to meet him if you want?'

I didn't know what to say. A voice in my head said no. The rest of me thought about Mum and me being financially comfortable for once in our lives, and I felt good about that. I imagined us never having to worry about money again.

I'd mused a few times about how easy it would be to make money selling drugs to my mates, but I'd never considered it seriously.

'I guess it could be worth thinking about.' I said the words with a strange, hesitant thickness in my throat.

'Okay, I'll take you to meet the King,' he said.

***

'Tommy,' Terry says. He's holding a glass full of whisky. 'The good honey,' he says.

Earthy and sweet, and a strong, warm kick. Tastes like heaven. The honey is full of natural sugar, energy.

'You've got about half an hour, d'you want something to punch? You need to warm up,' he says.

'Just another whisky, put a lot more honey in it this time. I'll warm myself up.'

Terry leaves me to it.

The bouncer wearing the denim jacket smirks, says, 'Fuck me, Donny, you hear that? Nobody talks to Terry like that, who's this kid?'

I shrug.

'You don't look like a fighter,' he says. 'What's your game?'

'Money,' I say.

'Prettier ways to make money than this, sunshine, you seen what they do in there?'

'I need money for my mum, a lot of it, she's ill. What they

do in there is nothing compared to what she goes through.'

He looks at his mate, rolls his eyes like I'm weird, says, 'Oh. What's she got?'

'ME,' I say.

'Isn't that the one when you're always tired? What you need that much money for? I'd love a day off just coz I'm tired, bloody hell.'

'No. It's the one where you wake up every day of your life feeling like you've been battered by Hammerhand,' I say.

He makes a strange whining noise. His colleague with the green bomber jacket has a bit of compassion on his face.

I look at the stars again, in awe. Incredible. But my heart sinks at the thought that everyone thinks people with ME are just tired. The emotion brings my mind back to Mum's PIP assessment. The assessor was supposed to confirm whether Mum was as ill as she claimed on the form. Yet, she was not a doctor. The doctors and Mum's physio had already supported Mum's application. You would have thought that was enough.

The assessor asked questions like, 'Can you walk fifty metres?'

The answer to that one is complex for people with certain illnesses, like ME. If someone put a gun to Mum's head, she could walk fifty metres. If she had to walk fifty metres every day, or several times a day, it would have a detrimental effect on her health. So, can she walk fifty metres? Not as often as she needs to. In the context of work, or social and day-to-day mobility, the answer is no. She should not have to literally work herself to death just to keep the cogs of our stupid commercialist, capitalist, materialist country turning.

The Tories hold a gun to your head and say, 'You will contribute to *our* society, or you will die.'

My favourite line of Mum's PIP assessment report read,

'She doesn't look tired.'

★★★

'Here you go, son,' Terry says.

The liquid in the glass is golden and gloopy. There's less kick this time, lots of honey, almost sickly. 'I'm going to warm up,' I say.

I don't want any distractions, so I go around the corner. There's not much space between the barn wall and the hedge. The shadow of a large metallic farm tool lurks ahead, twisted bits of metal and jagged edges. The ground is muddier than it is in front of the barn.

My warm-up starts with light movements from foot to foot on the balls of my feet, and shaking my legs and arms so they loosen up, rhythmically, gently. The darkness and the refreshing farm air make it easy to relax.

I know what I have to do. I know how to win. I have to let go. I have to trust myself.

As I warm and my muscles loosen, I start throwing technically sound shots in the air with my guard up, stance solid, relaxed, adaptable, feet moving fluidly. Everything is nice and slow, rhythmic, I imagine slipping past his big, awkward punches and delivering precise combinations on his chin. The moment you land a precise, well-timed shot to the chin, your opponent usually goes down. You don't need to be the strongest man in the world, just fast and accurate.

Awareness of the nervous, fiery sensation in my body, my breathing. It helps that it's dark, I'm functioning on touch, sound and smell.

I speed up, still flowing, throwing combinations merged with seamless footwork, and I build energy and excitement by letting go, letting everything happen without thought, without those cumbersome considerations we impose on the raw character of reality.

Now there's fire and my hands and feet are like lightning, my blood pumping with venom, a whipping sound with each punch, faster and faster with more tenacity, relentless determination, the culmination of everything I've learned.

'Showtime,' Terry says.

'Good luck,' the bouncer in the green bomber jacket says, pats me on the shoulder.

Terry and I walk through the crowd to the front. I put my bag down, take my jogging bottoms off, slowly, revealing the championship-red shorts. People laugh. Fuck them.

'Your opponent's strong but sluggish, and he doesn't like combinations, alright? He doesn't like getting picked off, either. Do the business, focus, and put some fucking power in, alright? And remember, if he hits you, it's going to hurt, like someone's set a firework off in your face, it's bare-knuckle.' Terry's words are a bit rushed. His breaths are slightly short. That means he's nervous. I wonder how much money he's bet on me to win.

'Great,' I say. An image of The Stallion's torn and bloodied face. Expel the thought. It won't get to that.

My opponent stares at me like I'm dirt, no respect. He's taller and stockier than me, must be about fifteen kilograms heavier, standing topless, abs and pecs bulging, small black shorts, big, thick legs compared to my skinny sticks. He looks about ten years older, eyes black, face unhealthy, a bit gormless, crooked. Big fists. Jesus.

Terry stands behind me, rubbing my shoulders. I'm sweating.

'Tommy,' Terry says. 'You've got to unleash hell. You're not here for tap-tap boxing. Every blow has to count, do you understand me?'

'Yeah.'

The nerves feel like a volcano of puke. No time to think, the good-for-nothing ref moves from the middle, I move in to tee off, find my range. No tap-tap boxing. He throws a punch, my feet get me out of the way. The swing, big, but he brings his hands back to his head, so he's not that shit. A shit boxer would drop his hands after he punches, a common bad habit.

He jabs, lunges a bit, misses, his defence slightly open. I don't jump on him, I'm too nervous. Don't fucking waste it next time. Make him pay. The crowd is cheering like fuck. I can't distinguish their words. Focus.

I shoot into range with fast feet and jab him. Lands clean but he barely notices.

'Christ, Tommy, give it some would you?' Terry shouts. I think he shouts it a few times, I can't tell. Forget about Terry, focus, flow, get in the fucking moment. The moment is without thought.

The guy is grinning at me, gritting his teeth. He launches a one-two, I step to the right and while he's off balance I launch a beasty right-hand over the top. His head cracks hard and clean on my bare knuckles. Throbbing sensation in the bone of my fist.

He laughs at me. 'All day,' he says. Launches at me, I sidestep again and crack him once more.

He's still laughing. 'That all you got?' he grunts.

Fuck.

He's athletic, fast, clips me a few times but I just about get out of the way before solid contact is made. I counter each time he tries going at me, just so he knows I'm not fucking about. His hands and arms absorb all my punches like I'm throwing foam at him. I need to turn on the rage, but I can't make mistakes while I'm at it.

I edge my way into range, head moving left to right, right to left, feet ready to get out if he attacks. Closer, closer, I jab, gets blocked, a right-hand of mine makes it through his guard, bangs his eye socket. I move out, he doesn't follow. In again with a flurry – jab, straight right, left uppercut, straight right, left hook. Some of those got through. He looks a little dazed. Crowd going mental.

'What the fuck, Tommy, finish him. Finish him, Tommy!' Terry shouts.

I go in for another flurry. He grunts, agitated, swings wildly. Bomb lands. Top of my head. Stings like fuck. Vision blurs. Ears ring like someone's fucked with the sound on a film. I raise my guard, tight, move legs fast. Don't let another one land.

Vision comes back sharp, he's chasing me like a bull, still grunting. His face is reddened where I hit it, his eyes are watering, they do that involuntarily when your nose or eyes have taken a significant blow.

My legs keep me safe, just out of his range. A few shots tap me, but nothing serious. I ping off at an angle and flurry with all my might, roaring, fire. Move out of range. He stops, recoups. I'm too far back to get in range fast enough. He starts coming at me again.

I fly in with a fast combo of straight punches. He gets his hands up, stops coming at me. None of my punches land. He drops his hands to see what's going on. I feint with my feet. He pulls his hands up again.

He launches at me, big hooks from all angles. I didn't expect that. One lands clean on my chin. A sickly feeling flashes through my body. White light flickers in my eyes. My legs are about to go, I grab him, hang on for dear life. My arms are around his, stifling his punches.

I gasp for air, try to get my mind back. He throws me into the crowd. I hit people and land on the concrete, next to feet shuffling out of my way. Elbow throbbing, wind knocked out of me.

People shouting, Get up, get up, finish him, fucking have him, things like that, jeering and laughter.

Dazed. Don't fuck this up, Tommy. No more losing. You can do this. I scramble to my feet, move quickly to meet him in open space. I feint a shot, he lifts his hands, I throw a huge right hook to the belly, hear his ribs crack as he gasps. Big left uppercut smacks his jaw. I'm roaring like a beast as I land a thunderous straight right. He's wobbling. I throw a flurry of punches so fast I don't even register which punches I've thrown.

Tunnel vision, all I see is anguish on his face. I keep smashing him until he's on the floor, and I keep going some more, until I realise how much of his blood I've got on me. I stop. Stand back.

He's dazed. Can't find his legs, fumbling about on the floor.

'Finish it. Finish it!' Terry shouts. He's got a horribly cold look on his face.

'He's fucked,' I say.

Turn back to see my opponent on his feet. Looks a little googly-eyed, face all over the place, but he's walking towards me, determined. Blood trickles from his mouth, down his neck, chest.

'Stay down you fucking idiot,' I say.

He laughs, spits blood on the floor. His front tooth is missing. Jesus.

In his incapacitation, he throws a punch from miles out, misses. His weight falls on me and drags me to the floor. He's trying to wrestle me, his grip is immensely strong, his body-weight hard to handle. I hit him twice on the chin while I'm on the ground, push my hips up, twist him with all my might, wriggle out before he can get on top of me properly.

We clamber to our feet. The crowd are going fucking mental, so excited, so animalistic.

My opponent is so tired and battered he almost trips over his own momentum as he comes for me. I sidestep to the right and, as the ball of my right foot touches the ground, I launch all the power I have through my hip to my upper body to my fist clenched tight on impact as it rumbles his brain unconscious. His head hits the floor like a baseball bat bouncing on concrete.

Chapter 6

Sammy is sitting in the dining room. The dining room is full of light. It is fairly long and narrow, with a big window running along it. The walls are not quite white, they have a slight hint of yellow and cream in them. One of my tall house plants with thin, lengthy leaves is in the corner of the room.

As I enter, I say, 'Hi,' awkwardly.

'Cheers for ditching us at IFOR the other night.'

'There were some guys after us, I didn't want them knowing we were with you in case they went for you.'

Sammy's face lights up. This is the first time I've given him honest insight into my other life. He says, 'I wish you'd told me, we could have had them. That what happened to your head?'

'Yes, but if anyone asks, that was Moose and me sparring. I'm sure you could have had them, but I didn't want to ruin your night. I'm sorry for being so shit this year. I've got one more thing to do in the next three weeks, and when it's done, I can tell you everything. Until then, how about you come on a little mission with me?'

'Everything? I'm buzzing, what's the plan?'

'Yes, everything. I need a lookout while I break into my tutor's office. I hid some drugs in there.'

'Brilliant,' Sammy says.

I've got the book I took from Tim's office in my hand. Sammy is by my side. We both have rucksacks on our backs, wearing casual clothes, looking like normal students. I wish I felt like a normal student.

There's a police car near the crossroads by the entrance to uni. I feel horrifically apprehensive walking towards it. Anxiety, heavy heartbeat, light sweat. Relax, Tommy, there's no need to panic. They've already made their arrests. They're just here to make the students feel safe.

What would Deano have said? No, policeman, I didn't attack that man you found, even though I was found near the scene with an accomplice and we both had the victim's blood on us. We got decked by two students – they are the ones who hurt that man. That man is our friend, trust us, honest, it wasn't us, it was two students. I feel safer playing that scenario in my head. The truth is, I have no idea what's going to happen. I just have to persevere.

There are plenty of people about, people going to the library, people coming from the library, no doubt all starting to worry about the exams coming up in a couple of months, and rushing to hand their essays in before all that. It will be a miracle if I pass this year.

The sky is grey, the thin parts of the trees above us are shivering lightly in the wind. To our right is the Arts and Social Studies Library. To our left, a mound of wet, dark-green grass, a few trees, a hedge.

'Tommy,' a voice from behind. It's Anna. Anna is a girl I sat next to in lectures in first year. Her skin is dark, her eyes brown, she's wearing glasses. She's dressed in a big, baggy chequered shirt, which is green, red and white. Her leggings are black.

Anna and a guy called Joe were pretty much my only

course friends. I haven't seen Anna at all during my second year. I never really got to know her outside of lectures. She was meticulously organised. Her notes were always colour-coded as she wrote them. She filed them appropriately before she left the room.

Anna says, 'It's nice to see you, Tommy. I thought you'd quit uni and left Cardiff, until the other day when someone spoke about you. I was in the library and two girls were talking about a Tommy who was a boxer and going out with someone called Isobel. I remember you talking about a lady called Isobel last year, so I knew it was definitely you they were talking about, but they said lots of particularly condemning things, all centring on the premise that you are a big, big drug dealer. I hope I'm not overstepping the mark telling you this, but when I saw you I thought it was only right you knew people are spreading rumours like that about you.'

'That's sweet of you, Anna.'

She eyes the cuts on my face.

Sammy says, 'He got those boxing—'

I butt in. 'If you come across anyone talking about me again, you should tell them you're my good friend, and that I tell you everything. Tell them I got those scars on my face because some terrible people are after me, because I owe a huge debt to the kingpin of Cardiff, and I'm probably going to be killed in less than three weeks if I can't pay it. You haven't seen me much this year because I've been running a huge drug operation, supplying kilograms of almost everything except heroin and crack to all of Cardiff. Actually, add the part about heroin and crack, and say I deal spice to the homeless too. Tell them I'm a millionaire, that I've got three houses, two businesses, and that once or twice, I've almost killed a man with my bare hands.'

Anna giggles, 'Oh, Tommy, you were always delightful.'

She rolls back the long sleeve of her shirt and checks her watch. 'Anyway, I'd better get a space at the library before they're all gone, see you soon maybe.'

'See you soon, Anna,' I say.

'How much of that is true?' Sammy says. 'I always hear random things about you, but I tell them it's all bullshit, I'm your housemate, and I would know.'

'Strangely, a lot of that was true, but it isn't like it sounds. I can tell you everything when it's all over, in three weeks. Whatever rumours you hear from now on, feel free to tell everyone you're the mastermind behind the whole thing. The more confusion, the further people will be from the actual truth.'

'I'm gonna make up so much shit. I'm gonna tell them you're my bitch, and I have a penthouse where I fuck coke-whores on beds of money while you clean the kitchen.'

'You're mental,' I say.

We reach my tutor's office. The corridor is empty. I knock on the door. Wait, praying, listening. No answer. Pray some more. Still no answer. 'You wait here, if anyone comes, cough loudly. If they attempt to go in the room, stop them at all costs,' I say.

'How am I meant to stop them?'

'You're a smart man, think of something!'

Sammy's face is like, True, I am a smart man, I will think of something, no problem.

I push the door open, it's still on the latch. Thank flying fuck for that. In I go, door closes behind me, like clockwork.

I glance over the room, looks just like we left it. It's lighter in here now. Except, a baggie in the corner near the door. What the fuck? How could we be so stupid. I swear we checked the room three times over. Jesus. I pick the baggie up, there's nothing in it, shove it in my pocket. Look around for anything else we might have left. Can't see anything.

I return the book to where I got it from. Quietly pull a chair under the roof tile.

The murmur of a voice in the distance. Loud coughing from Sammy. Shit! I move into the corner, stand silently.

'Hello,' a woman says.

I don't recognise the voice. I've got excruciating anxiety and a heavy heartbeat.

The sound isn't clear through the door. 'You're not waiting for Tim, are you? He's not back in the office until Monday.'

'Oh, no, I'm not. I'm just looking at these notices,' Sammy says. 'I want to see if there are any short story competitions advertised, I'm a top writer.'

'That's great,' the woman says. 'You know, there are great resources online for things like that, you could check out the National Association of Writers in Education competition listings for a start. What are you studying?'

'Actually, just Astrophysics, but I like to write. I wish I'd taken English Literature, they should have let me take both degrees at once really,' Sammy says.

Of all the times to take the piss out of someone, now's not it, Sammy! Wrap it up would you.

'That's lovely. Maybe you could do an MA in Creative Writing when you're done with physics,' she says.

'Astrophysics,' he says.

'Right,' the woman says.

Silence.

'Anyway, I'll leave you to it,' the woman says, finally.

I wait a while, hear the faint sound of a door opening and closing. Climb onto the chair quietly, cautiously, I have to stand on the arm for extra height, it's hard to balance. Slide the tile aside, feel around up there. Nothing. There's nothing fucking there. No holdall. Just tiles and wooden runners. Except, what's this? Feels papery. Pull it closer with the tips of my fingers, fiddle to get a grip on it. Small, blank piece of paper. Turn it over.

Meticulously fancy handwriting, 'You should have closed the blinds.'

***

We cannot control what life throws at us. There will always be opportunities and setbacks, and everything in between. Those who struggle in life respond to life's circumstances differently to those who don't. Rather than trying to control the wild world around you, your best bet is to control how you respond to the good and the bad.

A few years ago, and in this situation, I would have given up. With those drugs gone, my chances of paying Terry's debt are pretty much zero. I need every penny I can get. It took me over fifty boxing matches to learn that you should never give up. But that doesn't mean you should continue repeating the same losing mistakes over and over. That would be stupid.

I hadn't been going to the boxing club long before I started training for the championships in Cardiff. It was a long haul. I trained every day. That doesn't mean I pushed my body to its limits every single day. I had adequate rest days, I ate well most of the time, I trained my mental focus with meditation. I was ready to win.

Yet when I got into that ring, somehow, I threw it away. Something in me just didn't believe I could do it. Logically, I knew I was capable of winning. But I had a little sinking feeling in my heart that said, 'You're just not a champion, Tommy. People like you don't win, not in boxing, not in life.' I tried to push that thought out, to ignore it. That was the wrong thing to do. I should have faced the adversity head-on.

When you box, especially in an important match, your perspective becomes incredibly narrow. You barely hear the crowd, you barely see what's around you. Your opponent's face, their body language and their movements are all you focus on. You try to expel all thought and let your subconscious take over.

In the first round of my championship match, I managed to expel all thoughts, except one. The thought was, 'I can do this.' I came out against a great opponent and found I was fast and relaxed enough to hit him without being hit, and my reactions and defences were fast enough to get away from him when he tried to hit me. Yet I was still reserved, I couldn't let my shots go. I was worried about being hit, worried about making a mistake. This meant he threw more punches than me, and even though few of his punches landed, he just about took the first round.

In the second round, I started thinking, 'Fuck, although I could win, I'm going to throw it away, I just know I'm going to throw it away.' So, I was even more reserved. It was like a self-fulfilling prophecy. Because I told myself I might throw it away, I boxed in a way that ensured I threw it away. My opponent would make a mistake, I'd make him pay for it with fast hands and feet, and he'd retaliate with more punches, more bravery. I am not a coward. Something was preventing my bravery, my flow.

By the third round, I had given up on myself. I barely threw any punches at all. And yet he still struggled to hit me.

The match was close, even a shadow of my potential was almost good enough. If luck had been on my side, the judges might have picked me. They didn't.

I felt as if someone had died. I wanted to cry. I wanted to

die. I had worked so hard for it, and I had the ability to win. So why hadn't I won?

That boxing match felt like a summary of my life to that point, encapsulated in three, three-minute rounds. I tried so hard, tried and tried and tried, and yet somehow, life kept getting harder. There was no lucky break.

While I was depressed, in bed in my tiny little halls room, staring at the ceiling, shutting myself away from the world, I tried to blame losing on the fact I had to look after Mum, that I had to study, and I reasoned that the other competitors didn't have those troubles. I blamed myself for not training hard enough, for not having what it takes to be a champion boxer. But it was all bullshit. I knew I could have won. And I didn't know what I needed to do to fix that. I hurt so much inside and I knew that whatever it was I had to face, it wouldn't be easy.

Part 2

Chapter 7

Arlo and I walked along a road in an affluent area in Roath. It was dark, the street lights glowed softly. On both sides of us there were large, gated residences, neatly trimmed garden hedges, expensive cars. It was quiet.

Pangs of nerves put me on edge. I wondered what Arlo was thinking, he wasn't speaking. I worried the King would have a pile of cocaine on the table, that he'd shove my head in it as a test of character, an initiation.

We arrived at a honey-coloured, wooden gate. White walls protected the tall, white building. On the intercom, the lights from the buttons for each apartment glowed yellow.

Arlo dialled a call. He said, 'We're outside.'

My nervousness intensified. I worried the police were watching the place, or I'd do something stupid to offend the King.

A car whispered past, too slowly, as if it was watching us.

The arced gate opened electronically, parting from the middle. The drive was full of white, gleaming stones. The front door was white, with small square windows with artsy rippled formations in thick glass.

Although there was much white around us, the apartment was yet to be named the Whitehouse. That happened later.

There was a buzzing sound coming from the front door,

Arlo pushed it open. The buzzing stopped. We walked up five flights of stairs, no words, to the top floor. The King's floor.

There was a big, clean window from which you could see plenty of Cardiff. Mellow, static lights, hard-edged buildings, moving lights, blurry trees, shadows.

Arlo knocked on the apartment door.

'Come in,' a voice said. The tone was younger and friendlier than I expected, with a slight Welsh accent.

The room was spacious, with tall ceilings. The window blinds reached from floor to ceiling. I imagined it would be nice and bright in the daytime. The flush ceiling-lighting was ample, artificial, on the lower setting of a dimmer-control switch. The floor was formed of grey wooden tiles, of three slightly different shades. You could see the grain of the wood, faintly, through the grey varnish.

There were three black leather sofas forming three sides of a rectangle, facing a massive, ultra-thin screen on the wall, like a small cinema. The screen was being used as a computer monitor. There was a glass coffee table in the middle of the sofa formation.

The King was sitting in the middle of the short sofa, directly opposite the screen. He closed his laptop lid, the large screen went into standby. He looked as young as I was. Short, sharp black hair on the sides and frivolous, mid-length up top. He had a healthy facial structure. Stood to greet us with a strong, natural smile. There was no darkness in the skin surrounding his big blue eyes. 'How's it going, bro?' he said.

Arlo and the King greeted each other with a fist bump and a slip-out.

I couldn't help but admire the King's handsome facial structure. I remember thinking about something I'd read once, about mouth-breathers. Nasal obstruction due to various factors, including inflammation, causes breathing to occur through the mouth instead of the nose. This affects the shape of the mouth: the tongue drops, the face lengthens, the teeth position narrows. Your tongue is supposed to sit in the top of your mouth. I was overthinking because I was uncomfortable. The King was certainly not a mouth-breather.

'Tommy, this is the King. King, meet Tommy,' Arlo said.

'How're you doing, Tommy?' he said. His sporty-red trainers were almost luminous in the darkness. He was wearing smart black skinny jeans and a black T-shirt.

I was amused, having expected a suited, middle-aged man. Not a hipster.

'I'm okay, thank you, how are you?' I said.

'Good, I'm good, bro,' he said. 'Take a seat, d'you want a drink? Beer? Water? Smoothie? Orange juice?'

'Orange juice, please,' I said.

'Don't worry, I'll get them, you two talk,' Arlo said, disappearing into the kitchen.

Why do we usually associate mouth-breathers with bad looks? Is that cultural prejudice or is it natural selection? Natural appearance is a good indicator of health. Health is naturally attractive, animals breed with the strongest, the healthiest. But we're not animals any more, are we? Just relax, Tommy.

'Arlo tells me you're writing a book?' the King said.

'I am. Well, I'm trying … I want to, one day.'

'That's awesome, bro, what's it about?'

'I'm not sure yet. I want to write an epic fantasy, something really escapist and magnificent, but every time I start writing I end up writing *Lord of the Rings*,' I said.

Arlo put our drinks on the table, sat down opposite me.

The King smiled, said, 'I love reading that kind of shit, bro. You know, *Lord of the Rings* has loads of deep meanings in it, like when Saruman's Orcs chop down all the trees, that's all about imperialism, but it's also got environmental themes, about people destroying the earth for personal gain.'

'I must admit I've never finished the book, it's too long and slow for me, but I love the concepts, and the films,' I said.

'There you go then, bro, you could write the snappy version of *Lord of the Rings* so people who hate all those pages of description still enjoy its magic.'

'True, and I would love to write something with loads of political stuff in between the lines, Corbyn is Gandalf, don't you think?'

He laughed, 'Bro, Corbyn is more like Radagast. But who's May? She can't be Saruman, she's too fucking weak. I suppose she's just an Orc that was in the wrong place at the wrong time.'

'I guess Blair could be Saruman. He was a traitor, a warmonger for a higher power,' I said. 'But he's nobody now.'

'I heard he still makes a fuck ton of money advising organisations in the Middle East, and from public speaking and things like that, bro. He's an absolute war criminal. Funny how you get certain status and you're basically above the law.'

'I know, there's so much innocent blood on his hands, how does he sleep at night? I'd have to kill myself,' I said. 'It's everywhere though, the rich getting away with everything, like the bankers getting bailed out after crashing the economy,' I said.

'They're all psychopaths.'

We all took a sip out of our drinks in strange synchronicity. Arlo was quiet, looking, thinking, listening.

The King said, 'But you can't talk about this shit to normal people, they'll just call you a hippy conspiracy theorist.'

'There are loads of people who think like us, though. I think the media just makes out as if everyone believes their mainstream narrative; they have to, it protects their bullshit. If you got everyone who thought Blair was a war criminal to speak out at once, together, there would probably be enough momentum to have him at least investigated or something.'

'Divide and conquer, the war on free thought. We should unite everyone and expose the truth, how would you even start, though?' the King said.

'You'd need to gain some credibility first, make people realise not everyone who challenges the mainstream schools of thought is a hippy or tin-hat freak. Show that modern day hippies have some substance.'

'Bro, we should do a podcast, call it "Modern Day Hippy Talks", chat about these things and see whether we can change some minds.'

Arlo laughed, 'That would be epic.'

'Let's do it,' I said.

'Anyway, bro, you wanted to get some product?' the King said.

My enjoyment of the conversation disappeared. Even talking about buying and selling drugs seemed wrong. 'Possibly. I'm thinking about it. I just wanted to know what I could get, how much it is, that kind of thing.' I'd rehearsed that line in my head many times. Such a simple line, but a life-changing one.

'Well, I can do mud for three-fifty a Z, or flake for about seventeen hundred, it's primo Mexican. The mud's high grade. Or if you want pills, ket, acid, changa, 2CB, 2CI, 1P-LSD, grade, pollen, let me know and we'll talk prices.'

I didn't know what half of those things were.

'I think I need to start smaller,' I said. 'I'm skint, and I'm not sure how much I'll be able to sell, to be honest.'

'He's a good bloke, Mark, how about giving him a kicker?' Arlo said.

'Yeah, we can do that too.' He stopped to think for a second. 'How about I tick you an eighth of mud, and you can pay me sixty quid when you've sold a few bags.'

'When would I need to pay you back?' I said.

'Oh, don't worry about that, no time limit. It's only sixty quid, just pay me when you've sold some. A friend of Arlo's is a friend of mine. You can split that three-point-five into five lots of point-seven and sell them for thirty each. Pay me back, reinvest the profits and off you go. You keen?' the King said.

Everyone knows that being indebted to a drug dealer is a bad idea, but this didn't feel like that. The King seemed genuine, and down to earth. It didn't feel like I was getting into anything serious.

There was an ocean-green tint running through the glass in the coffee table. Darkness permeated the glass, except for at the edges, where the light concentrated and brightened. There was nothing on the table except for a thick, peach-coloured candle in a clear glass jar, and our drinks.

'Okay, yes please, I'll take that,' I said.

'Here's my current number.' He gave me a small piece of paper with the number printed on it.

'Thanks,' I said.

'Don't ring me with your personal phone, get a burner. You can get everything you need on City Road. I change my number every two weeks, never come here when you can't get hold of me, just wait and you'll receive the new number. Never text either, only call. I never have stuff here, so get hold of me tomorrow and I'll deliver to you.'

The door buzzer rang. He lifted the handset, said, 'Hello … Alright, bro, opening the gate now.'

'We better shoot off,' Arlo said. 'The King's a busy man.'

We said our goodbyes and left. On the stairs, we passed a

short bloke with a slouchy neck, double chin, and bowl of brown hair above beady brown eyes. Behind him was a thin blonde-haired bloke about my height, intense staring eyes, a bit jittery in the jaw. We all nodded at each other and carried on.

When the gate shut behind us, Arlo said, 'You see those blokes we just passed? The short one was Din. He's a big deal. The other was Connor, his right-hand man, he's alright.'

★★★

My halls room felt claustrophobic, as if the walls were slowly moving in on me. There was little daylight, except for the one window, which didn't open more than a few inches, probably to stop you from jumping out.

My money plant was on the windowsill, still small, but plump and sturdy. Rich, deep green.

I sat at my cluttered desk, next to my scruffy single bed. In front of me, a set of digital weighing scales, some small plastic baggies, an eighth of MDMA in a freezer bag, a metal spoon, and a small drinking glass. Pens, papers, my chunky, ancient laptop, a thick poetry anthology. I was looking forward to getting stuck into poetry.

You can never undo a crime. The moment you commit a crime, you are forever a criminal, but a crime is not intrinsically wrong. Still, I couldn't shake the feeling I was opening Pandora's box.

I was in possession of Class A drugs with intent to supply. Getting caught could result in life in prison. I would unlikely ever get that sort of sentence for handling an eighth of MDMA, but the fact it was even a loose possibility caused a heavy knot in my stomach.

I felt no guilt for what I was about to do. Barbs and her

mob of angry mother friends would say, No! How could he do it all without guilt. A Class A drug dealer, with no guilt? What a psychopath! Bring back the death penalty.

Come on, Barbs, it doesn't take a genius to realise MDMA is a lot safer than alcohol. It makes you feel a fuck load better too. Imagine having a bunch of people all lovey and wide-eyed when the clubs kick out, as opposed to those fucking boozy punch-ups that cost the NHS and police millions every weekend. Not to mention the cancer, liver damage and everything else alcohol brings.

I didn't think it was okay to go out gurning every weekend. I just thought that a bit of consistency would go a long way. Banning alcohol would at least demonstrate some integrity. But nobody would have that. Imagine a political party saying, we're going to be consistent, we want to protect your health, we shall ban alcohol. Everyone would go fucking mental. Inconsistent cunts, I thought.

I was getting fired up. I took a few meditative breaths to relax.

I told myself I'm not doing anything bad. I will only sell to friends, and it's better they get good quality MDMA from me than some sketchy shit on the street.

My heart raced, I picked up the MDMA and put it in the glass. I broke the main chunk of crystal with the spoon. The scent was a sort of fusion of bitter chemicals and a hint of aniseed. Arlo had told me that all good MDMA smells a bit like aniseed. The colour was yellowish-brown, glossy. The King had told me not to crush the crystals too much, because the crystal texture is a sign of quality. Nobody wants a fine, powdery MDMA.

I turned on the scales, the display glowed blue, put a few chunks on the pressure pad. 0.3 grams. Another chunk of similar size. 1.1 grams in total. That taught me the rocks varied in density, which meant estimation by eye would be nearly impossible.

I took that chunk off, put a smaller one on. 0.6 grams. I wasn't sure how pedantic to be. It took a while of fiddling around, adding and subtracting chunks of various sizes, to get the scales to read 0.7 grams on the dot. Creating five bags of MD of exactly 0.7 grams each took much longer than expected. I hoped the process would become more efficient as my experience increased.

I hid the scales and empty baggies under my mattress, and the five bags of MDMA in a shirt pocket in my wardrobe. And then I knocked on Sammy's door.

He said, 'Come in.' He was sitting at his desk, doing uni work. Flashy set of speakers next to his nice TV behind his sleek laptop.

'I need to know I can trust you,' I said.

'Mate, of course you can,' he said.

'I just got some MD, and I'm selling it thirty quid a gram. I'm desperate for cash, and I want to help my mum out. Next time you want some, come to me.'

'Bloody hell, mate, I never put you down for a drug dealer. Why the hell didn't you get me in on it? We could have been ballers, we would have got all the girls.'

'That's exactly why,' I said.

'Whatever. Where did you get it from?'

'Obviously, I'm not allowed to say.'

'It's all a bit risky, isn't it? Why don't you just get a job?' he said.

'I don't think seven pounds an hour would quite cut it. I'm caring for Mum every other week, got lectures, uni work, and by the time I've covered my expenses and given Mum some money, I'd be a zombie.'

'I work when I'm at home,' Sammy said. 'Minimum wage.

It's not that bad.'

I laughed, 'Your mum washes your clothes and cooks your dinner while you're at it.'

He looked a little embarrassed.

Don't forget that tidy little allowance, the presents they buy you, the clothes, and the food they stock the fridge with, I thought, but I wasn't ruthless enough to say it.

'Anyway,' I said, 'don't tell anyone I'm selling and, as you live so close to me, never ring or text me about it, just talk to me when I'm with you.'

'Okay. We're going out Friday, aren't we? I'll have one for that. You coming? It's gonna be sick.'

'I have to go to Mum's on Thursday. I'll get you a bag now.'

My first deal was as simple as that. I handed Sammy the bag of MDMA. He looked at it closely. 'Nice one,' he said.

The thirty pounds he gave me felt smooth in my hands, three ten pound notes, satisfyingly firm.

By the time I left for Mum's, all five bags were sold. Moose had two, Rosie had the other two, one for her, one for Bento. They all had a great night.

After I sold the eighth, I got an ounce. I paid for part of it with what I'd earned from the eighth, and I got the rest of it on tick. I sold strictly to my trusted friends only, so sales were dependent on them going out to the sorts of nights where you take MD, which wasn't all that often. Isobel and her friends also bought their stuff from me.

Between my good friends and Isobel's good friends, I was selling about half an ounce per week, which was a profit of around three hundred pounds. It was too easy. The risk was almost zero. It didn't feel wrong, and it didn't feel dangerous.

When I realised that there was a chance to make a life-changing amount of money during my time at uni, I couldn't help but spread my wings a little. I told my friends that they could give the number of my burner to other friends who wanted MD.

Everything needed to be done meticulously. There was no room for error whatsoever. Within a few days of allowing friends to refer other friends, my phone was ringing regularly, and I sold out fast.

People were never allowed to come to mine to buy drugs. I didn't want people coming in and out of my halls' room all the time. My housemates were none the wiser, except Sammy. So, I delivered. To save time, and to kill two birds with one stone, I always delivered by running to the location of the drop. That way, my fitness improved for boxing. I was literally running around like crazy, everywhere. Nobody would suspect a student going about their daily exercise routine in Cardiff University training gear of dealing drugs. Inconspicuous.

I changed my phone every two or three weeks. Each time, I made sure to go to a new shop. I went to ones that would not ask me for ID or proof of address when registering the phone to the network. I did not transfer the numbers from one phone to the other using the contacts stored on the SIM card, as most dealers would. Each phone has an International Mobile Equipment Identity (IMEI) number used to identify the device. When you put a SIM card in it, and that SIM card registers to the network, there is likely a record of that IMEI number paired to that SIM card. There is a record of every call that SIM card has made. When you put the old SIM card into the new phone to transfer the contacts from one to the other, the SIM card gets signal, registers to the network, and the new IMEI is associated with the old one. That leaves a trace of connection between each burner you use. All the calls on the old IMEI could probably be associated with the new

IMEI. Instead of using the SIM card to transfer numbers, I wrote them all out by hand, entered them manually onto a brand new SIM card in the new phone. Meticulous.

★★★

Everyone must have liked the way I did things, because they kept coming back for more, and referring more people to me. I gave anyone who referred their friend to me a referral bonus, usually a free bag of MD. I ran it as if I was running a business. I was always on time. I was honest about the fact they were point-sevens, not full grams. Reliable.

Some of my regulars, like Bento, who seemed to go out all the time, were clearly buying it from me and passing it on to their friends. The stupid thing was, he wouldn't even negotiate a discount. He'd buy five bags for a hundred and fifty quid. I told Bento that he'd be better off buying an eighth off me for seventy-five quid, splitting it into point-sevens and selling it on to his mates at thirty each.

He said, 'I'm not a fucking drug dealer, Tommy.'

I expected a bit of a condescending, negative response like that, so I calmly told him, 'Actually, you are. Supply is supply, whether you're making a profit on it or not.'

Bento took the initiative and started buying larger amounts and passing them on to his friends. Bento's network expanded nicely, and before we knew it, he was buying ounces from me regularly. With a little persuasion, many of my regulars did the same. That meant less running around for me, and more revenue per sale. Efficient.

Aside from business costs, such as buying customers a drink or two to show them my appreciation for their loyalty, taxis when I was running late, running shoes, training clothes, and so on, I kept every single penny; I covered basic living costs for me, and the rest went to help Mum.

Mum got better food, supplements, and cannabis in the form of CBD oil – the stuff that doesn't make you high. When she asked how I earned so much extra money, I told her part of the truth. I told her I was providing one of those on-demand delivery services, like Uber Eats. Technically, I was. People wanted drugs. I delivered them.

Funny how a morbidly obese person at death's door, with a severely dysfunctional junk-food addiction causing horrifically debilitating metabolic-disease symptoms can get a Maccies delivered any time they like, but delivering MDMA to a healthy scholar for sensible recreational use is a big no.

Yes Barbs, I did just compare food addiction to drug addiction. Both can ruin lives. One is socially acceptable. The other is not. But it's relative, isn't it? Something isn't inherently wrong. Drugs are not wrong by nature. Just like food isn't. The *wrongness* is circumstantial. I hope you see that.

The Oxford English Dictionary's definition of a drug is: A medicine or other substance which has a physiological effect when ingested or otherwise introduced into the body.

Food, a substance, most certainly has a physiological effect when ingested. Food is a drug. And food can have detrimental effects on our health. We just choose to view it in a different way.

I explained my theory of food falling under the definition of a drug to the King once. He liked it a lot. The King and I had short but sweet conversations every time he delivered the MD to me. I respected him a lot. The way he did things was inspiring. He was a full-time drug dealer. He changed his burner every two weeks. He had several safe houses for reducing risk. He also ran several legit businesses. He used those businesses to wash the drug money, so it was easier to spend.

The King's businesses were highly successful, even without

the drug money being pumped into them. The most successful was an import business. He'd get container loads of novelty items – like children's themed pens, pencils, notebooks, rubbers, rulers, things like that – for pennies from China, and sell them for fifty times the amount in the UK. He had a chain of ice cream vans around Wales, and a chain of fish and chip vans. Mark was the richest, most down to earth man I knew. I wanted to follow in his footsteps.

A day before I left Cardiff for the summer break, the King summoned me to his apartment. I hadn't been there since the first time we'd met. It was as pristine as when I was first there. We sat opposite each other on the sofas. We had a glass of cold, filtered water each, set before us on the coffee table. Mine had a slight smudge where my lips had been.

Mark said, 'I'm leaving Cardiff on Monday, and I want you to have my line. I'll introduce you to my suppliers tomorrow, and I'll call all my customers to tell them you'll be dealing with them from now on.'

'Just like that? Jesus. Why are you leaving?'

'When I started dealing, I promised myself that when I had five hundred grand cleared in my bank account, I'd quit and go travelling to find proper meaning. You'd have thought five hundred grand would be easy to save up doing all the things I do, but the more you earn the more you spend on life. And no matter how much money I make I feel empty, bro, I need to find something real, before I go mad.' He took a slow, composed sip of his water. 'Just yesterday I checked my Bitcoin investment, I bought a load of it a few years ago. I only cashed in half and I won't need to lift a finger for money ever again. You should buy a grand's worth the moment you leave this place, Tommy. Crypto is going to change the world. Hold on to it for as many years as you can, cash in when you've hit the million, bro.'

The thought of a million pounds was so distant, so alien, I couldn't help but smile.

He said, 'Anyway, that's a talk for another time. What about my line? I profit about five to ten grand a week on it. It's all yours, just say the word, I'll hand over tomorrow. I like the way you do things, bro, we're similar, you deserve it, you're the man for the job. You can have it all, Tommy.'

I turned the King down. I told him that Mum didn't deserve to spend a whole summer alone. Part of me also felt I'd fuck it up, that it was too much risk, that I'd end up in prison. There were too many unknowns.

★★★

I was home for summer. Mum and I were talking. She was in bed. Sunlight battled the closed curtains. The brightness was giving her a headache. It was stuffy, despite the windows and the bedroom door being open.

'So, you've finished a whole year at university. I'm so proud of you, how did your exams go?' Mum said.

'They definitely could have gone better, I wasn't as prepared as I could have been because I spent so much time training for boxing,' I said, thinking about the dealing, boxing, spending time with Isobel, and everything I did that distracted me from uni. 'But I only needed forty per cent this year. I'm going to try harder next year,' I said.

'Well, I'm sure you'll do brilliantly,' she said. 'I'm so sorry about the championships. What do you think happened? I wish I could have come to support you.'

'Yeah, that's why I lost, I didn't have support,' I said. 'Only joking. I'm not sure what it was, I just threw it away somehow. I was too reserved, I couldn't let go. I knew I could win, because the other guy wasn't any better than me. He wasn't stronger, faster, or smarter, but something stopped me moving like I should have. I'm just not sure what was holding me back.'

'How did you feel afterwards?'

'Like shit, obviously.'

'Yes, but what else, how did you really feel?'

A knot formed in my chest, and a thick lump clogged my throat. 'Like nothing can ever fucking go right, no matter how hard I try,' I said.

'I'm sorry, my angel, that's devastating to hear. You need to dispel that doubt in yourself, it will go right. And the harder you try the more it will, but you need to have faith in yourself, you need to really believe you can do it. Then everything will be different, and not just the boxing; once you recognise your own self-worth, everything will start falling into place.'

I didn't like that. I didn't like hearing I had no self-worth, and I snapped. 'Like it did for you, right?'

She scowled.

I walked out, sat on a bench on a hill that overlooked the sea. The sea was topped with white and grey, beyond that, dark blue. I focussed on the waves coming into the shore, no thoughts, just the sound, the sight, the movement. The waves were a good size for summer. Messy, with a strong onshore wind. They rolled in, deep and soothing.

When I got back, Mum was still in bed.

I said, 'I'm sorry. I didn't mean to snap like that.'

'It's fine, my angel,' she said.

'Go on then, how do I get self-worth? I don't want to live life full of disappointment and worry any more, I'm fucking sick of it,' I said, and I burst into tears.

Mum hugged me. Then she said, 'You have to change the way you look at things, and the way you look at yourself. You have to be good to yourself, and realise that you deserve all that you work for. One good way to start, is to gift yourself things as often as you can, tell yourself you deserve it. Something good, something you want – whatever it is – and receive each gift humbly until you learn that you truly do deserve them. Nobody deserves a hard time in life. Gifting is the easy bit, the nice bit, and you must make sure you do it. Do it daily.' Mum took a deep, laboured breath. Her illness made it strenuous for her to think and talk for sustained periods of time. 'Now, the hard bit: changing how you look at things. Remember when you lost in the championships? There were thousands of ways to look at that, yet you took all the negatives, you blamed yourself. You thought it was going to affect other parts of your life, and you felt it was going to keep happening – that feeling, that loss. If you didn't think that way, losing wouldn't have been so devastating. But you did so well anyway, you always do. You boxed a top boxer, that's amazing in itself, my angel.'

I wasn't sure what to say. My thoughts were conflicted. There is nothing amazing about losing, no matter who you lose to. Yet he was a great boxer, and the fact I gave him a good match must mean I'm a good boxer too. But I lost. I'm just not good enough.

Mum said, 'So now, whenever you face adversity you've got to try and look at it differently, try *not* to blame yourself. Tell yourself that nobody else could have done better in your situation, you did all you could. And don't go thinking it will keep happening, because it won't. If you challenge how you feel about these situations, if you take ownership of them, then you'll start overriding the pattern. And you have to see that they won't affect other parts of your life unless you let them. No one's judging you, and it doesn't mean you'll lose at other things, you have to believe that. Does that make sense?'

'Yeah, I suppose so,' I said.

'It's how you respond to each moment of adversity that will determine the next outcome, so you need to respond in a constructive way. And the beauty of all this is you can look back at any challenge you've ever faced, and change your perception of it just by viewing it differently. Life's all about that, about those shifts of perception. And the more fluid you are, the easier life is.'

'You're not as dumb as you look,' I said.

'You brat.'

We laughed.

★★★

During summer, I followed a daily routine. Every morning, I'd make breakfast for Mum and me. I'd write five hundred words. When Mum was well enough, about once or twice per week, we'd go for a short walk. Mum loved being outside. It killed me to see her in that bedroom almost all day, every day. In the afternoons, I'd make lunch. Everything we ate was fresh, and prepared from scratch, so it took much more time than just throwing something in the oven. Everything we ate was deliciously healthy. After lunch, I'd do the cleaning. After cleaning, boxing training. After boxing, listen to music. After music, I'd cook dinner. After dinner, I'd write another five hundred words. Bed. Well, not bed. Living room floor, or sofa. I think I preferred the floor. Sleep. Wake up. Repeat.

My novel was developing nicely. Instead of writing an epic fantasy, which would have taken years, I had decided to write about something I knew. I'd decided to take my own story and massively exaggerate it. The novel taking shape was about a student drug lord who would become the Escobar of Cardiff, he'd be more cunning than the King, more relentless than Flash.

Sometimes I would get writer's block. Forcing yourself to write every single day is difficult. When I had nothing to write about, I'd pick an adversity, like losing the championships, and I'd write about how it made me feel, and I would challenge all my negative responses to that adversity. I would write about and explore new ways of looking at it. Mum was right. Whether I had lost the championships or not, I'd done okay, I had boxed well against a formidable opponent, and that meant I could do even better next time. And just because I'd lost the championships, it didn't mean I was going to fail at everything else. I had great friends, I was at university. Those were both great achievements. Each time I challenged an adversity in my writing, I felt slightly better. Sometimes I had to challenge the same ones many times to make any changes in how I felt about them.

Mum's illness, coming to terms with losing the championships, turning the King down, and doing badly in exams were among the most difficult setbacks I'd had to deal with. Writing about them proved incredibly therapeutic.

★★★

One morning, Mum hadn't come into the kitchen yet. She was usually up and about by 6.00 am. I say up and about, but I mean in the kitchen, a bite to eat, and back to bed. I thought she was sleeping in. After a while I decided I'd better check.

It's funny how many thoughts ran through my head in the time it took me to get up from the sofa and walk five metres to her bedroom. What if she's dead, or killed herself, or fallen over and broken her back?

I opened the door, she was lying on her side, eyes open, seemingly unresponsive.

'Mum!' I went to feel her pulse.

'What?' she said slowly, not blinking, not moving.

'What's the matter?' I said.

'I'm fucking depressed, and I can't get rid of this migraine, I haven't slept all night,' she said.

I understood, and I knew nothing I might say would help her. This wasn't an indulgent depression, not like mine when I get miserable about life not going my way, this was depression from spending ninety per cent of her time in bed. The humanity was being sucked out of her.

'I can't take it any more, and I don't know what to do,' she said.

There was no point in suggesting a hobby or anything like that, this wasn't that kind of thing. She needed a fucking miracle. It wasn't just her mental state that was bad. She was pale and puffy, and there was lots of darkness around her eyes. A month ago, her tooth had fallen out. Despite all the supplements, treatments and dietary changes she'd been trying, and all the input from the specialist private doctor, nothing seemed to be helping. With all these costs, the money I'd saved up was disappearing fast. That's the shit thing about ME, they just don't know enough about it. There's so much trial and error. More research is desperately needed.

'I'm sorry you have to live like this,' I said. 'I wish I could help but I really don't know what to do. I can try and earn more money.'

'I just want a friend,' she said. 'I've spent the last decade with nothing, with no one, and I can't expect my son to do everything for me, you need a life too! I just can't bear the thought of going on like this until I die, what's the fucking point?'

'If I was in your shoes, what would you tell me to do?'

She smiled. 'I would tell you to meditate, but if you tell

me to meditate, I'll tell you to piss off. I've been meditating every day for twenty years, I just can't take it any more. I need to move, I need to do things for God's sake. I can't stay cooped up in here all the time. I need a garden.'

'I'll get you some CBD oil,' I said.

'This migraine is so sore I need a bong,' she said.

I laughed so hard. I didn't expect that. 'The combustion would be no good for you. I have an idea,' I said, 'but we'll start with more CBD for now.'

Mum's supplement cupboard looked like Holland & Barrett and beyond, stuffed into a small space. Magnesium injections, magnesium citrate, magnesium carbonate, magnesium threonate. vitamin B12 injections, vitamin B6 capsules, acetyl-l-carnitine, thiamine, riboflavin, niacin, folate, biotin, pantothenic acid, choline, coenzyme Q10, D-ribose, niacinamide, NAD+, acetylcysteine, bile acid, pancreatic enzymes, betaine hydrochloride, peppermint, dill, lipase, chromium picolinate, gymnema, berberine, kava kava, alpha lipoic acid, valerian, Chinese skullcap, gaba, sage, rosemary, phosphatidylserine, passion flower, lemon balm, tryptophan, 5-HTP, chamomile, Asphalia, melatonin, L-theanine, glycine, essential fatty acids, hemp oil, vitamin D, CBD oil, CBD balm, CBD crystals with terpenes, fermented cod liver oil, Thrive probiotic, Prescript Assist, kefir, Pro-Dental, inulin, resistant starches, Restore, glutamine, systemic enzymes, Golden Seal, neem, Tanalbit, bearberry, colloidal silver, clove, wormwood, black walnut, olive leaf, Lauricidin, propolis, oil of oregano, thyme oil, lactoferrin, resveratrol, bilberry tablets, cranberry capsules, pomegranate capsules, high phenolic olive oil, vitamin C as magnesium ascorbate and ascorbic acid, lysine, L-glutathione, liquorice root, ginger, Isatis tinctoria, Pueraria lobata, Lomatium dissectum, Rhodolia rosea, Idoral, iodine, natural desiccated thyroid, levothyroxine, triiodothyronine, pregnenolone, DHEA, zinc, Feverfew, maca root, selenium, calcium, bioflavonoids, shilajit, soya lecithin, and a fuck load more I can't be bothered to list. She'd tried everything!

Mum wasn't taking these things blindly, either. We'd read about them helping others with ME and, where we could, we'd researched studies that might relate to Mum's symptoms. Many of the studies were insubstantial, and even then, we found only a handful specific to ME. It costs millions to run a substantial study.

It is no secret the body needs nutrients. It's just unclear which ones might best help someone suffering from ME. Some of the supplements Mum was taking certainly helped, others didn't. The body is so complex, there's no one-size-fits-all solution, not when it comes to health. Until they understand more about ME, sufferers of the disease will simply have to experiment on themselves, like Mum has. It's better than doing nothing. Most doctors expect her to do nothing and suffer, or to take harmful, flawed approaches, like graded exercise therapy.

I returned to Mum with some CBD oil and balm, and some home-made, organic dark chocolate. I rubbed CBD balm into her temples.

She said, 'Thank you, my angel.' She could barely keep her eyes open.

'I'm going to get you something else, too,' I said. 'I'm very sure it will help your pain. In the meantime, take ten drops of this, and eat this chocolate.'

I called an acquaintance of mine who was a bit of a connoisseur of weed. He recommended that Mum micro-dosed an indica for sleep, and a sativa for pain during the day. He had some capsules with cannabis oil in them, which he sold to me.

I said to Mum, 'I've read a lot about cannabis for pain, and while CBD is all well and good, it might have more of a synergistic effect if you have some THC too, it's effects are more ... active. So, I got you some capsules. You don't have to smoke it, just take it as a tablet. My friend recommended you take one of these capsules at night, and one of these ones in the day. Would you like to try?'

She held her hand out, 'Am I going to be high like a stoner?'

I gave her one capsule, and some water to wash it down with. I said, 'No, these are tiny doses, I'm sure it will help.'

'Thank you,' she said, 'I'm going to try to nap now.'

★★★

Mum came out of her bedroom two hours later. She said, 'I feel much better, it's a bit strange, I feel lighter, maybe even a bit normal again.'

Every now and then, we find something that makes Mum feel better, almost normal again. But these things don't often last long. It's as if the disease adapts and finds another way to attack her. I made sure not to get my hopes up.

I said, 'That's great. While you're feeling good we should make the most of it, what would you like to do?'

'Let's walk all the way to Land's End.'

'There's no harm in trying,' I said.

Of course, we didn't get as far as Land's End. The coast path is concreted for about half a mile, it is well kept, for tourists and leisure walkers to enjoy. The shrubbery is trimmed, the vulnerable areas of the cliffs are fenced so that rocks don't hit you when the cliff erodes. After that, concrete turns into a well-walked stony path. It becomes rougher and rougher, the bushes wilder and the terrain less predictable.

We had to stop every half a mile or so, for Mum to rest.

The further we went, the happier Mum got. We both knew she was pushing herself beyond her limits, and that she'd suffer so much in a couple of days, but she needed to do this for her sanity.

After many miles, we got to a wooded area where the path was still evident, but it was nicely overgrown and everything was beautifully lush and green. The sound of the sea came from our right, the trees rustled above. There was nobody around. The ground was dry. Mum put her arms around a tree, and her ear to its bark.

I looked around awkwardly, hoping nobody would appear. 'What are you listening for?' I said.

'I'm not listening in particular, I'm just experiencing it all. There's a form of perception beyond the senses, like a fusion of intuition, all the senses and knowledge in one. It's like a *feeling*, and I'm trying to feel it.'

'The subtle fabric of the universe,' I said.

'Yes, exactly. We're all connected by it. It's the only thing that keeps me going sometimes, knowing we're all part of one big picture.'

'I wish I could understand it more,' I said.

'Put your arms around the tree, see what you feel.'

'Absolutely not,' I said.

She laughed, 'Come on then, let's carry on walking.'

Mum slowed to smell a bunch of bright blueish-purple flowers. She knelt right down and absorbed their scent. 'At least smell these, then,' she said.

They smelt as brilliant as they looked. It put a smile on both our faces.

Mum did indeed suffer in the days after our walk. Her body and head ached, and her mind was cloudy, so she couldn't think properly. It took about two weeks for her body to find some comfort again. The cannabis capsules and CBD oil helped with the suffering.

One afternoon, I was in the kitchen area making us a fruit salad. Mum was lying on the sofa so we could talk. She said, 'Are you going to see your friends at all this summer? Aren't you lonely?'

'You're my best friend, Mum, I'm happy here,' I said.

'Yes, but even best friends need other friends,' she said.

That cut me, because I knew she had no other friends. I said, 'You're right. Well, there is a big festival that Isobel and all my other friends are going to at the end of summer. If you're well enough, I'll go to that.'

'That sounds lovely, don't worry about whether I'm well enough, I'll be fine, especially if you freeze lots of meals for me to heat up. I think you should go, make it a big gift to yourself. What kind of festival is it anyway?'

I was slicing mango, the skin was green and red, the flesh, perfectly ripe. Orangey-yellow, gleaming with juicy sweetness. I cut it into squares down to the pip, ran the sharp blade down the pip to separate the squares from it.

'Music of all sorts, my friends say it's really good, and Ryan said he'll come so that will be nice, I haven't seen him in ages. One of my favourite artists is playing, he's called Lauer.'

The mango squares fell into the glass mixing bowl as I talked, joining slices of banana, strawberry and kiwi. The vivid green kiwi complimented the strawberry red.

'Oh, wow, that will be nice. Which one is Ryan again?'

'You definitely know him, he's the one I went to school with, the one I usually go out in town with. He's been to our house once or twice, his family has a farm in Torrington.'

'Yes, I think I know who you're talking about.'

Fruit is vibrant for a reason. It's full of good sugars, vitamins and minerals. It is frustrating that some well-read researchers say people with ME might want to limit their fruit intake to reach a beneficial gut microbiome status, and other well-read researchers say that you need lots of fruit to meet your body's energy demands. It's a fucking minefield. Some researchers say people with ME have a broken Krebs cycle, and that they're better off using ketones for energy over carbohydrates. Other researchers say the ketogenic diet is unsustainable and causes damage to your system in the long-term. A fucking minefield. But me and Mum, we try everything. You have to.

Apparently, sugars are good for things like converting thyroid hormone T4 to T3, which is the type your body uses most. Some say sugars will fuck with your insulin levels, some say fructose, the sugar in fruit, can help with insulin sensitivity. We hear fruit is good and we hear fruit is bad and how the fuck are we supposed to know what to believe?

I stirred the fruit in the bowl, sprinkled some blueberries on top, and squeezed some lime juice over it. It smelt sweet and citrusy. The lime was refreshingly light and cold on my fingers. Lime compliments mango particularly well.

'So, tell me about Lauer,' Mum said.

'He makes electronic music. I've been listening to lots of electronic music lately, one day I want to be a producer.'

'Wow, I bet you'd make a great producer,' she said.

'I'll play you my favourite song.'

I played the song for Mum from my phone. She smiled.

'It's called "Gammelan",' I said. I remembered the first time I had heard Gammelan – so beautiful, so perfect. And I looked around Mum's crooked little house, and I felt so torn between happiness and sadness.

'That is a nice song,' she said. 'I am excited for you to see him at The Festival.'

'Me too, more than anyone could ever imagine,' I said.

★★★

The end of summer was nearing, I was fucking excited for The Festival. There was a call from Arlo.

'Tommy, bro, how's it going, how's your summer been?' he said, sounding more energetic and confident than ever before. 'You know The Festival everyone's been talking about? I've got a proposition for you. I took over the King's business, he's gone. Summer's been mental, bro, you wouldn't believe how things have changed. I've got some mates willing to sell loads of MD and pills for us at The Festival, all we need to do is get it in there. I thought if there was anyone with the brains for how to do that, it's you, bro. I'll split the profits down the middle. I have as much as you think you can take in, ready and waiting.'

'All I have to do is bring it in?'

'Once it's through those gates, half the profit's yours. So many people get buzzed at festivals it's like a licence to print money once we've got it in there. It won't be easy though, bro. They search, and there'll be sniffer dogs, police, the lot. Most of it's there to scare you though, those dogs will be dumb as fuck. Have a think about it, bro, get back to me as soon as.'

He hung up.

I wasn't going to let the opportunity slip. I needed money, and I'd already let too many opportunities go. I should have considered the King's offer thoroughly and objectively. I shouldn't have let my self-doubt determine the decision. I could have stayed in Cardiff a week longer sorting everything out, then got Moose to take care of it all until I was back. I could have been in Cardiff weekends, and at Mum's five days a week. There would have been plenty of ways to make it work. I should have made it work. I promised myself that from now on, I would make everything work.

I spent many hours researching festivals, sniffer dogs, search law, and everything in between, including The Festival's forums, site maps, site rules and any other information I could find that would help me smuggle in enough drugs to make it worth it. I used an encrypted network browser so there would be no evidence of my search history.

Many options were considered. If I'd had more time, I could have gone to the countryside site way before The Festival was being built, and buried it there, marking the spot with GPS on my phone so I could retrieve the drugs once everything was in full flow. I considered flying the drugs in using a drone. Considered digging under the fence to get past security. Throwing them over the fence to be picked up on the other side. All of those left too much room for error.

You can't mask the scent of something a sniffer dog has been trained to get excited about – the scent of drugs, weapons, and so on – because the dog's nose will pick apart all the microscopic particles and distinguish its target no matter what else is in the air. The slightest trace of the substance will remain on you or the container, somewhere, unless you have industrial decontamination equipment. The best thing to do is to trick the security guards into thinking the dog is confused, which is highly likely at a festival where tens of thousands of people will possess drugs, or have been exposed to them in some way.

Dogs love food. If the dog triggered a search of my food bag, the security guards would probably think the dog was confused. Something like beef jerky would do the trick. What dog doesn't like the smell of meat? Even if the dog seemed confused, I needed to think of a way to hide the stuff – and loads of it – in the food bag, in a way that would go unnoticed by the security guards, even if they decided to search it thoroughly. That was the hard bit.

I examined every food item I had and I thought about

whether it was possible to hide drugs in them. I thought about making a big pot of chilli, or a lasagne or something, and hiding them in there, but security could easily put their hand into those sorts of foods and find the drugs.

I thought about cutting a carrot in half, carving the middle out and then putting it back together with metal pins. I tried this. The issue was the oxidation of the carrot. Once it had been cut, it browned around the edges within hours. Not enough time to get to The Festival and through security. And we would need hundreds of carrots to pull it off. Nobody goes to a festival with hundreds of carrots, unless they're in the food trade, which we certainly were not. We were just normal punters.

I started thinking about fresh food items I could open and stick back together without them looking like they'd been tampered with, and I ran through so many possibilities before I stumbled on the idea of a pineapple. After cutting the top off a pineapple and carving some space out of the insides, the walls were still firm. I filled the inside with stones as a test and put the top back on. Metal pins didn't create enough friction to keep the top attached to the bottom firmly. I was stuck brainstorming for a bit. I needed the top to seamlessly attach to the rest of the pineapple.

Toothpicks. Cocktail sticks. I whacked about a dozen thick wooden cocktail sticks a couple of inches long into the top of the pineapple's tough, green skin and through the flesh walls below. It didn't look like the pineapple had been altered at all. The wooden edges of the cocktail sticks sat flush with the green and yellow skin, nice and snug under the leaves. I held the top by the leaves and shook it. It was sturdy. I was buzzed. Nobody would think to cut the pineapple in half.

Each hour that night I woke and shook the pineapple to see how it would deteriorate. It was solid for the first five hours. During the next three hours it started getting a bit soggier and weaker. After about twelve hours it was mushy enough for some of the cocktail sticks to pull out under pressure. One hard swing and the top came off, all the stones flew out.

The drugs arrived via Royal Mail on the day of The Festival, via a 9.00 am guaranteed delivery. I wondered what someone like Barbs would think if she knew the Royal Mail was used to move Class A drugs. I suspected that millions of pounds' worth of drugs were distributed by the Royal Mail every year.

I put the drugs in sealed waterproof bags, and then I stuffed two hundred and fifty grams of MDMA into two pineapples, and a thousand pills into another two. Once I was done, I had four ordinary looking pineapples with tough green skin and some yellowing on the edges, and long, pointy leaves sticking out. You couldn't see the cocktail sticks. You couldn't feel the drugs inside.

The pineapples went into a big cool box with a range of other fruit, some drinks, a bottle of water, lots of beef jerky, some sandwiches, several tins of lager, and some other random items to make it look like I was going to eat and drink well at The Festival.

***

Ryan, Sammy, Rosie, Arlo and I stood in the queue to The Festival. We were at the top of a valley of fields and woods, and down in the valley and all around us you could see the giant, colourful festival site. Tall, flowing banners, thousands of tents, a huge arena with massive stages, big party tents, and other wonderful installations. I was insanely excited. Except for the thought of getting caught with all those drugs on me.

Apart from Arlo, nobody knew what I was carrying.

The queue would stop for a few minutes, everyone would put their bags and tents and whatnot down, and then the queue would move again, everyone would pick up their stuff, move a few metres, stop again, move again. I was carrying a big rucksack on my back, a tent, and the large, heavy cool box. I wished the queue would move faster. I didn't want the pineapples to deteriorate.

The atmosphere was brilliant. There were thousands of people around us eager to get through the gates and have the best time of their lives. Everyone was drinking, chatting, laughing. There were performers interacting with the crowd, dressed elaborately as fairies with flowing white fabrics and glowing fairy lights curled around them, entertaining us as we waited.

Ryan took a bottle of whisky from his bag, held it under Sammy's nose and said, 'Sip for mates.'

Sammy looked at him as if he were crazy.

I said, 'It's a thing we have at home. You have to have a sip now, unless you don't want to be his mate.'

Sammy took the bottle, cracked the seal, had a sip, exhaled the harsh afterburn. 'Sip for mates,' he said, passing it to Rosie.

The whisky bottle did its rounds. Every time I was challenged to sip for mates, I made sure I took in only a small amount. I didn't want to be impaired as I walked through security.

It was a hot, sunny day. The closer we got to security, the more nervous, sweaty and bothered I got. I told myself to relax, that my pineapples were too sophisticated for security to be suspicious about. I wasn't the only one who was nervous, I heard one or two people around us murmuring about security and their drugs. One guy said his was in his roll-on deodorant container.

I could see the dogs, and I wasn't easy about it.

'You alright?' Sammy said.

'I'm alright, just didn't sleep so well,' I said.

I imagined getting caught. Everyone would think I was an idiot. Isobel would probably split up with me for being so stupid. But a thousand pills made ten grand, and a bar of mud at forty quid for point-sixes, sixteen grand. The raw cost, about four grand max. Five would be spent on distribution. That would leave seventeen for Arlo and me to split. Eight and a half grand each.

I watched some people go through without getting their stuff searched at all. I prayed I was going to be one of those people. The dogs seemed so confused and disoriented, they ended up just moping about uninterested in anything.

Weighing up the pros and cons of drug dealing is not as simple as it seems. The question I could have asked myself was whether I'd take a few years in prison for less than ten thousand pounds? The answer is obviously, no. But that question was only valid if I was going to get caught. So, I had to weigh up the chances of that. The previous year, there had been forty-five drug-related arrests at The Festival. There were sixty thousand people at The Festival. I was assured that a significant percentage of those had taken drugs in with them. That meant my chances of getting in without being caught were at least reasonable. Plus, I had something nobody else had. Pineapples.

Security were choosing their victims at random. They'd stop you, make you put your bags on the table, and search them thoroughly.

The police were aplenty, and I saw at least one guy being led to them. They had a base set up in marquees nearby, with big signs saying, 'POLICE' on them to scare the shit out of us. Their vivid neon strips were the only unwelcome colours in the happy, colourful scene.

Our turn. We walked past the first security point, I was fucking sweating. There were cylindrical, blue amnesty bins for people to surrender their drugs without getting into any trouble. That was my last chance. I could have dropped the drugs in there, and nothing would have been said. Nobody paid the amnesty bins any attention, we all walked straight past. I couldn't use them, it would be throwing too much money away, and I'd have to pay Arlo back. I took a deep breath, swallowed the thickness in my throat. Flowed steadily with the crowd of people.

Past the dog, nothing. Relief. The dog was cute, I felt sorry for it, I doubt it liked being held on a lead, aggravated by the thousands of people walking past.

Towards the search tables. 'Bags on the side please,' security said.

Damn. I put my large rucksack, tent, and the cool box on the table. This is it. It's going to go wrong. They're going to find it. How could I be so stupid? No, relax, Tommy. You need to believe in yourself. You came up with a plan nobody would suspect. It will be okay. But what if it's not? I'm fucked. Fuck.

'Empty your pockets,' the security guard said. He patted me down while another security guard looked through my stuff. I had to play it cool. I saw in my peripheral vision the pineapples and other foods being put aside, the guy running his hand through the bag to make sure nothing was left in it. My nerves were frantic. I was worried I looked suspicious, too nervous. Sweat drenched me.

After I'd been patted down I watched security look through my big rucksack, and the tent bag. All the fruit from my cool box was still on the table. Security found nothing, put it all back in the bag and sent me on my way. The sense of relief, indescribable.

As we walked down a country path into the camping fields, Arlo said, 'Everything good?'

I said, 'Everything is in four pineapples in the cool box I'm carrying. When we've set up camp, take them.'

'You smashed it, bro. Consider this the highest paid weekend you've ever done.'

It's not over until the fat lady sings, I thought. If it seems too good to be true, it probably is.

The campsite got busy quickly, a dense collation of tents of all colours and sizes, and plenty of people. We put our tents in a circular formation with the doors facing a small enclosure for us to socialise in. We secured this space by scattering random items to ensure no one could put their tent there. A picnic mat, some foldable deckchairs Sammy had purloined while he was exploring, an inflatable mattress, bags of food, drink, and my cool box that had four pineapples missing from it. Not that anybody knew.

We spent the day at the campsite, drinking and chatting, waiting for the arena to open. The place was already a mess with empty cans, plastic bottles, food wrappers, wet wipes, and random other shit. I didn't like that, it made it harder to escape the real world.

We had a decent group of friends with us. Ryan, Isobel, and two of her housemates, Nina and Amy. Rosie, Bento, and two of their uni friends, Adey and Sarah. Adey was yet to become Shady Adey, he got that nickname about half a year later when he got heavily into coke, and a bit of side dealing. Moose, Daisy, Anthony, Flash, and Arlo were all there too. Banging!

'Oi, Tommy,' Sammy said, with a mischievous look in his eyes. He was going to try to be funny.

'Yes?' I said.

'How's that novel coming along?' he said.

'Good actually,' I said. 'I've been writing every day. Some of it is shit, but I'll get there.'

'Oh yeah?' Sammy said. He started laughing.

I smiled. I knew what was coming. Everyone quietened to listen to Sammy.

He said, in a high-pitched, patronising voice, 'Working on a novel, are you?'

'Go on,' I said. 'Give it to me, I deserve it.'

Sammy said, 'Gonna be a writer, are we? Got some romance, some heartbreak. A tough journey for the protagonist, is it? Little journey that makes him grow and reflect and become a better person? You're gonna self-publish some work, are you? Put it right out there on Amazon for the world to read, yeah? Make some book sales, and become a bestselling author, is it? Bestselling author, is it?'

There was nothing for me to say. Sammy's spiel, his whiny voice and all, was inspired by the famous scene from *Family Guy*. I knew it, and so did everyone else. Stewie takes the piss out of Brian about a novel Brian claims to have been writing for years. It's the funniest scene an aspiring writer, or anyone who knows an aspiring writer, can watch. Seth MacFarlane, Mark Hentemann, Steve Callaghan, and everyone else at Fox who worked on *Family Guy* managed to capture the sentiment of a wannabe writer so well. We all talk about the books we're writing. Few actually finish a novel. Even fewer come up with anything half decent.

Sammy had well and truly rinsed me. To top it all off, while we were all laughing, a soggy bread roll stinking of beer hit me in the face.

'That's it, you fucker,' I said. I picked up the soggy bread roll, dived over Sammy, rubbed it in his face and mouth, it squelched, he screamed, laughing and struggling to get his face away from my hand.

We all laughed a lot.

'Fair play, you cunt,' Sammy said once he'd spat it all out. 'Look at you thinking you're the big man now you punt a few pingers and got yourself a flashy haircut.'

'Sammy,' I snapped. 'What are you on about? "Pingers?" You're drunk.'

Everything fell quiet, I got a bit anxious. I worried what Ryan's response would be. I should have told him already. He's my best mate after all.

Isobel said, 'Oh, come on, Tommy, everyone here knows what you do. We're all friends here.'

Ryan said, 'Well, you got any magic beans for your old mate Ry?'

Arlo stood, he said, 'Never fear, the King is here,' taking a handful of pingers from his pocket and flicking them at everyone. We all laughed so much, I'll never forget that moment. It was fucking outrageous. Fucking illegal. Fucking amazing.

Spirits lightened, chatter loudened, it was hard to keep up.

Isobel and I couldn't stop looking at each other. She was sitting on a picnic mat just next to me, with her mates. She had glitter all over her face, her eyes were ocean blue, and powerful.

Paulo Coelho wrote something like, 'Your eyes show the strength of your soul.' I like that, because only a twat could think that all they're seeing is colour and form. There is so much more to it than that.

There was so much intensity in her eyes, what I was experiencing wasn't merely visual.

'You look good,' she said, looking at my jacket.

I had this wavy Adidas jacket on. Bright retro sports jackets were popular, but I hadn't seen anyone wearing anything like this one. The material was smooth and thick, it had vertically lined sections of white, and metallic maroon and turquoise, symmetrical both sides of the zip. Adidas and Ellesse T-shirts with the logos across the chest were also popular. Sammy was wearing an Adidas one that I'd seen dozens of people wearing. I wasn't into that, everyone wearing the same thing. Originality is everything. Diversity is key to the survival of any ecosystem.

'You look better,' I said.

Her eyes. Her skin.

Sammy said, 'Get a room. What's the plan anyway?'

And the moment was gone.

'Let's go to the arena,' I said. 'On our way, we'll go to that cocktail bar by the Lillyfields, I'm buying everyone a drink.'

'Cocktails are like, ten quid. Festival prices are ridiculous,' Isobel said.

'We're having cocktails and the cocktails will have pineapple in them. Tommy's orders, Tommy loves pineapple,' I said. I was feeling good, fucking loving it.

But it's not over until the fat lady sings.

We skipped and jogged and strode to the arena. Everyone was in a great mood. Festivals are fucking amazing, so many people so excited and music of all sorts booming everywhere, you can't imagine it until you do it. It's like another world.

There's something fascinating about sixty thousand people in a field who're there to love life, to forget about the shit heap of a hateful society we live in. Festivals are a testament to humanity, pure joy, escapism.

On our way to the Lillyfields we encountered some woods. Beside us were trees and a stream and small lakes and a waterfall, and all of it was lit by coloured lights shining onto disco balls. The atmosphere was so fucking elating, deep and mysterious and I felt like I was on another planet, one where everything is just … beautiful.

Colours and shapes, decorations, props, fantasy features, giant flowers, whacky sculptures, wildlands. Smiles, smiles, smiles, eyes, beaming eyes, crowds flowing in several directions. Time flying. Chatting. Dancing. Skipping about. Jumping to heavy beats. Smiling dancing laughing jumping, mood lighting softening people's features, intensifying the eyes. Loving it.

I said to Isobel, 'I want to do events, I love all this so much, I've never been happier.'

She said, 'You should, I bet your events would be amazing.'

Dance tents and strange enclosures, fiery stages and mental installations. Lauer, at the Temple, a fucking cool arena, literally designed to look like a fusion between Angkor Wat and science fiction, with smoke, lasers and atmospheric lights in warm green, blue and grey. The crowd all around us. Wild. Loving it.

Distorted glitches of memory, of pure euphoria. Smiles. Life cannot possibly get better.

Someone in the crowd shouting, 'Nice one bruvaaa.'

Someone shouting back, 'Niiice one.'

So many people in fancy dress. Dancing. Dancing everywhere. Tribal. Animalistic. Fucking banging.

Isobel, her smile, kissing. Soft skin. Glitter. Glistening. 'Gammelan.' *Da na na now,* those bass synths, yeahhh. Intense lighting. Decor. Smoke. Confetti. Faces. Cheering. Chanting. Whistling. Buzzing.

I also remember a horrible feeling, staring at the Temple stage, all those lights, those colours and textures, the haze, thinking about Mum and how I wish she could experience something as amazing as I was experiencing, and I thought about her loneliness, and her shitty excuse for a life, and that made me more sad than you could ever imagine.

I woke up on the Monday morning of The Festival with my emotions all over the place. The sun penetrated the thin skin of the tent causing daylight levels of brightness. I was in Isobel's tent. She was fast asleep. The tent was small and stuffy, and I felt there was a layer of dirt and sweat covering me. I had a headache, and my body was starved of nutrients, drained of energy. All the MDMA and alcohol we'd consumed over the weekend made me feel toxic.

People were already moving around outside. I checked my watch, it was 8.00 am. Ryan would be driving me home, he'd said he would like to leave at 9.00 am, so I had to get up and get on with it. I shook Isobel to wake her up.

She looked a bit confused. I kissed her cheek, said, 'I have to get up now.'

The thought of leaving her made me incredibly emotional. She put her arms around me, we hugged tight.

She kissed my cheek. 'I'll miss you,' she said.

'I'll miss you too,' I said.

'Don't forget your jacket,' she said. She'd been wearing it, the metallic white, blue and maroon one, the sickest jacket in the world. The one I'd been wearing when it had all started, just four days before. I knew The Festival had changed me. I wasn't sure exactly in what way, but I felt different, I felt more optimistic that life could be great, and that there was plenty of love in the world, despite the heavy comedown.

I kissed her once more, 'See you soon,' I said.

She nestled back into her sleeping bag.

'Is that your voice I hear, Tommy?' Ryan said.

'Yeah, I'm up,' I said.

'You okay, mate? You going to miss Isobel?'

I could hear Sammy, Arlo and Moose laughing.

'Fuck off,' I said.

Arlo shouted, 'Tommy, bro, come here I've got a present

for you, bring your bag.'

'It better be good,' I said.

Arlo had a small pop-up tent. I unzipped it and climbed in. His hair was all matted and frizzy, sticking up a bit, as if he'd had an electric shock.

'How's it going, bro, you enjoy yourself?'

'It was mind-blowing,' I said.

'Here's the cherry on top,' he said. He passed me four stacks of notes. They weren't significantly large stacks, and they weren't the neatest of stacks. He whispered, 'There's eight grand there, it was a pleasure doing business with you.'

As I put the money in the bottom of my bag, I worried I would get searched on the way out and that the money would get confiscated, or that someone would steal my bag somehow, or that I'd lose it. These worries were intensified by the comedown.

'Thank you, Arlo,' I said quietly.

'No, bro, thank you,' he said.

'Ryan and I are heading off soon, I'll see you when I'm back in Cardiff.'

'Yes, bro, can't wait, we should have a sesh at mine.'

'I feel so rough that I don't think I'll be seshing for a while,' I said.

Arlo laughed. He said, 'We'll see.'

Ryan and I dismantled and packed his tent. Some of our group were rising out of their tents, everyone as rough as each other, yet still excited, still buzzing from the best weekend ever. I couldn't stop looking at my rucksack to make sure it was safe. I wondered whether anyone noticed me doing so.

Once Ryan and I were all packed up, we said our emotional goodbyes to all who were awake, and we made our ascent up the hill. The devastation of the campsites made me think of Armageddon. Hordes of zombies trudged the paths towards the exit gates. The atmosphere was like another world from when it had all started. I felt like crying.

The only thing keeping me going was all that cash in my bag. I had money again, and at that point that was a rare and beautiful feeling.

'You alright?' Ryan said.

'Yeah, I'm just taking it all in. I can't get over how good it was.'

Ryan said, 'Merts.'

'Merts,' I said.

Merts means the best of mates.

It was nerve-racking leaving the site, walking past police, security and stewards, but my fears were unfounded because before we knew it, Ryan and I were on the open road, heading back to Mum's. When I opened Mum's door, I felt so great and yet so empty. I wanted to throw the cash on the floor and roll in it, but I had to keep it a secret from Mum.

Chapter 8

Back in Cardiff for second year, I went to see Arlo. I wanted to get business going as soon as possible. I had grand plans for expansion. The first step was buying everything cheap, in bulk.

Arlo had moved into the King's apartment. I waited outside the gate. The driveway stones gleamed in the darkness. The gate screeched as it opened.

I wondered where the King had gone since his retirement. I pictured him in a small cave in Tibet, meditating.

The buzzer for the front door sounded loudly. I pushed the door open. The buzzer stopped. I climbed the stairs slowly, only my footsteps to be heard. I knocked on the apartment door.

'Come in, Tommy,' Arlo said.

The lighting was dim. Arlo was sitting on the sofa opposite the big screen. Professional boxing was showing, muted. The apartment was deteriorating. There was a chip in the floor by a leg of the coffee table. The air smelt musty, a bit like dust and weed.

Arlo said, 'Welcome to the Whitehouse, bro.'

The coffee table was covered with crap. An ash tray, a bag of weed, a silver grinder, some half-empty mugs, two pint-glasses with dubious residues left inside, scraps of paper, which were probably debt lists, and a bunch of other things under piles of rubbish, like a plastic bag with half a takeaway box hanging out of it. I imagined some chips or scraps of cheese getting stale in the box.

I said, 'Why's it called the Whitehouse?'

'Because I'm the bloody president. And all the white stuff that goes through here,' he said. 'Sit down, bro.'

I took a seat on the sofa adjacent to Arlo's. There was a cigarette burn on the cushion. 'So, what's it like sitting where the King once sat?' I said, for want of something to say.

'Honestly, it's so stressful,' he said, 'but the perks are worth it. I have so much money now, and we have a lot of fun up here, good parties and that, you know, and it's going to get even better now all you students are back. I wanted to talk to you about that, Tommy. I've been thinking, bro, I want you to be my right hand man. I'm so busy I can't do it all, and I can't think of anyone better to help me than you. I'll pay you good money, and I'll rent you a nice new place to meet clients at. These aren't the sorts of people who'd come to your student house.' He laughed. 'I'll make sure you're well looked after, come on, bro, we'll run Cardiff.'

'What will I be doing?' I said.

'Mate, it's literally distribution, logistics. We speak to clients, make deals, take some weight here, some money there, you know how it is. You're doing it all already, except this time we're talking boxes and bars, not Z's. It's worth it, bro, what were you making before summer?'

'I made a couple of grand a month. It was almost completely risk-free, all to mates, and mates of mates, all students, just mud, it was perfect really. I plan on expanding this year, and I've got boxing, and I want to do an event, I'm not sure I'll have time for your errands as well.'

'I'll pay you ten grand a month.'

Ten grand. Jesus. He knew that would get my attention, I could see it in his face.

He said, 'And you can carry on doing everything you were doing, just get someone underneath you to take care of all that, you'll have so much money you won't know what to do with it.'

Ten grand. Jesus. I said, 'I'll think about it, Arlo.'

It should have been me sitting where Arlo was sitting, offering to pay someone ten grand a month to run dodgy errands.

Arlo's phone rang, he said, 'Hello … Nice one, coming now.' He got the door.

Flash entered with a girl. She wore a short red dress. Her skin was tanned. Her eyes, dangerously attractive, dark, with well-defined edges.

'Sup, geez?' Flash said. He fist-bumped Arlo, fist-bumped me. 'Tommy, geez, this is Olivia.'

Olivia smiled, teeth as white as cocaine. She slipped off her sandals, her bare feet were thin and longish, like her legs. She looked out of place, a celebrity among the riff-raff. 'Pleasure to meet you, Tommy,' she said. Charming Welsh accent.

Flash and Olivia took a seat on the sofa opposite me.

Arlo said, 'What can I do for you, Flash, my man?'

'Just up for a Q of flake, mate,' Flash said.

'Not a problem,' Arlo said. 'This stuff is *the one*. You got time for a sample?'

'Time for a boomer? Time for a boomer? When haven't I got time for a boomer?'

Arlo went into another room, returned with a black rucksack. He took a large airtight container from the rucksack and put it on the table, popped the clip-lock sides of the lid, lifted out a freezer bag full of cocaine, placed it on the table.

Jesus. That's a lot of cocaine, so pure it pierced the darkness. I felt uneasy, couldn't take my eyes off it.

Arlo rummaged through some items on the table, plucked a small glass mirror from the mess, handed it to Flash. Arlo pointed at the cocaine, said, 'You have the honours.'

'Oi oi,' Flash said. Flash took a card from his wallet and scooped a chunky white clump of cocaine onto it. He said, 'Go get us a hot plate love.'

Olivia stood, pulled her short dress lower, strutted into the kitchen. The lights were off in the kitchen, there were vague outlines of dishes cluttered on the counter. A red light flashed on the water and ice dispenser on the fridge. The microwave hummed.

Flash said, 'How's it going then, Tommy, bro? Heard about your little earner at The Festival, man, that was some intense shit. Fair play to you, mate. I'm here punting Q's and you're fucking walking about with a fat stack, how's that come about?'

'Just a bit of luck,' I said.

Arlo didn't seem to notice my discomfort, he smiled at Flash and me, and yet he knew I didn't want anyone to know that I took so much weight into the festival.

Olivia returned with a blue plate. Flash put his clump of cocaine on the plate. Pressed down with his card. The heat of the plate helped the cocaine become softer, finer, less clumpy. The cocaine was a flat white spread. Flash scraped it into a mound with a swift swipe of his card, began chopping into it with the sharp corner of the card. Repeated the process a few times. Transferred the white stuff onto to the mirror.

Olivia was watching him. She sat on the sofa lengthways, her back resting on the sofa's arm. She lengthened one bare leg towards Flash, the other bare leg, bent at the knee.

Flash split the mound into four large lines. He passed the

mirror to Arlo. 'President first,' he said.

Arlo took a note from his wallet, rolled it tight, snorted the whole, large line, tilted his head back, sniffed some more, expressed a heavy sigh of relief. 'This stuff's banging,' he said.

Flash received the mirror and the note. Snorted his line. When his airways were clear, he said, 'Oi oiii.'

He passed the mirror to Olivia. Olivia took the mirror and the note elegantly with her long, slim arms, sniffed lightly, airily, no victory chant. She looked directly into my eyes, held me there. 'Pass this to Tommy, would you Flash?' she said, her eyes not moving from me.

I said, 'No, I'm okay, thank you.'

'Come on, geez, when in Rome,' Flash said.

Arlo said, 'Go on, Tommy, why not? Treat yourself.'

Olivia's eyes.

I shook my head. 'You lot have it.'

'Go on then,' Flash said, 'don't mind if I do.'

Olivia passed Flash the line.

She returned her attention to me.

I forced myself to watch the boxing, anything but her. The intricate movements, both men delivering and avoiding punches with tenacity. One of the boxers took a heavy punch, it rocked his legs to jelly but he managed to grab the other boxer and hold on for dear life.

I wondered whether boxing was any good for me at all. A few more seasons wouldn't hurt. This was my year to be the champ. I promised myself that. I had to prove myself.

That horrid sense of defeat, of not being good enough, was no longer in me. I had trust in the bigger picture. Losing and learning humility is equally as important as winning.

Time passed. The cocaine kicked in for Arlo and Flash, they talked a lot of random shit. I kept as much of my attention as possible on the boxing. I could feel Olivia watching me.

World-class boxers are incredible human beings. The negotiation between explosive movement and balance takes over a decade to master. The physical state they get their bodies into is hard to believe until you've tried to get somewhere close to it yourself.

Arlo's voice caught me, he was laughing hard at his own chat. 'Mate, I had two freshers down here the other night, fuckin ket whores. Literally came here before a night out, getting some gear, in these little shorts, wavy jackets, those fuckin little legs like, wow, and they were giving it all the chat about how wild they were. So I said, Let's have a threesome if you're that loose, and they started getting all yap-yap trying to call my bluff, like, No way you wouldn't do that with us you haven't got it in you, so I started getting a little hecked up and I got a fucking wad of cash out and was saying, Don't underestimate the fucking president, and I flicked a couple of grand of notes at them bam bam bam saying, Get undressed you fucking whores, and next thing I knew I had one handcuffed to the bed fucking her in the ass, while the other fucked her with a dildo. Fucking mental. Money gets the girls.'

'Money gets the girls,' Flash said.

'I made them wear their wavy jackets the whole time too, just so they knew they were nothing but ket whores to me.'

Flash and Arlo laughed and laughed. Olivia stayed silent, disinterested, eyes fixed on me. I couldn't help feeling torn between disgust and wanting to experience something like that. The image of fucking Olivia in the ass, handcuffed to a bed. I shook my head to get rid of the thought.

Flash said, 'This chop's really the one. What do you reckon, one more for the road?'

'Go on then,' Arlo said.

Flash started racking up on the mirror again. 'You know

what, Tommy,' he said, 'if you're not touching this stuff, man, you should be selling it. The profit's not like mud but it flies out. Only reason I'm not getting rid of bars is coz I'd sniff it all.'

Flash and Arlo guffawed.

'I am happy with what I'm doing, to be honest. It feels less risky,' I said.

'It's all Class A, Tommy boy, you've got to be in it to win it, rinse it, yeah?'

Arlo's phone rang. He said, 'Serious?'

The room was awkwardly silent.

Arlo said, 'What the fuck are you waiting for then? Get down here and pick me up and tell the boys to meet us at Jason's.' He put his phone on the table. 'My so-called mate Jason's gone and fucked me over, now I gotta go down there and shake him up a bit. You two coming?'

'Buzzing,' Flash said, 'you know how much I like a bit of a move around.'

'What did he do?' I said.

'His was my safe house. He's been stealing gear, thought I wouldn't notice, I'm gonna fuck him up.'

'I'll pass,' I said. 'Can't handle the violence.'

'A grand says you'll come with us,' Arlo said.

'I wouldn't do it for all the money in the world,' I said.

'We'll see about that,' Arlo smirked.

★★★

I was at Moose's new house. He had moved into a place with Daisy. They'd both graduated and were in full-time work. Daisy was at work. Anthony was next to me on the sofa. Moose, on a chair by the table. The place was clean and fresh, except for the slight hint of weed in the air. The colourful, cultured decor made me happy.

Moose said, 'Go on then, Tommy, what's the plan?'

I said, 'We're going to bring in a lot of money this year, and we need to figure the best way to handle it all: what's going to be safest way to move stuff around, which roles we'll fulfil, and so on. I have quite a lot on my plate, so the more you can help with, the better. We'll split everything fairly.'

'How much work we talking?' Anthony said.

'I reckon we'll be turning over almost ten grand a month if we work together. We're going to do it properly, wash and tax the money, safe houses, burners, discipline. My best idea so far, is getting a shop in one of the arcades, buying vintage clothes at kilo sales, and reselling them for way more than we bought them for. People go mad for vintage stuff. We can record fake cash sales all we like. And I'll put a load of it through my event accounts too.'

'With all those costs, we're not going to clear a lot, you sure it's worth it at this stage?' Anthony said.

'Definitely. It puts us in a position to grow properly, without as much risk. All those other dealers are ticking time bombs, I don't want to be like that. With any luck, we'll make good profits on the businesses and won't have to be boosting cash flow with dodgy money for long.'

'Yeah, I'd definitely go legit as soon as possible, I have a bad feeling about Arlo and that lot,' Moose said. 'Although, I'm not sure how much I can help, my shifts are dire. I might just be a burden, to be honest.'

'How about we use yours for the safe house, me and Tommy can make the moves, you just help out where you can. I got time, haven't I?' Anthony said.

'I don't want either of you picking up from Arlo's, it's sketchy as fuck down there now. You've got to talk to him, Tommy,' Moose said.

'I'll talk to him. So, we're good? We need to find a place in one of the arcades, any chance you can do that, Anthony? I'm going to get on with planning the event. I'll register a company for us to do the books through. Just let me know when you find something, there'll be cash waiting in the business account ready to go. Find out when one of those kilo sales are on too, and buy whatever looks fashionable, loads of it. Moose, I'll get Arlo to send someone to deliver half a box of mud and some pingers here. I've got to shoot off, got a workshop.'

'Let's make it happen,' Moose said, holding his clenched fist out in front of him.

We all fist-bumped.

★★★

I was excited about the creative writing workshops that second year had to offer, and I thought it was a good idea to get into a habit of going to them regularly. I was five minutes late, and I opened the door to a chatty room of people who quietened a little to look at me.

The tutor, Sibi, smiled pleasantly. She had short hair, messy in a stylish way. The tables and chairs formed a rectangle. Sibi was at one of the short ends of the rectangle, nearest the whiteboard. There was nothing written on the whiteboard. She had that whole short side of the rectangle of tables to herself. Every seat along the other three sides was occupied, except one, opposite her at the far end of the room.

Behind me was a wall painted white. To my right was a girl with a studded denim jacket. I nodded vaguely. To my left, a guy with a blue Adidas T-shirt, the logo large over the chest, white. The same T-shirt everyone was wearing these days. I smiled vaguely. The chatter died out completely.

Sibi said, 'We're going to break the ice today by going around the room and each of you telling the class one thing that's on your mind this morning. It can be anything: something pleasant, a worry, or simply what is in your head at the time. Although, from experience, that can be dangerous.'

Everyone laughed.

What was on my mind was that I had a lot of money from The Festival, and I was poised to make a lot more. I couldn't stop thinking about how much money I had, how much money I could make, how much money I would need to spend on the property in the arcade, how much money we could spend on vintage clothes, how much money the next box of mud would cost, wondering whether I would ever be a millionaire. The heaviest thought of them all, which kept coming back to me, was that I'd made my decision regarding Arlo's proposition.

Fuck, my turn already. 'Um,' I said. 'I have a ...' I froze. And then it came to me, a normal people worry. 'I'm worried I don't spend enough time with my girlfriend.'

The tutor was intrigued. Everyone else smiled. I wondered if any of them knew I was a drug dealer. I kept worrying that they were looking at me in that funny way.

The girl next to me said, 'I'm worried about sharing my writing with the class.'

Everyone agreed. When you write, you expose yourself. That takes a lot of balls. As young, novice writers, we all had a long way to go. Sibi assured us it was all par for the course, and over time it would become much easier, and eventually we'd enjoy sharing our work, and criticism would be our friend.

We read a short story about a woman kept in a nice house in a suburban area. Sibi prompted us to find meaning between the lines. I was amazed at what we found. There were metaphors for World War II in there. Things like buns in the oven, which we all assumed to mean pregnancy, were actually referring to extermination ovens, and so on.

I wished I could do that with my writing, wished I could hide meaning to provoke thought. But I felt mine was too frank, too full on. I hadn't written a thing since I'd returned to uni, and I hated myself for that, but I knew I needed to stop hating myself for it, because people with self-worth find a way to embrace their feelings as part of who they are, and forgive themselves for it.

When the class finished, I put my notepad in my bag, and I smiled, because I wasn't putting any drugs in there. I was being a normal student, a proper student. The class chattered as they left. I had no one to chatter to.

I said, 'Thanks,' to Sibi, on my way out. She smiled.

I walked to my student house with a strange sense of satisfaction, I'd enjoyed the class. And I hoped I would enjoy more classes to come.

Later, Arlo and I were in my bedroom. The door was locked. It was a bit messy, but not chaotic. The money plant was on my windowsill. The Wandering Jew was on the shelf above my bed. It was light and frail, only a few leaves.

Arlo was wearing a green Adidas zip-jacket with blue stripes along the arms. I remembered having a jacket like that from a charity shop when I was about six, when we lived in a council flat in London. Back then, I slept on cushions on the floor. Mum couldn't afford an extra bed.

Arlo said, 'Richard delivered that gear to Moose's earlier, you lot are gonna be busy, Tommy, you're doing well. You saving any time for yourself? Having any fun?'

'A little fun, I got that houseplant with Isobel, that was pretty good, and we've planned to do something next week.'

I pointed at the Wandering Jew.

'Living the dream, Tommy,' he said, chuckling. 'What is it with you and plants?'

'They make me happy, and they don't ask for much in return. What more could you want?'

'A tree that literally grows money,' Arlo said.

'I suppose that would save us a lot of grief,' I said.

'Anyway, bro, you know what I wanna ask you, so tell me what you've decided,' Arlo said.

I said, 'If I work for you, I need it to be a complete secret, I'm not even going to tell Moose and Anthony, and definitely not Isobel, not a single soul. And I'm going to go by a different name. I don't want anyone to know anything about me.

'Okay, bro, that's no problem, I got you covered. I know you're doing alright already, but this way you have a bit of security. It's only a matter of time before someone takes the piss. You get robbed once and you're back to square one. Working for me, nobody's gonna touch you. You keen then?'

'Can you advance the first month's pay?' I said. Ten grand seemed too good to be true.

'Tell you what, bro,' he said, pulling a clip of notes out of his pocket, counting twenties. 'Here's a grand, and once you've found a nice new place for the new Tommy, whatever his name's gonna be, ring me and I'll sort the deposit and rent and all that. I'll do it legit so you don't need to worry about anything, and once this month has gone well, I'll give you ten grand cash on top. Can't be fairer than that, can I?'

I was quiet. I was thinking about how nobody in their right mind would turn down ten grand a month just to move a few parcels around. I thought about how the King never got caught, and how I could pull it off if I stayed smart. I could help Arlo make his operation safer, that would benefit us both.

'What if I decide it's not for me?' I said.

'You know me, bro, I'm not gonna make you do anything you don't wanna do, as long as you're not going off to work for someone else, or stealing my customers, you do what you gotta do. Stick this uni year out with me and I'll sort you out so well you'll be laughing for life.'

'Yeah, go on then,' I said. A year flies by, how bad can it get?

'Good man,' Arlo said. 'As soon as you've sorted that place, I need you to meet Din. He knows the cocaine guy around here. I've never met him, he works for a man called Terry, he's like Terry's Messenger or something. Terry runs Cardiff, he basically controls everything that comes in here, except the bud the Turks shift, that's their own, grown here, but everything else, Terry's got a hand on it.'

I felt a strange yearning for that sort of power, and at the same time, a massive, uncomfortable apprehension towards it.

'Get this, nobody's ever met Terry. Din's been buying flake off him for five years, but it's always been through the supplier, who Din can't name, and who is adamant he's working for Terry. The best thing is, they get this shit straight off the boat and nobody touches it, driven straight up here, Din doesn't cut my shit and I don't cut it for you lot so it's fucking premium, the best.'

'I wonder what this Terry bloke is all about,' I said.

'Everyone knows about Terry, everyone high up in this business anyway. They say he's ruthless, absolute psycho, but he gets the job done, everything he does is perfect, like some kind of control freak and all that. I dunno, but I do know you never piss Terry off. If you work well with him, he'll sort you. Only reason the Turks are allowed to move their own bud in this city is coz Terry gets a huge cut. Must be a fucking billionaire.'

'I guess we're high-ups now,' I said.

'Tommy, mate, this time last year we were penniless in chess club drinking orange squash, now I've got a fucking gold-plated china set that I've never used. Anyway, bro, I gotta shoot. Here's a little present, do what you want with it.'

The present was a freezer bag with about an ounce of flake in it. Before I could protest, Arlo left. He pulled my door closed three times, each time it wedged stuck at the bottom. He gave up and left it open. The front door of my student house closed loudly.

A thousand pounds and a freezer bag with about eighteen hundred quid's worth of premium cocaine lay thin and bland on my desk, next to my chunk of handwritten novel and accompanying notes. I put the money in between the pages of the heavy dictionary on my bookshelf.

★★★

I felt *odd* about working for Arlo, as if I was doing something terribly wrong. I couldn't work out whether I felt guilty because I distrusted him, or whether it was because I was sour that I could have been in his shoes. Whatever it was, it spurred me to do everything properly. I wanted to be impeccable. I refused to lose again.

To secure my new identity, I purchased stolen ID documents from the Dark Web. I didn't want to use my own laptop for doing that, just in case there was any traceable evidence of the transaction that could be linked to me, so I bought a crappy laptop from a second-hand shop and used that one. I used the Wi-Fi of a random coffee shop on Crwys Road to ensure the activity wasn't being linked to my home network.

I sat on my own in the corner, with the laptop and my back facing the wall. Light-hearted dance music sounded from a portable speaker in the corner. The wall was beige, with small, black-and-white stags sketched on it. A stag horn protruded from the wall. I wondered if it was real, or if it was just a wooden carving.

The waiter wore black jeans and a knitted black cardigan. I ordered a cappuccino. A student with books and his laptop out tapped away at the opposite end of the room. The other small, square tables were empty. I appreciated the ambience. Quiet, but not dead.

The problem with the Dark Web is that it's completely unregulated. Some sites are trustworthy, but most are there to scam you out of your money, and they use fake reviews and forum posts to make themselves look as legitimate as can be. It's not as if you can complain to the police when you've been ripped off trying to buy a fake ID. On the Dark Web, you can buy drugs, prostitutes, murders, counterfeit cash, and almost any other contraband you can think of.

The waiter put a mug of cappuccino on the table. It smelt rich, intense, the top was foamy, white and brown, and there were darker ripples where they'd poured the liquid and shaped the foam in a fancy way.

Using encrypted messaging, I contacted a seller and asked about an ID for a UK resident with a reasonably normal name, aged somewhere between twenty-one and twenty-eight. The seller replied promptly. He had what I was looking for. He sent me a photo of a provisional UK driving licence, and a passport, in the name of Leon Reddick. Twenty-four years old. Address in Surrey.

To ensure the fraudulent ID was not associated with my student house, I told the seller to send it to a made-up name, Michael Morris, and I gave him an address on Dogfield Street. It was an address I'd sold drugs at in first year, and I knew the old tenants had moved to a new house so it was unlikely anyone there now would recognise me. My plan was to turn up pretending I'd once lived there, and ask for any post for Michael Morris.

On my way home, I put the laptop I'd bought into a random bin. I walked through the door of my student house, and Sammy called for me from the living room.

Lilly, Ellen, Mickey and Sammy were sitting on the sofas in the living room, curtains closed, film about to start, currently paused. Sammy said, with a cheeky smile, 'Watch *Harry Potter* with us, Tommy, you could be head boy of Hufflepuff one day.'

'I'd never want to steal your place,' I said.

Everyone laughed.

'Come on, you never spend time with us any more,' Sammy said.

I said, 'I know, I'm sorry. I'm just so flat out starting a business, I haven't had time to breathe.'

Lilly said, 'No way, that's so cool, what kind of business?'

'I'm going to sell vintage clothing at one of the arcades in the city centre.'

'That's amazing,' she said. Her eyes bulged with genuineness.

Sammy laughed. I wasn't sure if he suspected it was a front for the drug money, or whether he was laughing because people like me don't start businesses. People like me are not usually successful. The world is stacked against the underprivileged.

I said, 'Start without me, I've just got a few emails to send and a quick errand to run. I'll be with you in half an hour.'

'See ya later,' Lilly said.

'In a bit,' I said.

The film started, I went into my bedroom and locked the

door. I could hear the *Harry Potter* theme tune clearly. I hated how the walls were paper-thin. I closed my curtains.

I realised that I didn't *actually* have anything to do. That felt weird. Anthony had the burner and was shifting the mud. I didn't want to look for a new place on my normal laptop, so was going to buy another cheap, shitty one to browse anonymously with. I thought about watching *Harry Potter*. Yes, I will treat myself to a nice evening before everything gets too hectic. I invited Isobel over.

We were watching the *Prisoner of Azkaban*. I was agitated. Couldn't relax. My mind kept crunching figures, and then flowing onto other thoughts. I love stories where the underdog rises to the top. Orphaned Harry is the best underdog you can get, so innocent and naïve, only to become powerful and ultimately, prevail.

'Tommy, get us some popcorn,' Sammy said.

'Only if you suck my dick,' I said.

Everyone laughed.

'Tell you what, screw popcorn, who wants pizza?' I said.

'Oh, I can't afford it,' Lilly said.

'Yeah, I'm skint,' Sammy said.

You lot don't know the meaning of skint, I thought. I said, 'Don't worry, my treat. To say sorry for never being around.'

The pizza smelt rich with cheese, garlic and grease. Everyone was delighted. I gifted myself one slice, and the others ate the rest. The pizza you get delivered is generally soaked in shit oils, the dough is hard to digest, the cheese is crap, and the tomato sauce, not merely tomato. That kind of pizza is not conducive to good health. I wanted to be healthy so I could box again and win the championships.

Isobel and I cuddled on the sofa next to Sammy. She was warm and light and soft, and she smelt fresh, like her moisturiser or her shampoo had fruit in it. It was a nice evening.

Two days later, I went to the address on Dogfield Street to pick up my post. My heart raced when I knocked on the door. The main risk was that if the Dark Web purchase was a police set-up, they'd be watching the house, but I thought that if that was the case, it would take them much longer to deliver the letter with the fake ID in it, and so if the letter was there already, there was nothing to worry about. Plus, the police have much more to worry about than a fake ID. A rounded lad, breathing heavily, answered the door.

'Sorry to bother you,' I said. 'Um …' I paused. For fuck's sake, don't hesitate. 'I lived here last year. A friend of mine said they accidentally sent a letter here the other day. Do you have it by any chance?'

'Oh, well, we usually just put them in a pile, which gets thrown away after a while,' he said. 'I'll see if it's around.' He disappeared back into the house, door half open, the wall I could see was white, the floor, pale laminate.

He came back with a pile of letters, he said, 'Pass them on to your old housemates, would you?'

'Thank you so much,' I said.

Walking home, I sifted through the letters. Mine was near the top, a brown envelope addressed to 'Michael Morris'. The name and address were printed in a standard font on a sticky label. I threw the rest of the post in the bin. Inside the envelope was a blank piece of paper with a driver's licence taped to it, and a passport. Leon Reddick had dark hair, like me. His fringe was down to his eyebrows, unlike my hair, which was pushed back. His face was slim and clean shaven, like mine. His eyes were dark, unlike mine. Nobody really scrutinises IDs anyway.

***

The apartment I found overlooked the water of Cardiff Bay. It was spacious and full of daylight. As nice as the Whitehouse, but smaller, so Arlo's ego wouldn't be provoked. It was a thousand times cleaner, and I felt good in it. The estate agent and I stood in the middle of the open-plan living room and kitchen. The large windows from floor to ceiling in the living room boasted a breathtaking view of land and water. We were high up, on the seventh floor of a ten-storey building.

The sun was out, shimmering over crinkles in the water's surface, flickering, fluid; it reminded me of diamonds, except this image was better, rarer, more powerful.

The kitchen area gleamed. Glassy-black surfaces, not like the plastic shit at home. Six spacious cupboards along the wall, more underneath the glossy black worktops. An empty wooden wine rack on the wall marked where the kitchen ended and living room started. The double fridge-freezer had a water and ice dispenser built into it.

The overall look of the place was flashy, but not outrageous. The floor tiles, five different shades of light sand to dark brown, rectangular and of varying widths and lengths, all fit together to make a bold yet elegant floor design. There were more light tiles than dark.

The sofas, long, leather, slimline, bright red; I wasn't sure about the colour, a bit too kitsch for my liking, but the floor made up for it. An ultra-flat TV, about fifty inches, mounted to the wall.

The rug under the coffee table was thick and soft, white. White is impossible to keep clean. 'Could you get that in a darker colour?' I said.

He looked at me a little funny. 'Why not,' he said.

My suit did the persuading there. Slim fit silvery-grey trumped his frumpy charcoal.

I could get used to this. No, don't. It's only temporary.

You're going to quit as soon as you can.

He showed me to the bedroom. The four-poster bed was giant. I threw myself onto its firm, comfortable surface, landing flat on my back. Aaahhh. In-breath. Deep. Out-breath, relaxing.

'Ultra-high-quality memory foam,' the agent said.

Ultra. I wonder who regulates the scale of quality. Ultra seems to be better than super these days, and super better than premium. Maybe they need to start branding the drugs as ultra-premium. I smiled at the thought. Ultra-premium platinum-gold cocaine.

'I love it,' I said.

He opened the en suite bathroom door. The shower had a wide, circular, chrome head. The whole room was shiny and tiled, black and white, perfectly clean.

'I'll need to speak to my uncle this evening when he gets back from the office. We'll apply first thing tomorrow morning. Remember, we're paying six months' rent in advance, so be sure to wait for our offer,' I said, smugly, like some preppy whose family is actually paying his rent. I felt like a dickhead doing it, but I had to play the part so there was no suspicion. The agent looked at me exactly like I was the twat I was pretending to be. I smiled and held out my hand.

He shook it lightly, a bad handshake. 'We'll hear from you tomorrow then,' he said. His skin was blotchy and pale, unhealthy.

I went and sat by the water's edge, everything felt surreal. I was horrifically nervous and absolutely buzzing.

This is my lucky break, I've finally made it.

But there was a sour worry in my gut that it would all go wrong, that it was all too good to be true.

Someone like me can't be rich, it just isn't possible. It has to go wrong, it always does.

I realised what I was thinking was too negative, and not logical.

You deserve it. You've worked harder than anyone you know, and smarter. Take the reward.

I taxied back to my student house. Opened the door to see Sammy in the hallway. He said, 'Bloody hell, you're dressed nicely.' He was wearing a black hoodie, blue skinny jeans, white trainers. Standard.

'Had a business meeting,' I said. Still in my suit.

'Cool,' he said.

I wasn't sure what to make of his facial expression. He seemed a bit *off* with me. 'How's it going, everything alright?' I said.

'Yeah, all good. I've got a lecture. Better get on.'

'Alright. See you later,' I said. Stepped aside to let him past.

'Doubt it,' he said. He closed the door loudly behind him.

What am I supposed to do? We don't all get things handed to us on a plate. Sammy doesn't realise that.

I had planned to meet Isobel, so we could walk around Roath Lake together. The lake was *our thing*. We loved it. I changed into normal clothes. Adidas trainers, black skinny jeans, a stylish white T-shirt, a faded blue denim jacket. Headed for the lake.

Isobel was sitting on a bench on the bridge. Her gaze was fixed towards the white clock tower that looks like a mini lighthouse. The bright blue paint on the door of the clock tower stood out, unnatural against the soft greys, deeper blues and greens of the lake. On the other side of the bridge, the children's play park was empty. The grass and paths surrounding it, empty, except for the trees and shrubbery. Epic.

Isobel must have heard my footsteps. She smiled at me. Her smile was stunning, as always. White teeth. Lovely, welcoming eyes. I wished I could enjoy her smile every second of every day.

'Hello, sweetheart. You look wonderful.' I said.

'Sweetheart, that's a new one.'

'I was talking to the lake.'

'Is that so?'

'You look better than wonderful,' I said. Isobel was wearing a pale pink jumpsuit. White trainers. Very trendy.

'Thank you. As do you.'

I kissed her on the lips, and on each cheek.

'Would you like to sit here, or walk?' she said.

'Let's walk,' I said.

Isobel and I held hands as we walked. Her touch was gentle. We walked slowly, enjoying the view of the vast lake beside us. The lake looks different every time you see it. It absorbs and reflects everything around it. Everything around it is predominantly natural. Trees, grass, shrubbery, the sky. Beyond the trees: a road, and houses. The lake reflects the streetlights and houselights at night.

That day, the lake was reflecting a light bluish sky patched with grey clouds. All that infused with the reflections of the greenery to form the darker blues, greens and greys. Everything changed, continuously yet slowly, as the water, the clouds and our positions changed. Flux.

There were plenty of ducks, geese, and pigeons toddling along about their daily business on the concrete path we walked, and on the lake's grassy edges.

'What have you been up to today?' Isobel said.

I really didn't want to lie to her, but I had to. If she didn't know about it, it didn't exist to her. And if it didn't exist to her, she couldn't be involved in it. 'I had a business meeting with Anthony earlier. That's about it. How about you?'

She slowed her walk a little. 'Oh,' she said. Apparently deliberating for a second. 'That's strange. I bumped into

Anthony in town earlier. He never mentioned it.'

Fucking hell. What are the chances. 'Yeah, that *is* strange. He might have had a lot on his mind, what with the business tasks and all that.'

'You're all very busy, aren't you? Are you managing alright?'

'It's pretty full on, but we're getting there.'

'I miss you, you know. It's frustrating barely ever seeing you. I'm supposed to be your girlfriend, after all.'

'I love you very much,' I said. 'I wish there was more time in the day. I won't be busy forever.'

'I hope not,' she said.

'What were you doing in town, anyway?'

Isobel switched sides to avoid walking close to a large swan; took my other hand, held it slightly tensely. 'A swan could tear your arm off,' she said.

'I think they just tell kids that to make sure they don't provoke them. These swans are so friendly. It's nice, don't you think? When animals and people walk together. We're all enjoying the lake, just the same. No torn arms in sight.'

'True, it's lovely. I was just shopping. And I met Nina for coffee.'

I felt anxious. Imagined encountering Isobel and Nina in town one day; one of Arlo's associates by my side, both of us carrying rucksacks full of money and cocaine. I couldn't introduce Isobel as my girlfriend, I wouldn't want to put her in any kind of danger. Isobel would probably sense my discomfort. She would wonder who my new friend was and what we were up to. I'd have to tell more and more awkward lies. The worry kept me silent for a while.

'Are you okay?' Isobel said.

'I'm okay,' I said.

On our way back, walking down Wellfield Road, I saw

Gary in an alleyway. Gary is the homeless guy I met before the Rhetorik and Friends night. Since then, we had bumped into each other on the street here and there, and had had a short conversation every time we did. There was a man sitting cross legged next to Gary, lifeless. 'You two alright, Gary?' I said.

'He's just had a smoke, that's all.' Gary's teeth were all gone. His mouth no longer looked like death, the gums were a much more normal, light reddish colour. He looked a lot better than before. But his teeth were all gone. Fuck.

'Spice?' I said, trying not to look at his mouth.

'Always spice now,' he said. 'Not me, though, still clean now, I am. I'm gonna get a room to sleep in every night, and some fuckin new teeth, maybe. Gonna take me a while, but you know how it is.'

I held back tears. Fucking hell. That's not what you want to hear your mate say. I wished I knew how to help him. Not to give him money here and there, but really, how to *help* him. Nobody did, else he wouldn't have been there.

'Here,' I said, handing him a tenner.

'I've got some too,' Isobel said. She gave him her spare change.

'God bless you both,' he said.

'This is my girlfriend, Isobel,' I said. 'This is Gary.'

She shook his hand.

'We'd better get on, mate,' I said. 'Good luck, I hope it works out for you. I'll see you soon.'

'See you soon, Tommy,' Gary said.

As we walked away, Isobel said, 'You're a sweet man, Tommy.'

I couldn't reply because I was too sad. Sad because I knew that the tenner I'd given Gary would only get him half way to a bed and breakfast for one night. Sad because despite

Gary's high hopes, I was sure that the next time I saw him, he'd still be homeless and toothless.

***

It was my first day taking care of Arlo's business. I was waiting for Din at the Bay House. I had turned the sofas to face the big windows so I could see the marina, not the giant TV. It was a grey day, the wind roughened the surface of the water.

My fringe was down and ruffled, my hair flat, like that of Leon Reddick in the photo. I was wearing contact lenses that made my eyes brown. I wanted to ensure Leon Reddick was as different from Tommy as possible. I wore grey slim fit suit trousers and a fitted black shirt.

I wasn't sure how nervous I should be. I remembered the time we passed Din on the stairs, leaving the King's place. He was small and rounded. When Arlo had said that Din was a big deal, I'd found it hard to believe. He was too normal-looking. This was not like the films.

I sat there wondering where the King was. I imagined him getting bored of the cave in Tibet, and moving on to a full moon party in Thailand.

The higher up the ladder you go, the more disciplined you need to be. Terry, whoever he is, is moving serious weight without even touching it. I admire that. Why doesn't everyone aspire to that? Most people just try to do it all themselves, but that's not conducive to rapid growth. It's riskier too. I'm handling some of Arlo's business, but he's doing his own thing too, isn't that just unnecessary?

He's got drugs at the Whitehouse all the time, that's so sketchy it's not worth it. If he left me to it, I could do it all safely, intelligently, so nobody would ever get into trouble. He'd make serious money without lifting a finger. What's to stop me going off and doing it myself? Not enough capital. And loyalty.

Is twenty grand a month much worse than forty? When does it end? You need to be modest. Nobody has the self-control.

The buzzer. I sprang off the sofa, darted to the door.

'Hello,' I said, through the intercom.

'Din here,' he said.

Din, Connor, and another guy entered the Bay House.

'Hello, welcome, come in,' I said. Why so formal?

Din shook my hand first, 'Hello, Leon, mate. How you going? Alright?' he said. Strong Welsh accent. His grip was firm, he was composed, relaxed, confident.

'Nice to meet you,' I said.

'Connor,' Connor said. His eyes darted about the place, as if he was wired. It was only 11.00 am.

The other guy introduced himself as Jonno.

'Leon,' I said.

Jonno had thin, receding hair. Unfortunate, unhealthy. By the rest of him, I assumed he was no more than a few years older than me. His skin was smooth and pale. He was tall and skinny.

The quality of someone's hair is a good sign of what's happening inside their body. Not enough nutrients, hormonal imbalances, and the hair goes shitty. That's why Mum's is grey and slowing, edging backwards, poor woman. Not fair considering she eats more healthily than Olympic athletes.

'You got a tidy place up 'ere you 'ave, Leon,' Din said.

'I'm very happy with it,' I said. 'Can I get you a drink? Beer, coffee?'

'Why not. I'll 'ave a beer,' Din said. He pointed at the other two. 'Beer? Beer?'

You could tell he was sharp by the way he moved. Despite

his short neck and stubby head, he commanded the room with his body language.

The boys nodded. I got three cold bottles of premium lager from the fridge, popped the lids, a light steam wisped from the neck. Din lingered at the window a little, then took a seat. I sat opposite him. He gazed out of the window some more.

'So, you're taking care of Arlo's business now,' he said. The way he said it was not as if it was a matter of fact, but more as if he was intrigued by the idea. 'And Arlo took after the King.'

He deliberated. You could feel his thoughts were calculated, purposeful. I liked that about him, but he was drinking beer in the morning, that wasn't rigorous.

'You after the usual?' he said.

'No. We're expanding. We need two boxes,' I said. Two kilograms. Each gram gets sold at one hundred pounds on the street. Mental money. Not that we'd be selling it in grams. We'd be selling it in bars and ounces. I hesitated in the silence and said, 'If that's alright?'

Din looked at me with a curious grin. Connor made a whistling noise, the sound of surprise at the quantity, the magnitude.

Jonno sat quiet, expressionless.

'Great mate, great,' Din said. 'How much you paying up front?'

Even if Din got five per cent commission on the sale, this was a three-grand meeting for him.

'We've got twenty ready right now,' I said.

That was less than half the total cost. Even though someone like Arlo was bringing in shitloads of money each week, his overheads were high, and he needed cash flow for all the other substances we dealt in. It wasn't as if every penny he made went into the bank and stayed there for later use. This meant he was always getting drugs on credit, selling them, paying the debt, getting more on credit, and so on.

'Twenty?' he said. 'Bluddy 'ell, he won't like it, and Terry won't like it, not at all, hear, not at all. How long you want that for?'

'A couple of weeks maximum,' I said. I hoped Arlo had done his maths right.

'I'll get him to do it, but 'e won't like that, 'e won't like that at all,' he muttered the last bit. 'But for Arlo, we'll do it. D'you want that delivered here?'

'No, no gear here. No cash either. I want to be able to sleep at night. How about we meet at Artigiano's tomorrow, that little coffee place in town? You could hand over the two kilos there. I will drop the cash to you tonight.'

'I understand, good call.'

I was worried that my inexperience was showing. I wasn't sure what someone in my shoes should say when it comes to sleeping at night. I was worried I was showing weakness.

'A coffee shop. Public. Inconspicwas. I like it. You're a smart man, Leon. Most 'ave gone complacent in this game, me too at times, you know, me too. It's so easy these days, we're all takin' the piss. I'm careful enaf, but it won't be long until most of these fuckers get caught.' He stood up, 'You're going to do just fine 'ere mate. Two o'clock okay for you tomorrow? This Artigiano place … never been, hope the coffee's good. See you there.'

'Two is fine,' I said.

Handshakes and goodbyes.

Once they'd gone, I changed into black jeans and black T-shirt, took out my brown contact lenses so my eyes were blue again, and pushed my hair back. I was Tommy again.

I slumped on the sofa, tired from the nerves. The clouds had let a bit of sun through; it glistened as it moved on the rougher patches of water with a relaxing rhythm. Mum would like the view, but she'd hate the decor.

It dawned on me that Leon had no friends, and he knew nobody except Arlo, Din, Connor and Jonno. Less than a handful of people. I wished I could show Sammy the Bay House. He'd go mad for it. I imagined his face so excited to be associated with the big guns.

After lying on that sofa and thinking about how surreal my life had become, and worrying about how ten grand a month was too good to be true, I arranged to meet Moose and Anthony to check how things were going with them.

★★★

We all sat at Moose's dining table. The dining table had some cool candle holders on it, with cream coloured wax candles in them. Each candle holder was made of metal engraved with intricate, abstract shapes. The colour of the metal ranged from dark, oily grey to light, matt grey.

I said, 'So where are we with the shop?'

'I've found a place on Castle Arcade. It's not big, but it's a nice little space. Massive glass windows, rustic brick finish on the walls, nice wooden floor. You wanna come see it tomorrow?' Anthony said.

'I promised Isobel I'd see her tomorrow,' I said. I paused, I felt terrible lying, but I didn't want to tell them I was working for Arlo. 'I trust you. If you like it, get the paperwork and I'll sort it. How're you doing with clothes?'

'We went to a few kilo sales, got a couple of hundred items, sports jackets, jeans, denim jackets, sports tees,' Anthony said.

'Perfect,' I said. 'And ask Coach Jimmy if he wants a rail for his Rhetorik stuff in there. Give him whatever deal he wants, don't mention me, you're the manager remember.'

'Yes, sir!' Anthony said, saluting me.

'Yes, boss,' Moose said, saluting me. They saluted each other, laughing hard.

'Fuck you both,' I said. 'Right, what are we going to call it?'

Moose piped up, 'Wannabe hipsters like you would love a little name like Vintage and Vinyl, wouldn't you Tommy?'

'Quirky,' I said. 'I know you're taking the piss, but that'll do nicely. And how's our side-business going?'

Moose said, 'That flake Arlo gave you went in a day.'

'Jesus,' I said.

'And the mud and pingers are going steadily,' Anthony said.

'Tommy,' Moose said, 'we want to sell coke and ket now. There's no point punting Class A's if we're not going to make the most of it. We'd double our takings and that means we can quit sooner, and while we're ahead. I only wanna do this until I've got enough for a house or something.'

I didn't feel great about it, but I didn't want to be a hypocrite. I saw how people got addicted to coke and ket way quicker and easier than to MD, and the MD crowd were so much more reliable. I thought that dealing coke and ket meant more room for error. Yet, I was picking up two kilos of coke for Arlo the next day, and I was lying about what I was doing, which made me feel so wrong. The addiction issue made me particularly uncomfortable. I convinced myself I wasn't selling the stuff to the end user any more, I wasn't actually buying or selling it at all. I was just handling it. And if Moose and Anthony wanted to sell it, that wasn't me selling it either. So, I wasn't doing anything directly against my morals. I said, 'I'll get some delivered. Just be careful, and no selling to addicts.'

'We wouldn't,' Moose said.

***

I was at Artigiano's, waiting for Din and two kilos of cocaine. The nerves were ten times worse than anything I'd experienced before, even during a championship boxing match. I was trying not to sweat, but my white T-shirt was already thick and sticky. Why the hell have I worn white? I thought.

I sipped my strong black coffee. Sweat cooled on my forehead. The sweat was making everything worse, I couldn't stop thinking about it. Couldn't stop thinking that I looked weird, out of place, suspicious. I felt sick.

The café was busy. It was better that way. Less focus on us. People occupied most tables, chatting, laughing, working, consuming, enjoying their overpriced coffee.

At least the coffee is Fairtrade. Fairtrade cocaine? Obviously not. Stop being a hypocrite. Get some integrity. As soon as Mum is sorted, quit and do something real, something to help the world. Make the world a better place.

The thought fired me up, got me excited, made me feel alive.

Connor entered. He saw me and waved, big smile on his face. He was dressed casually, blue skinny jeans, white trainers, black T-shirt sticking out of the bottom of a grey jumper. He had a green rucksack on his back. A rucksack with seventy grand's worth of gear in it. Class A. That horrible feeling returned to my stomach.

Surely, we can't get away with this so easily?

I was expecting Din. I didn't like the inconsistency. I stood and embraced Connor as a mate. Less suspicious. It was all pre-planned, no discussing of business here, no checking the merchandise, no names.

'You alright then, mate? Having a good day? I'll just get a drink, alright,' he said.

I sipped my coffee, it was cooling fast, but still tasted good. Strong. Rich. Kick. The caffeine stimulated me, made me feel more capable, energy coursed through my veins alongside the nerves.

Connor returned with a large, frothy drink in a big round mug. There was cinnamon sprinkled on top.

Nice. Cinnamon is good for circulation.

'How's it going?' I said.

'All good mate, busy, working all day you know,' he said. 'Here, I've got your bag for you.' Handed me the bag. Two kilos of cocaine.

It felt lighter than I thought it would. All the weight was in my head. Two kilograms is just a few bags of sugar, but when it's Class A drugs, it drags your whole body down. I wanted to look inside the bag, but I put it beside me without a glance.

'Thanks, can't believe I left it at yours,' I said. Not sure why, nobody cared. Nobody was listening. That's how these things go unnoticed every day.

'Not a worry, mate, no worries at all,' he said.

'Thanks, I appreciate it,' I said.

'Anyway, I gotta shoot back to work now.' Connor chugged his drink down, wiped his mouth with the back of his hand, sprang up off his seat and strode away.

So there it was. Me, a rucksack, and a couple of boxes of cocaine. A million thoughts hit me at once: what if the police were following Connor, what if they're outside, or in here undercover, what if this coffee shop is bugged, what if I get stopped for some reason walking to the safe house, what if I get run over, what if someone noticed how quick our coffee date was and got suspicious … for fuck's sake so many things could go wrong.

After a few weeks of regular large transactions, the nerves

subsided. I got so numbed to the idea of moving big weights around I barely thought about it, it was as if I was moving bags of overpriced sugar.

Chapter 9

Regrettably, my visits to Mum became less and less. The money I sent to her became more and more. I'd told her I was running the fashion business, and she understood that I couldn't come home as much. The money paid for a carer and a cleaner a few times per week.

Mum and I were sitting at the dinner table. The flat was cleaner and tidier than I'd seen in years. Mum's posture was a bit better, and her smile bigger than ever.

'Would you like some yerba tea?' I said.

'That would be lovely,' she said. Yerba tea has dozens of different vitamins and minerals in it.

I put the kettle on. 'How've you been?' I said.

'I'm having the odd good day now, it's lovely. And to have a cleaner and carer in has been a blessing. The new doctor I've got is amazing, we did so many tests. God, it cost thousands, but now I'm being treated properly, she's put me on some medicine and helped me hone my diet. I'll be better in no time.'

In her face I could see the years of doubt and anguish. Neither of us believed she would ever truly be better. We'd been fighting a losing battle for years. It was impossible to imagine Mum living a normal life again.

'I hope it works, imagine having my own mother cook me dinner for once!' I said.

'You brat,' she said.

'Only kidding, I like looking after you.'

She smiled. It wasn't a pure smile, it was a resigned smile. She hated the fact I had to look after her.

I had to hold back the tears. I said, 'Anyway, my good news: my business is doing very well.'

'That's wonderful,' she said. 'I hope you're not overdoing it. Are you still at university?'

'I'm trying, yeah,' I said.

'I always knew you'd do brilliantly. Just please, look after yourself. Stress is so unhealthy, you don't want to end up like me.'

'I know, I know.' I paused. 'Anyway, it's going so well that I want you to look for a house, one with a garden and a spare room so you can get a float tank.'

A float tank is also known as a sensory deprivation tank. You lie in a solution of water and Epsom salts that is so dense it makes you feel weightless, the tank is pitch black, and it is heated to your body temperature. You see and feel nothing, so you can meditate, relax and recover. Just what Mum needs, to heal, to recover.

'Oh, that's lovely of you, my angel, but you know there aren't any nice houses for rent around here.'

'Fuck renting it, Mum, we're buying it. I'll be ready to pay for it by Christmas. Merry Christmas, I guess.'

It felt so strange saying those things. It felt weird having something go right, and then another thing going right, and then more things going right. It was in those moments where I started to realise life doesn't have to be a series of disappointments, that everyone deserves a break, and it happens. You have to fight for it, but it will happen, and that makes it all worth it, every single fucking setback. Just keep going and trust the bigger picture, that subtle fabric of the universe that our little brains will never completely comprehend.

★★★

Moose, Anthony and I were inside our lovely little shop in Castle Arcade. Vintage and Vinyl was about to open to the public for the first time. Anthony and Moose had done a great job. The walls were painted a light bluey-grey, with vinyl records stuck all over them, some were highly collectable, framed. There was lots of rustic brown wood all over the place, the floor, the shelves, the bannisters. Rows and rows of vintage clothes hung in themed batches. There was a special section for Rhetorik clothing.

Alex was setting up his vinyl to play a funky disco set. There was a decent-sized queue of people outside, mainly students, many of whom I once sold drugs to, many of whom Anthony sold drugs to still. People were fascinated by the hype, they weren't sure whether the place was truly owned by drug dealers or not. To some we were big characters, to others it was all exaggerated rumours, and they all loved the idea of vintage clothes and vinyl records in one shop.

The music started, uplifting eighties synths on top of a kick and a hi-hat. I unlocked the door, said hello, hello, welcome, welcome, and left them to shop our outrageously overpriced second-hand clothing. There is already so much clothing in the world, I felt good recycling the old stuff. I felt even better that people were willing to pay a premium for it.

With advice from a discreet accountant, the company was registered as Vintage and Vinyl Ltd, and Anthony was the sole shareholder and director. I was an employee of the company, with a contract and everything. This way I could go to the bank and get a mortgage, easy. My job title was Innovation Manager, and I was paid four grand a month, enough to get a mortgage and more.

By the end of the day we'd taken many thousands of pounds legitimately, and we'd also washed a lot of cash through the books, taxes to be paid and all. Vintage and Vinyl was a success.

***

Time flew by as it always does, and before I knew it, we were about to open the doors to Emp Col for my big event, Frenzy. I was at the bar with Isobel. She seemed a bit distant, a bit off, staring at her drink as if it might give her something I couldn't.

'Are you okay?' I said.

'Sure,' she said, taking a sip of her drink. 'You've done so well, Tommy, it looks amazing. I've never seen anything like it.'

'That means a lot to me, thank you.'

It meant a lot to me because I never really felt like anything I did was that impressive. It meant a lot because I'd put so many hours into making sure the night would go well. From orchestrating the decor to getting more lighting, to booking the artists and promoting the event on social media and on posters around Cardiff, to managing ticket sales, guest list, and everything in between. Most of all, it meant a lot because Isobel had come to mean a lot to me. What she thought about me mattered a lot.

For the decor, there were tree barks and animal skulls attached to the walls and hanging from the ceiling, all painted intricately with lines, dots, circles, squiggles, zigzags, and complex geometric shapes, in an array of neon colours: blue, green, purple, yellow, orange, red, pink, white. These colours glowed vividly under UV light. Everything else was soft in the darkness. The room was filled with depth and vibrancy. It was ominous and energising.

At the far end of the room, Sarah, a mate of a mate, was playing deep, minimal house, ready to warm up the punters as they passed through the doors. An elaborate laser, strobe and beam lighting set-up was flashing through the empty room with the music. The doors would open in ten minutes.

Isobel continued to stare at her drink.

I wasn't sure what to say. I said, 'Do you want a bump of coke or something?'

'No, just don't ignore me all night, alright?'

'I won't,' I said.

There was a chill-out room for staff and friends beside the bar. Anthony and Moose burst through the door laughing and chatting, rubbing and sniffing the scrapes of coke from their noses.

'Yes, Tommy! Tonight's going to be huge,' Moose said. 'Anything you need doing before we open?'

'I think we're all set,' I said. 'You two just be ready to do your thing.'

Their role for the night was to discretely sell as many drugs as possible.

'Nice one, bruvaaa,' Moose said, in the accent of Danny Dyer in the film *Human Traffic*. We'd heard it at the festivals and now everyone was doing it.

'Nice one, bruvv,' I said, same accent. I wondered whether Justin Kerrigan knew that people were still paying homage to his work almost twenty years later. What a classic! And it seemed so fitting that this was happening in a club, in Cardiff.

Moose said, 'I said, nice one, bruvaaa.'

I said, 'I said, nice one, bruvvvaaa.'

We laughed.

Isobel said, 'See?'

'What do you mean?' I said.

'Never mind,' she said.

Robin, the manager of Emp Col, appeared from upstairs. He said, 'Shall we turn that music up and open the doors?' Robin was tall with long, black curly hair. He looked tired and stressed.

'We shall,' I said.

I was nervous for the success of the night, but I couldn't stop smiling with excitement.

Some of the first through the door were Sammy, Rosie, Laura, Bento, Daisy, and Isobel's housemates, Amy and Nina. They were all dressed wonderfully colourfully and had lots of glitter and gems all over their bodies. Wavy jackets, skinny jeans, short shorts, skirts and playsuits. Bright sporty trainers.

We all said our hellos and discussed how cool it all looked and how fun the night was going to be, had a drink together and dispersed. Isobel went off with Amy and Nina.

People came in fast and plenty, the looks on their drunk, high faces were priceless. The chatter got louder, the movements wilder, and the night was in full flow. Banging!

A hand pressed on my shoulder, I turned to see Arlo, Din and Connor.

What the fuck are Din and Connor doing here?

'Nice to see you all, how's it going?' I said.

Arlo said, 'Everything's great, excited to be here.'

Din and Connor nodded.

I wondered whether they'd noticed I wasn't wearing the brown contact lenses I always wore when I was Leon, and that my hair was now slick, pushed back.

'Nice event you got here, mate,' Din said. 'We 'erd you 'ad an event on here and Robin's a long term client of mine. Thought I'd finally come get that money he owes me.'

'Do what you need to do,' I said. 'Arlo, can I have a word?'

'Certainly, my man,' Arlo said.

We went aside. I said, 'What the fuck are they doing here?'

'Relax, alright, mate? I told them they can't let anyone know they know you, I can't stop them coming, can I, public event and all that.'

'This is going to fuck it all up, they'll hear someone call me Tommy, and they'll want to know about it.'

'Tommy, bro, honestly, you're worrying too much, if anything like that happens I'll make sure they don't tell anyone. Me and Din are close now, we're doing loads of business and it's all going really well.'

I was fucking pissed off but there was nothing I could do. I should have quit working for Arlo there and then, because once discipline is breached, it's a slippery slope. But for ten grand a month … I was prepared to let a bit of discipline slip.

'Fine,' I said. 'Take this wristband, it'll get you free drinks and green room and all that.'

Arlo said, 'There we go, and make sure you enjoy yourself tonight, Tommy.'

The sight of skulls, UV paint, branches, so weird and wonderful, cheered me up. And the lights beaming, the music booming.

I spent the night making sure everything was running smoothly, saying hello and thanks for coming to everyone, and listening to them tell me how they were loving it, absolutely loving it, all in awe of the set-up, the sound system, the environment, the enchantment, and I must admit I fucking loved it too, immersed in potent colour and beautiful dance music.

Olivia and Flash by the bar. Flash wearing a slick white tracksuit jacket, sharp and athletic as always. Olivia wearing a black lace top, light denim shorts, very short, her well-shaped arse curving out of the denim.

'Oi oi, Tommy boy,' Flash said. 'How's it going, mate?'

'Loving it,' I said. 'Take these, for green room and free drinks.'

'My man,' Flash said. Flash took a wristband from me.

Olivia held her arm out. Her wrists were slim, her fingers long, elegant. I felt like she was staring at me the whole time, I kept my eyes fixed on her wrist and the silver wristband.

'Why, thank you,' she said.

We made eye contact, I felt a pang in my chest. Lights flashing all about us, a bit of haze in the air, and the delightful music. As much as I wanted to enjoy those sensations forever, I said, 'I'd better go check everything's alright at the door.'

Flash said, 'Stay and have a drink with us, Tommy boy, surely you got time for one?'

I didn't want to be rude. I said, 'Yeah, if we're swift.'

We got gin and tonics, with plenty of real lime.

'This one's to you, Tommy boy. Cheers!' Flash said, holding up his drink. He seemed a little agitated.

'Cheers,' I said.

'Cheers,' Olivia said. Nice smile.

We clinked our glasses and took a sip of our drinks.

Flash said, 'What you sayin then, Tommy boy, you having a big one with us tonight?'

'I can't get too fucked, but I'm definitely going to have some fun, especially after last entry at midnight and when I know everything's running smoothly.'

'Want a bump to get you going?' Flash said.

'No, I'm good, thank you.'

'What about you then?'

'We just had one,' Olivia said.

'Fuck it. Well, I'm havin' another, I'll catch you two losers in a minute.' Flash headed for the men's room.

'Charming,' Olivia said.

'Is he alright?' I said.

'I think so. He's been acting a bit weird. It's probably just mood swings from sniffing too much. He's doing it almost every day now. Since he finished uni he hasn't worked, he just sits at home selling little bits here and there and sniffing what he can.'

I wanted to say, Why are you even with him? I said, 'Have you had a proper word with him?'

'Do you think Flash listens to anybody, Tommy?'

'I see what you mean,' I said. 'So, what do you do? While hc's doing all that?'

'I'm a presenter on a YouTube channel, we review make-up and beauty products.'

'Good move,' I said. I meant it too. The world is just one massive machine of consumption. People lap all that stuff up, making them buy products because it excites them, and when you have a *genuine* person giving you *genuine* reviews, you feel empowered to make your own purchasing decision. Not that you're really empowered to do anything, you were already going to buy something before you even clicked the link.

'You're mocking me,' she said.

'I assure you, it's ingenious.'

'Thank you,' she said. 'As is this event, and …' She paused. 'Oh. He's back.'

Flash was cleaning the drip from his nostrils with tissue. He said, 'Now we're talking, oi oi!' much livelier and more smiley than before. 'Come on then, babe, let's go have a dance,' he said.

'I haven't finished my drink yet,' Olivia said.

'Put it down then, get another later. They're free.'

'I'll catch you two later,' I said, and headed for the entrance.

Robin was at the door with his girlfriend, Millie, who was scanning tickets and taking cash. Millie was wearing a long flowing jacket with sequins all over it. I liked it a lot. An intricate pattern of body gems gleamed on her face. Two of the security team were standing by the front door letting in a few people at a time.

Robin, looking a bit dishevelled and suspicious, said, 'Tommy, I forgot to mention I'll need that venue fee in cash, you don't mind if I take it from the door money, do you?'

He was lying. He'd already told me we could settle the fee after the event. This was something to do with Din.

I said, 'Okay, no problem, just make sure you invoice me for it.' I couldn't see any reason why not. Whatever amount we took on the door, I was going to put another few grand of the drug money through the accounts too. I was paying Robin, the artist, the guys who enhanced the sound system, and the lighting guys in cash, just so I could get rid of some of it. When you earn obscene amounts of money illegally, one of the biggest problems you have is making it seem legitimate so you can spend it without suspicion.

Ryan turned up. I had thought he couldn't make it due to having to work late, and he had said it would take too much time to come from Devon.

'Surprise, and all that,' Ryan said. He got his wallet out to pay for entry.

Millie said, 'Ten pounds please.'

'He's my best friend, he's not paying,' I said.

'Oh, come on let your old mate Ry support your event would you?' Ryan said.

'Absolutely not, and take this wristband,' I said.

'Fine,' Ryan said. He handed the tenner to Millie. Millie

took it, put it in the till.

'If Ryan's going to be like that,' I said to Millie, 'take his tenner as a tip for yourself.'

'You're such a gent, Tommy,' she said.

'Not me, thank Ryan,' I said.

''Tis a pleasure,' Ryan said. 'We gonna go upstairs and get fucked or what?'

He was interrupted by a loud young guy coming through the door with a few mates. 'Oi, look, it's Tommy, this is his event,' the guy said. 'I know you from boxing.'

I didn't know his name, didn't really recognise him.

'How's it going, mate?' he said.

'It's going well,' I said.

He said, 'This is Chantelle, Mike and Zaz.' His friends smiled, the girls gave me a hug, Mike shook my hand.

'I hate to be rude, but we've got to go sort something out in the office,' I said, leading Ryan upstairs.

'I'll catch you later, nice to see you,' the guy said.

I was too polite and embarrassed to tell him I didn't know who he was.

We walked up the stairs and Ryan said, 'Look at you, Mr Popular.'

I said, 'Nah, they were probably trying to blag free entry or something.'

As we entered the main room, Ryan said, 'This is decent.'

'I love it,' I said. The UV, the colours, the lights, the people smiling and dancing, and the beat.

We passed the bouncer into the green room. Isobel, Nina, Amy, Arlo, Din, Connor, Flash, Olivia, Moose, Anthony, Sammy and Alex the DJ were sitting on the sofas. They looked like an edgy, fun bunch in their wavy retro jackets and the glitter and the sequins and the skinny jeans all sprawled about laughing and chatting and bopping to the beat, which was muffled in here because the door was closed behind us. The sofas faced each other. In between them, a wooden coffee table with loads of lines of flake racked up on it, and glasses of cocktails, beer, champagne, and more.

Moose said, 'The man of the moment. Sit down and relax with us, and how about a boomer?'

'I don't know,' I said. I didn't like that Din and Connor were there. I didn't like that Olivia was there. I made sure not to look at her.

'Come on,' Ryan said. 'Let's do one together.'

'Do you want one?' I said to Isobel.

'I'm okay,' she said. Her voice was bitter.

I felt uncomfortable.

Ryan handed me a twenty pound note, already rolled. 'Go on, Tommy, you deserve it, this is your night.'

Din and Connor didn't seem to react when Ryan called me Tommy. Everyone was looking at me, expecting me to sniff the victory line. The lines looked fluffy and smooth, brilliant white. Large. Daunting, even.

'Go on, you put all this together, treat yourself,' Moose said. 'Tommy … Tommy … Tommy, Tommy, Tommy,' he chanted.

Everyone else joined in, except Isobel, who stared ahead blankly. They were chanting my name and jumping about and going mental chanting faster and faster and louder and louder so I took the note and I sniffed a line from the table. It went up smoothly, and it didn't burn my nose like I expected it to. That was my first ever line of coke. I don't think anybody realised that it was, except Isobel, who clearly wasn't impressed.

They chanted and they chanted.

Arlo had madness in his eyes, he sprang to his feet and pushed the table over, all the coke fell with it as it crashed down on its side, almost hitting me.

'What the fuck?' Moose said.

I was speechless.

'I fucking own you,' Arlo said. 'Don't ever forget that!' His face was big and red, his forehead bulging with ferocity. He stormed off.

Flash followed him, 'Alright, geez, what's the matter?' he said.

Everyone else was awkwardly silent.

Din made a whistling noise, and said, 'I wonder what's in his knickers?'

'He don't want Tommy getting all the attention,' Moose said.

'I s'pose you've got to know your place in these things,' Din said.

'Arlo put that coke on the table and we didn't give him enough respect,' I said, hoping nobody was catching on to what was really going on.

'Fuck him,' Anthony said.

'Looks like Arlo's got a mutiny on his hands here,' Din said. 'Terry won't like that.'

'Don't worry about it, I'll make sure Arlo's alright,' I said.

Ryan said, 'Give me that note.' He got on his knees, put his face to the floor and started sniffing huge chunks of dusty, mucky coke off the ground, ensuring he was loud and dramatic. 'There we go, problem solved, no coke wasted.'

Everyone laughed and cheered and clapped as he sat up with a face full of flake and muck.

Ryan and I put the table back to its original position.

Olivia said, 'Are you okay, Tommy?'

'I'm fine, just a bit shocked,' I said. 'Let's get more drinks, and somebody put some bloody coke on the table, would you?'

Isobel scowled at me. I wasn't sure why she was being so cold. I was worried Din had said something about my work with Arlo while I wasn't there.

Chatter and whatnot resumed. I sat next to Isobel on the sofa. I said, in a quiet voice, 'Are you okay?'

'I'm fine,' she said. 'Nice to see you so friendly with everyone. I didn't know you knew Olivia.'

Olivia was no longer in the room.

I felt anxious, and a bit excited. That was the coke. 'What do you mean by that? She's Flash's girlfriend.'

'I know, she introduced herself a moment ago. I saw you talking to her at the bar.'

'Flash ditched us for a line, I didn't want to be rude.'

'Sure,' she said. 'We're going for a dance, you can get wasted with this lot.' Isobel stood up, as did Nina and Amy.

'I'll come,' I said.

'It's okay, I know you've got work to do, people to please and all that,' Isobel said. She turned her back before I could get another word in. My anxiety intensified.

'Line?' Moose said.

'I'm a bit anxious,' I said.

'Honestly, do more, it gets rid of the anxiety.'

Fuck it.

I went for it.

***

We went to Anthony's for the after-party. Student after-parties are grotty, drawn out affairs. I'd been to loads before, but I'd usually shoot off early, using boxing as an excuse. This time, I didn't have an excuse, and I wanted to have some fun, let loose a bit, celebrate the success.

We'd already had a decent night, but we were so buzzing,

nobody wanted it to end. We were chasing something impossible, trying to prove that what goes up might not necessarily have to come down. But it does.

It was 6.00 am. Isobel, Ryan, Sammy and I were on the sofa. Everyone else was on the floor, with blankets and cushions.

Music coming from the TV.

Moose, Daisy and one of Moose's course mates, I forget his name, were sitting with their backs against the sofa, nestled between our legs. Moose was rolling a joint. Flash and Arlo were slouched on the floor by the wall by the dining table. Flash had calmed Arlo down, and they'd joined us again. Nobody had mentioned Arlo's outburst since we left the green room. It was as if it had never happened. I didn't like that.

Flash was racking massive lines of coke onto a DVD case. Nina, Amy and a guy called Jake lay halfway under the table.

The room was stuffy, my body was already breaking out in a detox sweat. I felt clammy and tired, but my mind was wired. I was overthinking, about everything. I said quietly to Isobel, 'I'm sorry I didn't spend my night with you.'

'You were busy, I get it, I understand,' she said, and she swiftly changed the subject. 'Can you hear those two?'

Martin and his mate Harry were standing at the kitchen sink, chatting. The distinct sound of a line being snorted. Martin was saying, Raving is a state of mind, and Harry was saying, I know I know, man, I know exactly what you mean, like, you can't understand raving until you've done it. Another line snorted.

Isobel and I smiled at each other. People chat so much shit when they're high, and it gets even worse when they're tired.

Flash's phone rang. ''Ello, geez,' he said. 'I'll be out in a second.' He handed the precious DVD case with coke on it to Arlo. In less than a minute he was back with ten boxes of

NOS, each box with twenty-four canisters in it. 'Oiii oiii,' he said. 'This one's on me, boys and girls.' These days, you can get NOS delivered any time you like.

Everyone perked up. The canisters clinked as he put the boxes on the floor next to Arlo.

Arlo began the filling of the balloons.

Tttttssssshooooowww.

Martin and Harry followed the sound from the kitchen like zombies, perched themselves next to Arlo.

'Fucking fiends,' Moose said.

Arlo filled the balloons one by one, passing the full ones around the room.

Once everyone had a balloon, we said Cheers, touching our balloons together. Then we started inhaling the NOS from the balloons, and exhaling it back into them; my balloon was yellow, the scent and taste, mildly plastic. Inhale again, exhale, inhale, exhale, the room got slightly blurry, throbbing, my hearing reduced to wom, wom, wom, wom. I was still thinking coherently, which made it more weird. I was thinking about how weird it was that I could somehow put thoughts together when everything was all wom, wom, wom, wom, and the room was pulsing. I wondered how that was possible: two cognitive faculties so strangely presented, almost opposites, wom, wom, wom, mixed with coherent thoughts.

This is fucking weird, I heard myself saying to Isobel. And I could have sworn she said, I know, it's so weird, isn't it? But I wasn't totally sure. My heart raced and my body pulsed, and I couldn't help but laugh, laugh, laugh so hard I let my balloon go and gasped for air.

Everyone was laughing, coming out of their trip.

'Did we just have a conversation?' I said. My voice was weird, inflated.

'What?' Isobel said.

'Didn't we just talk about how weird it all was?'

Everyone laughed so hard.

'Nobody said a word, Tommy,' Moose said.

'I could have sworn Isobel and I were talking,' I said.

'You were tripping sacks,' Ryan said.

'That would have been difficult with a balloon in my mouth!' Isobel said.

'You donut,' Sammy said.

I shrugged.

That sound of NOS squeezing into a balloon again. *Tttttsssssshooooowww.* Everyone turned towards it. Arlo was sorting the second round.

'Give me that controller,' I said, so I could choose a tune.

I went for Fatima Yamaha, *What's a Girl to Do*, because I love the cut-back simplicity of the synths, and the raw vocal sample.

'Yes!' Martin said. 'I fucking love this track.'

Moose said, 'Anyone wanna blow some bud into their balloon?'

'Me, I wanna do that,' Sammy said. 'But let's have that boomer first!'

'Oiii oiii,' Flash said. He rolled a tenner tightly. Snorted the first line. Fluffy white cocaine moved seamlessly into the crisp note into Flash's nose into his bloodstream. Flash edged the DVD towards Arlo, but Arlo's hands were tied, firing up the balloons.

Tttttsssssshooooowww.

'I've got responsibility here, Flash bro, I am the chief facilitator of nitrous oxide consumption. You're going to have to drive that line for me or something.'

Moose said, 'Go on, Flash, stick that fucker up his nose.'

Flash poked the note in Arlo's right nostril, put his finger over the other one, and placed the DVD close to the note, lining up the white stripe of cocaine with its free end. Arlo sniffed, stopped, coughed and choked, cocaine blew everywhere, everyone laughed so much. Arlo, somehow, never let go of the balloon.

Tttttsssssshoooowww.

So much laughter. Cocaine all over the place.

'Fuckin 'ell, there was an eighth on that DVD,' Flash said, rolling on the floor laughing.

I'd never heard so much laughter in one room. I thought, Maybe these moments are what life is all about. No worries, just laughter. But we wouldn't be laughing so much without the drugs.

Arlo passed the balloon to Moose.

Sammy started scooping the cocaine from the floor with his student card. The Cardiff University red and white got smudged with oily, dust-infected cocaine.

'Take this,' Anthony said, and threw his baggie with what was left of his coke in it to Flash.

'And this,' Arlo said. He handed Flash a bag with a massive chunk in it, about half an ounce.

'Oi oi, geez, nice save,' Flash said. 'We've got enough to fuel a rocket now.'

What the fuck is life? I thought. A green balloon full of NOS entered my hand.

'How about this joint then?' Moose said.

'Everyone has to do it,' I said. I'm not sure why, it came out involuntarily. I didn't even want to do it really, although I was a little curious. I'd smoked a bit of weed before, I really liked how it made me feel. I liked how balloons felt, so I thought that combining the two could be epic.

'Yes!' Moose said. 'Toke, pass, hold it, and we'll balloon the fucker together, when everyone's got some. Tommy's idea, he starts.'

'Jesus,' I said. 'You lot better be quick about it then, else I'll literally suffocate and die.' I was genuinely worried that might happen. 'Moose, you're right next to me on this one.'

He handed me the joint, squeezed himself in between me and Isobel on the sofa. He was warm, with a slight tang of body odour.

I toked, quite a big one, passed it to Moose, who did the same, passed it to Isobel, and so on. My throat dried and my lungs felt irritated. I wanted to exhale but I couldn't ruin it. The joint kept going, person to person, one by one, my heart pounded harder as it tried to get more oxygen around me. I grunted, shook my head, telling Daisy to hurry the fuck up.

'Fuck me, he's still holding,' Flash said. ''Urry up, you lot, he'll be blue after this.'

Flash was last in the queue. My lungs clutched for air, my chest jerking, trying to breathe, but I stopped myself exhaling the smoke. I wanted to prove a point. I could fucking do it. The joint reached Flash and he sucked with a swift smooth swoosh.

I exhaled into the balloon, gasping on the inhale and getting a sketchy helping of NOS straight into my oxygen-starved body, and as I thought about that I realised, wom wom wom wom, wom wom, definitely, wom, wom, not, wom, a good idea. Fuck. Blackness.

I was in a dark room, everything quiet. I knew I'd just smashed a balloon, but I didn't know where I was. This isn't fair, I said, or thought. How did this happen? I said it in the darkness. I couldn't see the four walls trapping me in, but I knew they were there. This is fucking weird. So fucking weird. Is this another dimension? How do I get out? That thought panicked me. I'm trapped here forever. How do I get out? How is this even possible? Shit! This isn't fair. This wasn't supposed to happen.

I heard laughter and talking and, Tommy, you alright? The sweet sound of Moose's voice.

'That was fucking weird,' I said.

'It's not fair, is it, Tommy?' Moose said.

Everyone laughed so fucking hard, me included, it hurt my stomach.

'That was so fucking weird,' was all I could say. I didn't want to tell them about the dark room. It felt too real for my liking, like one of those moments when your whole perspective on life could be shattered and from that moment you'd look at everything differently, perhaps too differently to cohere with the common social fabric, only to find you're now a bit of a madman.

'Fair play to him though,' Arlo said. 'Holding that bud all that long must have been heavy, and then ripping it into a balloon, fucking hell.'

'Tommy's master of the sesh, who'd have thought it? Who'd have known,' Flash said.

Everyone laughed.

The worst part of it all was heading home in broad daylight. It was 10.00 am. Everyone else was still going. Isobel and I waited for the taxi outside Moose's. The air was cold and moist, and I couldn't stop shivering. My mouth was so dry no matter how much water I drank, my head was aching, and I felt like I hadn't slept in days. I kept wondering whether that kind of damage to my body was worth it. So much fun, but fucking hectic.

When I woke, Isobel was sitting next to me, looking a little moody, scrolling on her phone.

'Hi,' I said, my throat in pain.

'I can't do this any more,' she said.

'What?' I said.

'I'm sick of being second to everything else you're doing,

and I'm sick of your shit.'

I didn't know what to say. 'What shit? I'm doing my best okay. I have so much on my plate.'

'You *put* most of it on your fucking plate, Tommy. You've clearly got money now, why don't you just tone it down and live a normal life for a bit? You don't need to have it all, I just don't get why you have to push for more and more. You don't look at me like you used to, you don't talk to me like you used to, do you even like me any more?' she said.

'Of course I do, I love you with all my heart,' I said. 'And some people *do* have it all. They have money and friends and a girlfriend and a healthy mother, and a father too, and probably some fucking grandparents on the side. Why can't I have just a bit of that? This is just the teething stage, it will be better once I've streamlined everything. I'll sell the businesses in less than a year.'

'That'll be two shit years I've been strung along, I'm not having it any more.'

I had never seen her so furious, never seen her cry so much. I tried to hug her. 'I'm sorry,' I said. 'I'll make it up to you.'

She pushed me away and sobbed. 'Just fucking leave,' she said.

'I'm sorry,' I said, so heavy.

As I was leaving, she said, 'Tommy.'

'Yes?'

'Don't do anything stupid.'

***

Stupid is relative. It's not as if you think what you're doing is stupid at the time. At the time, it makes sense. You justify it to yourself. I wanted peace, so I taxied to the Bay House. I was still a little wobbly from the after party.

I was hurting, so I had a bottle of whisky delivered, drank it with ice. I sat on the sofa. The room was horrifically bright. I couldn't be bothered to close the blinds. I messaged Ryan, told him Isobel had ended it with me. He said he was at Anthony's still, asked where I was so he could head over.

I rang Moose. 'How's it going?' I said

'Still going,' Moose said. 'Buzzing.'

'Who's there?' I said.

'Just me, Anthony, Ryan, and a couple of girls Anthony knows. Their afters finished so they came here. Everyone else left, Daisy went to bed as well.'

'We have names, you know,' one of the girls said.

'I have something to show you,' I said. 'Bring everyone who wants to party. Bring supplies.' I gave Moose the address to the Bay House.

Through the peephole, I saw a small mob of Anthony, Moose, Ryan and four girls. I opened the door.

'Oi oi,' Moose said.

'Make yourselves at home,' I said.

'Whose place is this? It's tidy as,' Moose said.

'Long story. Get that flake out,' I said. 'We've got some fun to have.'

'Oiii oiii,' Moose said. 'Taking a liking to the flake aren't you, mate?'

'It's alright, I haven't made my mind up yet. Just can't keep pinging all day.'

'Nice one, bruvaaa,' Moose shouted.

I followed with, 'I said, nice one, bruvaaa,' louder than Moose.

Moose followed, louder than my last one. 'I said, nice one, bruvaaaa!'

'You're that guy who ran last night,' one of Anthony's mates said. She had a posh London accent. The four girls were sitting on the sofas. Anthony perched on the floor by the coffee table.

'I am,' I said.

'Sick night,' she said. She had wavy brown hair, and the most immense glassy blue eyes. She wore a sleek black top, split from the middle of her stomach, opening wide by her shoulders, only just covering her nipples. The curve of her braless tits in full flow. Light denim skirt, short. Stockings with lace on the thigh. Jesus. Slim, athletic, dancey body. Decent.

'Who wants a line then?' Moose said.

Everyone wanted a line.

'Just rack loads on the coffee table so everyone can help themselves,' I said.

The girl who had complimented my night moved over so I could sit next to her. 'My name's Claire,' she said.

She smelt of perfume. I could feel the skin of her arm on mine. She wasn't clammy. I worried I was over-clammy. My hand rested on her bare leg.

'Claire . . . Like the Guy Gerber track,' I said.

'Who?' she said.

I put the track on.

When the trickly synths kicked in, she said, 'This is beautiful.'

Involuntarily, I said, 'You're beautiful.'

She looked at my hand on her leg. Smiled.

Ryan said, 'Go on, Tommy, where'd you bury the owner of this place then?' He eyed the wine rack. I'd filled it with expensive wines, to look the part. I had figured my associates would respect me more.

I said, 'Straight in the bay.'

Claire said, 'Is it Airbnb?'

'Something like that,' I said.

Claire said, 'This is Lauren,' pointing to the girl next to her. Ryan had nestled between Lauren and the arm of the sofa. Lauren had blonde highlights in her fair hair. Her teeth were large when she smiled. Her eyes lit up, perhaps slightly artificially.

Claire said, 'And this is Mary, and this, Sian.'

They were all petite, pretty.

'Tommy,' I said. 'Nice to meet you all.'

When Claire returned to the sofa after a line, she clutched my arm. Coke can make you a bit like that. Lots of built-up tension, anxiety. She appeared to be experiencing a mixture of euphoria and anxiety. Her eyes said, This is intense, but I like it.

Anthony, Moose, Mary and Sian were chatting in full flow. Their voices were animated and sometimes they talked over each other so it all blurred:

Seriously, right, houses on the bay are cheaper than town and twice as good; You can speedboat on the water as well; The train to town is decent. You get it free most of the time, they never check tickets; Yeah, just look at this place, it's peng; Yeah, peng. So nice.

'Who lives here?' Moose said.

'It's complicated,' Anthony said. 'I feel someone's been snakey.' He said that so quietly I barely heard.

I felt horribly anxious. 'Oh God,' I said. 'I'm starting to think all those lines were a bad idea on two hours of sleep.'

'Get two more down you then, snake,' Anthony said.

Did he just say snake? Surely not.

I snorted two more lines, sat down again.

'How do you feel now?' Claire said.

'Yeah, much better,' I said. Uplifted. She ran her hand on the skin on my side, just underneath where the T-shirt met the jeans.

'Is this your place?' she said.

'Something like that,' I said.

'Show me around,' she said.

'Well, as you've gathered, this is the living room,' I said. 'The living room is attached to the kitchen. Have you seen my wine rack?'

'No, I must have missed the wine rack, show me.'

We inspected the wine rack, full of expensive wines I knew fuck all about. 'This is the, um, fuck knows, some posh wine anyway, it cost five hundred quid. Want some?'

'I'd love some,' she said.

'Anyone else want some posh wine with that cocaine?'

I poured some glasses and handed them out.

'Cheers,' Claire said. We clinked glasses in the kitchen. The walls wobbled around me. Light glistened on her plump lip. She put her glass to her mouth, sipped the red, eyes on me.

'Shall we continue our tour?' she said.

'This is the master bedroom,' I said.

'Master,' she said. 'Bet you like that.'

'Something like that,' I said.

I locked the door.

Claire slipped onto the four-poster bed. I dimmed the lights. Everything became smoother, sexier, more luxurious. Those glassy blue eyes! And her skirt was riding close to her groin, legs stretched long, the stockings semi-transparent, the lace on her thigh, incredible. Her back was straight, her shoulders rolled back, chest out. 'This is comfortable,' she said.

The covers were silky, black with white abstract lines running vertical, seemingly random in width.

Part of me wanted to open the door, go back to the sofa. The rest of me wanted to stop thinking, to let go. Seize the moment.

She said, 'You got coke or ket on you?'

'Both,' I said.

She pulled her top down. Her tits stood firm, curving out from her toned stomach, her exposed ribs. She lowered her head onto the pillow.

'Rub coke all over me,' she said, circling her fingers on her hard nipples.

Jesus. It was at that point I knew I was in too deep. Too intoxicated. Too convinced I was a film star, and this was my destiny. Like a fucking film star.

I put a clump of oily flake on her nipple, started rubbing and pinching. She squealed. Her hips pressed up, pulled down. I kissed and licked her nipple. The coke made my mouth numb. I put some flake on the back of my hand. She sniffed it smoothly, licked what didn't go up her nose, took four of my fingers gently into her mouth, I could feel the back of her throat, she slowly peeled her lips off my fingers, grinning.

'Buzzing,' she said. 'What do you do to have a place like this?'

'Events and fashion, things like that,' I said, kissing her lips, feeling only a cold, numb tingle.

'I'm so numb,' she said, tugging at my T-shirt.

I took it off.

She said, 'You're so hot.' She unzipped my jeans, pulled my cock out. Put some ket on my stomach. Sniffed. Gave me some. I sniffed. She pulled her skirt up, her knickers aside, climbed on top of me, guided my dick into her narrow body, we both gasped. Started rhythmically, slowly, sensually, all cokey and ketty and loving it.

After ages of different positions and intensities, I said, 'I can't fucking finish.'

'How about you get me a drink, and while you're doing

that I'll speak to Lauren. If you can't finish with both of us, there's something wrong with you.'

'Fucking … how about yes,' I said.

Moose and Anthony were gone. Ryan and the other girls were drinking wine, they'd opened a few more bottles.

'Where have the others gone?' I said.

'Home,' Ryan said. 'I don't think they're very happy with you.'

'Fuck them,' I said, 'I'm their fucking boss.'

I poured a few whiskys.

Claire whispered in Lauren's ear. They took their drinks and went into the bedroom. I followed. It was everything I'd imagined, and more.

★★★

I surfaced about two days later, burner ringing, head aching like hell. It was Arlo. 'Where the fuck have you been, Tommy?'

'Isobel ended it with me, I needed some downtime,' I said.

'Downtime? We've got gear to move, and I need you to back me up. Some fucking lowlifes caught me alone in town last night and threatened me with knives. The scumbags marched me to mine and made me give them everything there, we lost twenty grand and half a box of flake.

'Jesus,' I said. 'I'm sorry, Arlo, but I'm in no state for that right now, and you know it's not my thing.'

'Not your thing, Tommy? What the fuck do you think you're into? Half of that twenty grand was your payday, and if I'm half a box down, that means you're not getting paid for four months. You haven't got to do anything drastic, just make sure I don't get hurt.'

I knew there was no point arguing. I was in a shit situation and it was my fault. I needed the money. I couldn't lose everything I'd worked for. Mum was finally off benefits, she had her own house, things were too good to ruin.

Arlo, Richard and I led the pack. Richard was one of Arlo's good mates. He was tall and stacked. Behind us, Flash, grinning, buzzed for the action. Behind Flash were Connor and Jonno. Din had sent them as a gesture of goodwill, and to make sure the flake was recovered so that Arlo's tab with Terry was more likely to be settled.

We marched to a house on a scruffy terraced road in Splott. Some parts of Splott are rough compared to Cathays and Roath. You don't get many students in Splott.

Arlo kicked down the shabbily painted green door in two swift smashes. The hinges gave way, wood splintered over the worn, greyish-blue carpet. The hallway was a mess with junk mail and clothes that had fallen off the radiator. It smelt as if it hadn't been hoovered in months.

We burst into the living room. Living room was also a mess, weed scattered everywhere over the table. Sofa had tears in it. Flashy widescreen TV. A bloke in grey joggers in a panic, caught off guard. Arlo curved a metal bar over the guy's head. I had never heard a metal bar on a skull before. The sound is indescribably shocking. The guy hit the floor with a disgusting limpness that you don't often see in a creature of flesh and blood.

Commotion in the hallway. Connor and Jonno screaming. Guys coming down the stairs, kicking and punching, a bit of a scuffle. Connor's lower body rolling through the doorway, his head on the ground being kicked in the hallway.

I saw red. I barged my way into the hall, flattened a guy with a straight right. Flattened another with a one-two. Took a hefty blow to the back. Winded. Fuck. Gasping for air. Nausea. The motherfucker had a baseball bat.

Arlo smashed him on the back of the head with his metal bar. I got on the guy, smacked his face, over, and over, and over, furious that Mum lives such a shit life, even with her new house and her money, angry that Isobel left me, that I cheated on her, that Anthony and Moose hate me, pissed off that no matter how hard I try, everything goes to shit. Whack, whack, whack, fuck this fuck that life's a heap of shit anyway. The guy was so battered by the end it wasn't even satisfying hitting him.

One of the others was wobbling about on the floor. I dived over, cracked him clean on the jaw. Drilled a few extra for good measure.

'Tommy, get the fuck off them, that's enough,' Arlo said, 'Flash is finding the shit they stole and we're getting out of here.'

There was blood everywhere. I was coughing it up. My hands were covered in it. Connor's face was swollen and soaked with red, unconscious. Jonno was trying to resuscitate him, shaking him, shouting at him. Arlo's voice had taken me out of my rage. The strange numbness of shock, and the reminder that what has been done can't be undone. Jesus. I've gone too far.

Of all times, my personal phone rang. It was Mum.

'Hello?'

'Hello, son, were you boxing? You're breathless,' she said.

I stood and walked out the house calmly, like a bit of a psycho with no remorse. Shock does that to you. 'Yes, Mum, just had a tough session,' I said. I coughed. Phlegm and blood.

Mum said, 'I hope you're looking after yourself. I'm guessing you forgot about today. I bought tickets to that concert, remember, you were going to take me?'

'Fuck,' I said. 'I'm so sorry, I've not been myself lately.'

Mum was silent, I could feel her disappointment. I'd

fucked up, badly.

She said, 'I'm devastated.'

Police sirens.

'Mum, I've got to go. I'll call you as soon as I can.'

Part 3

Chapter 10

I'm in my tutor's office holding that piece of paper: 'You should have closed the blinds.' Without that stash, I have no chance of making anywhere near the money I owe. I jump off the chair, slip the chair close to the desk exactly where I found it, flick the latch on the door back to normal. My heart is pumping and I feel like punching something, but I'm not going to let it get to me. I will figure it out.

'What happened?' Sammy says. 'Where's the stuff?'

I pass him the note.

'Oh, fuck,' he says.

'Time for plan B,' I say.

'What's plan B?'

'There isn't one yet.'

'We'll figure it out,' he says.

'I've got to get money out of the business account, and some cash from Vintage and Vinyl, you wanna come?'

'Can we do something baller after that?' Sammy says.

'Like what?' I say.

'I dunno, let's go and blow ten grand at the casino. And then get cocaine and strippers and all that.'

'When I've sorted my little problem out, we'll do something baller.'

'Wicked,' he says.

As we walk to Vintage and Vinyl, I phone my bank for a large personal loan. I tell them I need to buy a car, some white goods for an unfurnished flat, and that I need a long overdue holiday. I manage to secure twenty grand without much fuss, only 3.5 per cent annual interest, the whole debt needs to be paid back in three years. Since Vintage and Vinyl technically employ me with a healthy salary, and I have the mortgage on Mum's house, credit cards and more, my credit rating is good. I'm worried about the repayments now everything's fucked, but now's not the time for that.

As I put the phone back in my pocket, Sammy says, 'Even though you've been an antisocial twat this year, I'm going to miss you next year.'

'What do you mean? I'll be around,' I say.

'Yeah but I've got that internship year in industry at PwC, haven't I?'

'What? PricewaterhouseCoopers? You never told me about that.'

'Whose fault is that? Yeah, I'll be in London most of next year. I'll miss you, mate.'

'What will you be doing?'

'You do loads of stuff. They teach you industry knowledge and skills so you have a chance of joining them after uni. It's an unpaid internship, which is a bit shit, but Mum and Dad will help me out, and the woman who runs it all is my aunt's best friend so I'll be well looked after. Quite lucky really, this particular internship programme only had ten spaces available to students across the whole country.'

I fight the image of a giant skyscraper with an erect penis sticking out of it, Sammy's mouth gliding over corporate cock. 'Congratulations, I'm happy for you,' I say. I feel so guilty about being such a shit friend to Sammy this year, I feel like crying. 'Hopefully we can do something fun in the summer, before you start.'

'Yeah, we should go to Vegas and fuck loads of birds. Or Columbia,' he says.

'If I'm not in the bottom of a river tied to a rock, why not? You can have all the girls though, I'll make sure of that,' I say.

'Fucking wicked, let's be sure you're not murdered then,' he says.

Written upon the windows of Vintage and Vinyl is: 'Clearance: up to 50% off' in white and black. I barely ever have the chance to come here, I'm always too busy. Disco music is playing from the record player in the corner. The walls have Rhetorik T-shirts pinned to them, next to the collectable vinyl records in frames. That particular Rhetorik print was made especially for us: the T-shirts are black, the prints are white, and in the shape of a spinning record.

Mika is at the counter waiting to serve customers. Mika is attractive, androgynous, fluid. Black, textured hair, roughened fringe slightly wet-looked, mid-length at the top, short on the sides, super sharp. Well-groomed face, youthful, healthy skin with well-defined cheeks and jaw. Always fashionable. Today, Mika is wearing a low-cut white top, revealing a flat, hairless chest. Vintage, acid-wash-grey dungarees.

Mika once made a great point about fluidity to me. At that time, Mika's voice was higher-pitched, a characteristic you'd associate with a more feminine side of Mika's personality, which fluctuates openly, identifying neither as male nor female, or anything else, just Mika. Mika said, 'Fluidity is about being adaptable. People get stuck in their own heads and think they're this immutable entity, you know? They say, "I'm just this way, or that way" and they don't really realise that everything changes, especially people, and change is a good thing. So now I try to be fluid about everything, you know: gender, personality, politics, taste, fashion. I like to stay open and receptive to how I feel, and to change, always embrace change, I'm happier that way.'

I liked that. I wish I was more fluid.

There are two customers looking through rails of jeans near the back of the shop. One of them is saying, 'This is sick, look at how sick this is, sick sick sick.'

I hate how overused the word is.

Coach Jimmy is eyeing Rhetorik items on a rack. He's wearing tracksuit bottoms and a sporty T-shirt that don't match. He's always got a look of seriousness about him. He's not intimidating, yet not completely welcoming. I remember when they told me that Coach Jimmy is known as the Dark Horse. I never found out why.

Jimmy says, 'How's everything?' The look on his face makes me fear he knows more than he should.

'Everything is good,' I say. 'I'll be back at training soon.'

'That's good to hear,' he says.

'I might come along too,' Sammy says.

'Great,' Jimmy says. 'You and your mate Anthony did a good job on this place.'

'Thank you, it's been hard work.'

'I have no doubt it was, with many unexpected challenges, I'm sure.'

I can feel him scrutinising the scratches on my face, the bruises on my knuckles. 'Many,' I say.

'Tommy, if you ever need anything, just let me know.'

'Thank you, I will do,' I say. I wonder about the extent of the offer.

Mika, with a deep, commanding voice: 'Tommy, Sammy, you ignore me all day?'

'Never,' I say. 'How are you?'

Mika hugs us both. I never know whether to call Mika a

he or a she, but all I do know is that Mika doesn't care. That's the beauty of true fluidity. Things offend you less.

'I'm good, excellent. I play all my old disco records, and I'm love it.' The voice, a bit higher-pitched, more eccentric this time. When Mika applied for this job, the personal profile was full of creative and professional traits any employer would want from an employee. The final sentence read, 'Not your average corporate cocksucker.'

Anthony, Moose and I had liked that a lot. We laughed so fucking hard our abs ached. We'd arranged an interview right away, Mika started work the next day. The corporate world is a joke. True life is about people, the earth, community. Local businesses can stay true to that. Real people. Not robots. Not drones. Not sheep. Not slaves. People not profit. The planet, not profit. Imagine if those were the priorities, and profit was a secondary goal. I wonder what the world would look like then.

'How's the clearance sale going?' I say.

'It's good, people are love jackets just twenty-five pounds, you know? Even some strange man come here earlier and he buys this colourful denim embroidery, really nice thing, but he doesn't look like a man who wears fashionable things, you know, he looks a bit tacky and boring. So he takes the jacket, two hours later he come back and returns the jacket, no reason, just he doesn't like it any more, and he say, Make sure Tommy knows about the return, okay? So maybe he your friend or something, because I didn't think anyone else knew you were the boss, you know?'

I am uneasy. 'Where is the jacket?'

'Upstairs with the other returns, it's XL, reworked, you'll see all that colourful embroidery, all the patterns we put in, go check.'

Upstairs there are two rooms. One is for stock, the other

is an office. There are no windows. We are in the stockroom. The lightbulbs are bright. There are rails and boxes of clothes everywhere. The returns pile is small. A couple of T-shirts, and the jacket. I like the jacket a lot, it's denim with lots of little feathers in all colours embroidered on the back. I am wary about the return.

In the inside chest pocket, there's a note, 'You can't run, you can't hide. Set Terry up.'

'What does it say?' Sammy says.

I pass the note to him. I say, 'Terry is the kingpin, you can't set him up. Arlo wants me to set him up so Arlo can go free, he's trying to threaten me.'

'I can't believe Arlo would do that,' Sammy says.

'Me neither, but it seems desperate times call for desperate measures. Let's get the cash and go.'

There's just over a grand in cash in the safe. I take the cash and requisite banking documents so we can head there next.

On the way out, I say to Mika, 'What did the man look like?'

'He was big, had bald head, bit like fat egg. He never tell me his name.' The voice deepens now, 'He have bruising on his face, like he been hit or something.'

Deano. I thought he'd been arrested. I wonder if he got bail. Surely not for a violent crime.

On our way to the bank, Sammy says, 'I still can't work out whether Mika is a man or a woman.'

'Neither, and both,' I say. 'It's complicated.'

'But sometimes she's so fit, I dunno if I can fancy a man, she must be a woman.'

'I suppose you could fancy a person at times and not at other times, it doesn't have to be so *defined*, does it?'

'I dunno.'

'I think that's what the whole fluidity thing is all about,

taking things on a moment-by-moment basis. One minute you're this, the next you're that, and there are no set boundaries.'

'I don't really get it,' Sammy says.

'Me neither,' I say.

There's a long, frustrating queue at the bank. I've never really understood banks. I wish I could use a nice little community bank, one that reinvests in good causes. I don't think many exist any more, the bigger financial institutions probably muscled them out. I assume a nice guy can't just go and start a bank, too many regulations and whatnot. Regulations are good, but not when the regulating institutions get lobbied by the guys being regulated. It's foolish to think that sort of thing doesn't happen, it's natural. Humans like to protect what they have. Institutions like to protect themselves. How many bank bosses are good friends with Tories?

I withdraw every penny from the business account, in cash. I have a feeling the bankers are somewhat suspicious, but I don't seem to have any real problems, it's not really that much money.

All the cash is in my rucksack. Sammy is beaming with joy.

'I have to do something alone now,' I say. 'Can you take this home safely?'

'I'll come with you,' he says.

'This is going to get messy, I can't take anyone with me, and we need to protect that cash.' I hand him the rucksack.

He unzips it, looks at all the cash, smiles. 'This is so gangster. I want to go and put it all on red. I won't though, you can trust me to get it all home safely. You're not going to go and do a robbery on your own or something, are you?'

'No. I'm going to go see Isobel'

'I definitely don't want to come with you to do that, good luck,' he says.

I only half-lied to Sammy. I have one thing to take care of before I go to Isobel. First, I have to try find Gary. I haven't seen him in months. Part of me doesn't want to find him. He keeps telling me he's on a waiting list, and that they're going to help him soon, first with a home, and then his teeth. He'd often say, 'Tommy, my brother, the day you don't see me again is the day I'm sorted out or the day I'm dead. I'd probably be happy with either, you know. So be happy for Gary.'

Being around Gary had always been hard. It reminded me that no matter how hard we work to get somewhere in life, if we don't all work to help others as well, there will *always* be suffering. The, *Every man for himself* model that the UK subscribes to is one of the dumbest and most isolating I've ever encountered.

I find Gary sitting in an alleyway with a smile on his face. Not sorted, not dead. His lack of teeth is still hard to look at. We often talk about homelessness and how hard it is to get from the street back into normal life. Speaking with Gary confirmed for me that it takes ten times the courage, energy and luck to get from homelessness with absolutely nothing to piss-poor and homed, than it does to get from rich to richer.

Anyone who is that proud of themselves for managing to get from rich to richer is deluded. Going from comfortable to more comfortable is also not much of an achievement at all. I'm sure Barbs was quite proud of leaving school with half decent grades and going to a half decent uni; over the years, growing from middle class to slightly more middle class, with more crap on finance and a slightly bigger mortgage. But with all that support from her parents: dinner cooked for her every day after school, a car to drive to college with, the allowance at uni, help with rent while she was on her grad scheme, help with the deposit on the house… she practically had it handed to her on a plate. And that's a fucking good thing, Barbs, don't get me wrong. I am very happy for you. Sincerely. The only thing I'm not happy about is your willingness to perpetuate the misconception that someone like Gary doesn't try hard enough. That he somehow deserves his misfortune. That you could do what you did with no help at all.

'Tommy, my brother, where've you been?' Gary says.

'It's a long story I'm afraid. Anyway, mate, I've got something for you.' I give him a twenty.

Ironically that twenty will go nowhere. It costs a lot of money for a homeless person to get a bed for the night. You wouldn't have thought it, but being homeless is expensive. You can't buy raw ingredients and cook a healthy meal. You can't grind coffee beans and make a cheap coffee. Not that the homeless are worried about good coffee, but you get the idea. You can't rent a decent room spreading the cost over a monthly payment, like most who rent do. The economy of scale you're working with means you pay a premium on everything. Barbs would have never thought about those things. That's why her understanding is distorted. It's not her fault. They don't teach the economics of homelessness in the papers. Why would they?

'Cheers, ma brother,' Gary says.

I sit on the pavement next to him, by the entrance of the alley. In a low voice, I say, 'Remember that time I said if I ever saw a dealer trying to sell drugs to a homeless person I'd put their jaw in the back of their skull?'

Gary laughs, 'That'd be too good, eh? They're still always coming around offering me a fiver of spice on tick. Still clean though I am, I am, yes, brother.'

Gary and I high-five. His hands are dirty and cracked, perhaps from malnourishment and dehydration.

I hate seeing his toothless mouth. I feel his desperation, his struggle, his lack of self-esteem. It's funny how they teach you maths and English for over ten years in school, but not once do they develop your self-esteem, or your relationship-building skills. Gary wouldn't be here if he had been taught self-esteem and relationship-building skills. That's the bottom line. Society has failed him. We've all failed him. And now he's got no teeth. Fuck!

'You know what, mate, have this,' I say. I give him another twenty quid and I promise myself that when this is all over I'll try and do whatever it takes to get him off the streets once and for all, whether it's private counselling, or a nutrition and cookery class, whatever it takes. I want to cry, but I force it all back in and I say, 'Take me to the dealers.'

'You serious? Now? No way, Tommy man, those are ruthless they are, they'd stab us both.'

'A favour for me,' I say. 'You don't have to hang about, just show me where they sell their gear.'

Gary walks with a bit of a limp. He got beaten up by drunk men on a night out. His right leg was injured badly while they kicked him on the floor. They beat him up because he was smiling at them the wrong way. It's quite hard to smile the right way when you have no teeth.

Who the fuck would beat a homeless man? Reminds me of that posh cunt from Cambridge University on the news, who burnt cash in front of a homeless man. I wonder if he was a Tory? Members of the local Conservative Association were filmed laughing their heads off about the incident. Says it all really. Or am I being prejudiced? I wish it was merely misplaced prejudice. I wish it was pure cynicism with no basis in truth at all. I wish Theresa May truly cared for the poor. I wish our whole country cared for the poor.

'Down there, take the next right. That's where you can get spice or anything like that, any time, but you're a fuckin nutter if you go down there, Tommy, a fuckin nutter.'

We're on a street I've never been down, the pavement and road are scattered with rubbish, it smells a bit sketchy, like smoke and rotting food, the buildings on both sides are dilapidated, ghostly. It's a bit industrial down here, not so many houses as warehouses and old commercial buildings.

My adrenaline starts firing, like I'm about to go to war. I take a deep breath to calm the nerves. I've got to be impeccable. One mistake and I could be murdered. I've been wanting to do this for a long time. I never had the guts before, I never believed in myself.

'You'd better go back now, thanks for showing me here, Gary,' I say.

'I'd do anything for you, Tommy, my friend, you know that.'

I approach with soft footsteps, hyper-alert. There are guys talking with strong Welsh accents. I have the element of surprise on my side. But my body is throbbing, I'm too fired up. I take two giant, deep, slow, controlled breaths. Turn right.

There are four guys hanging about, chatting to each other. Indistinct hip-hop is coming from one of their phones. I can't see the phone. One of the men is sitting on the pavement. They appear to be in their mid twenties, early thirties.

'How much for a gram of spice?' I say. Spice is the dirtiest new drug out there. It turns people into zombies. The homeless and the lower-class drug addicts zone out on the sides of the pavements in the city centre and beyond as if there's no tomorrow. Gary tells me that spice is the new heroin. It gives you an intense high, and it's cheap. At least the rich can afford more socially acceptable drugs, like MDMA, and cocaine.

'Who the fuck are you?' a guy says. He's got short, curly, ginger hair. A rough, pale face, stubble, a bit of acne.

I take a twenty out. 'I've got money,' I say.

'Get him his bag then,' the curly-haired guy says.

One of them runs off to get the bag. He's stocky, wearing black cotton tracksuit bottoms and a mucky white T-shirt.

Curly-haired guy says, 'You gonna give me the cash then, or what?'

I approach him slowly. Standing to his left, there's a skinny guy whose blue Adidas T-shirt doesn't quite hang over his waist. He's slouched, definitely the weakest link. The guy sitting on the pavement looks stronger, he has a better posture and his face is a bit more switched on.

I hand the cash to the curly-haired guy. While I hold it towards him, I relax my legs, slight bend at the knee, raised rear heel. The moment his hand grips the note, I transfer all the weight from my leg into my fist and I uppercut him clean on the jaw. Bang!

The crack is horribly satisfying, I've been wanting to do that for a long time. For a split second, there's silence. In that split second, he looks confused, a little shocked, his brain and body don't know what's what. The other two are so surprised, they don't react. I push the guy wearing the Adidas T-shirt off balance. Step back to gain the advantage of long range, and a good stance.

Curly-haired guy's head hits the ground like a coconut on concrete. Clockwork.

As Adidas guy tries to gain his balance, I crack him in the ribs, he screeches. I follow with an overhand right to his jaw. I hit him so hard it feels like I've punched a brick wall. My knuckles tingle. He crumbles to the ground.

The pavement guy grabs my leg from behind, buckles my knees, takes me down. Crafty fucker, I didn't think he'd take the initiative. He's heavier and stronger than me. I throw punches at his head but I can't get the leverage or range needed to make impact. He pins me down, sitting on my waist. Hits me. Nothing. Can't punch to save his life. Tries to hit me again, I slip the punch, he hits the concrete, growls.

While he's confused about missing, I push my hips up, rotate him off me. Spring to my feet. Wait for him to stand. The moment he's on his feet, I knock him out cold with a big, heavy right. BANG. It's like a fucking film, except it's real, because this is what happens when extraordinary people do extraordinary things. I am extraordinary. Impeccable.

All those boxing matches, the wins, the losses, they were all worth it, because I've achieved something more meaningful than a useless medal: the fucking cunts who sell drugs to the homeless are finally being taught a lesson. I'm so happy right now.

'What the fuck?' The guy who went to get the spice. He drops the baggie. From his back pocket, pulls out a little flick knife. He is scared, I can see it in his face, I can sense it in his body language. He is rigid and jittery. Doesn't want to come near me.

'You fucking coward,' I say. 'Come on then!'

He won't approach me. Flinches as I move towards him. I stop just outside his range. He's pointing the knife at me, but I know he can't reach me from there. I must stay relaxed. I cannot make a mistake. Cannot close that range prematurely.

I feint a jab, he flinches, launches the knife towards me, misses as expected. My second jab knocks his head back, my rear hook cracks his cheek.

I rummage through their pockets. They're not out cold, but they are incoherent, their movements uncoordinated. They have just less than a grand in cash on them. One of them has car keys in his pocket. The car is a charcoal-greyish, old banger. In the old banger is another grand in cash. These guys are the epitome of everything that is wrong with society. They are no better than Theresa May and her cronies stamping on the faces of the poor every time they try to rise.

My hands are throbbing, my adrenaline still pumping hard. I wish I'd worn a mask. The guy who had the flick knife is coming round, back to reality. I hit him again, hard, this time he is out cold. I take his flick knife, press my thumb on it, flat so it won't cut me. It's sharper than I thought it would be. It has a fancy serration pattern on the base of the blade.

I carve 'Scum' into his forehead. I knock each one unconscious once more, and I make the same incisions on all their faces. Scum.

***

I'm walking to Isobel's, still buzzing from the fight with those drug dealers. I am torn between being fucking proud of what I've just done, and worried that two wrongs don't make a right. You can't please everyone. Not everything is clear-cut right or wrong.

There's a florist ahead. I should buy her some flowers really, that's always a nice gesture. I should have bought her flowers more often when we were together.

It smells nice in the shop, lightly floral, with the odd hint of soil. Everything is well presented, clean. There are white and yellow roses in separate bunches in metal vases. There are other flowers of all colours, neatly ordered, well arranged. I don't know their names. I prefer wild growth, a bit of dirt and unpredictability, like real life.

The lady at the counter says, 'Can I help you?' She's elderly, with curly white hair, her smile is pleasant.

'I'm looking for some flowers for my girlfriend,' I say. I know she's not my girlfriend, but what else can I call her? I wish I'd given her the attention she deserves. I'm not ready to let her go. I will fight for her.

'Okay. Well, what does she like?' the woman says.

I realise I don't really know. 'Um, well, I don't think she likes red roses. She would probably prefer something with white roses in, and other flowers, the more vivid the better.'

The lady fashions a bouquet with plenty of bright little blue flowers, some fluffy yellow ones with hundreds of tiny little petals, and some large, white roses. It looks great.

On the corner of Isobel's road, with all the terraced houses and the bins and the rubbish on the pavement as you see everywhere in Cathays on certain days, I find Adey, lurking conspicuously.

'Everything okay so far?' I say.

'I've been watching over her all day every day, mate, and when I needed sleep I got my mate on it. Please forgive that debt, Tommy, I'll do anything.'

Adey looks tired, his hair is scruffy and his face is cracked. I appreciate his efforts.

'Stick at it and we'll come to some kind of arrangement,' I say. 'I'm here for at least ten minutes, go get yourself a drink and some food if you're hungry.' I hand Adey a twenty.

'Thank you. You're a good man, Tommy.'

'I'm not so sure,' I mumble, or think out loud, I'm not sure whether anything comes out of my mouth because I'm deep in a flash of thoughts about whether I'm a good person or not. I'm walking towards Isobel's. I'm definitely not the worst person in the world. They all say that though, don't they? Maybe I'm just as bad as the rest of them.

I knock on Isobel's door. I'm more nervous than when I went to beat those guys up. Am I supposed to hold the flowers out towards her, or just keep them close to my chest until she reaches for them? Does it matter? I know they won't make her happy, we're too far gone. I hope they're better than nothing. She answers the door.

'What?' she says.

'I'm sorry,' I say.

'Sorry for what?'

'I'm sorry I lied to you. I'm sorry I disrespected you. I'm sorry I put you in danger. And I'm sorry I didn't prioritise our time together, even though it was the nicest time I ever had, and the only time I felt like a normal person. I was the luckiest person alive, to be with you. I got you some flowers.'

'Come in,' she says.

We're in her room, lying on top of her neat bed. The ceiling is smooth, slightly creamy white. The sound of her breath is soft. She says, 'It was sweet of you to get your mate to look after me.'

'I'm guessing he wasn't that subtle?'

'He's a fucking idiot. He's been following me everywhere, and you can tell by the way he looks about he's trying to do a great job, like he thinks he's a high-profile secret-security guard or something. Oh, yes, and the girls said Flash knocked on the door while I was at uni, he wanted to talk to you about something very important, he said it changes everything. Apparently, he was really sketchy, like he was scared someone would see him there. He left a number for you to ring.' She hands me a piece of paper with a number scribbled on it.

'He probably wants to get at me,' I say, 'lure me out.'

'What if it really is important? I think you should phone him and see.'

I phone the number. There's no answer.

'I'm really sorry, you know,' I say.

'I know, Tommy.' She puts her hand on mine. Her touch is light. 'I can't magically trust you, this is going to take time. I don't even know if you're the man I fell in love with, maybe we've both changed, it happens when you're young.' She's crying.

I feel sick. The synths in 'Gammelan' are running through

my head but they're all distorted and sad now. I have to change the subject before I cry. 'You know how I always said I wanted to beat up the scum who sell drugs to homeless people?'

'You didn't?'

'I finally did.'

'I'm proud of you,' she says.

We hug for a long time.

'Do you want to come with me to visit my mum next week?' I say.

'That would be lovely, I miss her,' she says.

'Me too.'

I get a text on my personal phone. 'I'm outside. Get in the car.' It's Terry's Messenger.

Fucking cunts invading my privacy all the time. But what can I do?

'Terry's lot are outside. They want to talk to me. I'm sorry, but I have to go.'

'Be careful,' she says. 'When will you be back?'

'It depends on what he wants. I'll be okay, I promise.'

It's a white Audi with blacked-out windows. The driver opens the back passenger-side door for me. I slide in. The Messenger is beside me. The door clicks shut smoothly. The car pulls off. It's comfortably warm in here. The air seems a bit artificial, a bit dry. I catch a glimpse of Adey gawping at the car as we cruise past.

The Messenger says, 'Terry wants to talk.'

★★★

I'm in Terry's office. The lighting is warm and dim and it softens everything. I wonder what he does in here. Probably just summons people, deals with them, sends them on their way. Terry is less dissatisfied than usual. He says, 'You did well the other day, that was a good fight.'

'I did what I had to do.'

'I know you did, son, I know. There's another fight, a big one this time. I'll wipe twenty grand from your debt, all you have to do is box him until the fourth, then take a dive.'

'There's no way I'm going to take a dive,' I say. 'I don't lose any more.'

'As much as I have faith in you, Tommy, son, this is about money, a safe bet. I can't go with a tip if I don't know it's guaranteed, can I now? This guy's an ex-England-champ as well, has a pro record. It's white collar, but it's proper boxing. It won't even be easy to go to the fourth, he'll be fit, he's been training for a long time for this one. I know you've got the skill, but this isn't the time for a battle, just go down in the fourth, and take twenty grand.'

'I'll do what I have to do.'

★★★

Isobel and I arrive at Mum's new house. The front is rich green and overgrown, there are vines wrapping around the gateposts and a huge blanket of leaves along the wall, with bits overlapping the kitchen window. Mum's silver Peugeot estate is parked near the house.

'This is cool,' Isobel says.

'Mum wanted something with character,' I say.

I knock on the door. Mum doesn't know we're coming.

The door opens, Mum takes a second look. 'Tommy! You bloody brat, you're not supposed to surprise me like that.'

'Sorry, Mum, we thought a surprise would be nice. Since you said you were doing a bit better now, and all.'

'It's nice to see you both,' she says.

The porch has rain jackets, wellies and walking boots in it, and leads straight into the kitchen. The kitchen is dimly lit by daylight. It is small, cute, and it has character. The kitchen floor is tiled with what looks like slate. To my left, the overgrown window. In front of me, a sink, and a wooden surface with about enough space for two chopping boards. There are wooden cupboards below the sink and the surface. To my right, one more surface with two more cupboards below. The kitchen is three or four strides long, at most.

'This place is so cool,' Isobel says. 'I'm sorry I haven't visited you here yet, how are you?'

'I'm sorry too,' I say. 'I should have been here more.'

'No, don't be sorry, I know you're both busy. It would have been nice to see you more, it's a shame we live so far apart. But I am a bit better, thank you. It's still a struggle, I'm far from well, but I feel like I have a small part of my life back, and maybe I'll be able to visit you in Cardiff sometime soon.'

I've always wanted Mum to come visit me in Cardiff. The place has defined me. And what parent doesn't want to see where their child lives once they've flown the nest? I bet it kills her to see such a small part of my life. I want to cry with joy with sadness, with every emotion I have. And in this moment it all feels worth it, every fucking bit. The risk. The struggle. The blood. The sweat. The tears. For Mum.

'That's amazing, what have you been doing?' Isobel says.

'I go for long walks and I can drive again, so I go to a yoga class. If I carry on improving I think I'll be able to work again.'

'Don't bother with work, Mum, I've got you covered. You just enjoy yourself.' She has many years of wasted life to catch up on. I'll pull something out of the bag after Terry's shit is sorted. Maybe I'll write a book about it all.

'Oh, you don't need to worry about that,' she says. 'I've been isolated for so long, I think a job will be nice, it kills me to feel so disconnected from the world. Do either of you want a horsetail tea?'

Yes please, we say.

'What have you two got planned while you're here?' Mum says. She lights the gas on the stove and puts the kettle over it. The metal sings softly.

Mum's posture as she stands by the stove is better than I've seen it in so many years. She's still hunched, and a bit frail, but she's much more poised than before.

'We really want to go for a walk at dawn tomorrow, it's more exciting at dawn. Do you want to come?' Isobel says.

Mum thinks for a moment, says, 'No, thank you, I'm saving my energy to dip in the sea as many days as I can. The cold-water therapy seems to be helping me lots.'

'What's that?' Isobel says.

Mum says, 'You can boost your immune system by going into cold water, and there are some breathing techniques I do to make the cold more tolerable. There's a guy called the Ice Man, he can sit in ice for ages without bother. It's so cool, and a bit supernatural. He's so fit and healthy too. Usually you just need to turn the shower cold after a normal shower and endure it for a while, but I much prefer the sea.'

'I couldn't handle the sea right now,' Isobel says.

'Me neither, not without a wetsuit. You're doing well, Mum,' I say.

'Yes, I love the sea so much. It is bloody cold though, I wonder what it will be like doing it in winter!' She's excited. I've not seen her this optimistic in a long time.

'That'll be mental in the winter,' Isobel says. 'Surely it's not just the cold water that's helped you so much?'

'It's been a mixture of things really. I've been doing a lot with my doctor, she's one of the best in the field. We ran a thousand tests, we made sure we fixed my gut, we made sure my body was getting the right energy, and micronutrients, I had to take all sorts of things. The worst part is we still don't know how to take it further, we've tried everything. She said it usually gets better and worse and better and worse throughout an ME patient's life, so I'm probably going to be stuck a bit like this forever.'

I say, 'Don't worry, it won't be long until they fund the research properly, they can't ignore it forever.' But I know these things take decades, and that nobody really cares about people with ME, not in the bigger scheme of things. It's easier not to care.

The kettle whistles and Mum pours hot water into a teapot. She scoops a few teaspoons of horsetail leaves into the water. It smells mildly earthy, and super healthy.

***

Isobel and I have just got back from our walk at dawn. We ended up walking for hours, along the coast and back. The air was refreshing and the sound of the sea was calming. The soft tinge of the early sun on the landscape was worth a million dollars.

It's 9.30 am. On the dining room table, there's a large bunch of blood-red roses. Their leaves and stalks are rich green. The vase is clear glass. There's a message on a card taped to the vase. The water has small, light specks of something floating in it.

'They're nice,' Isobel says.

'Yeah,' I say.

I wonder who they're from.

Mum is meditating in her room. She's not asleep because she's slightly poised. She opens her eyes. 'How was your walk?' she says.

'Refreshing,' I say. 'How are you?'

'I'm fine, and thank you for the flowers, they're beautiful.'

'I was worried they'd mess the order up to be honest, the website was a bit all over the place,' I say. I'm thinking on my feet, I don't know where the flowers are from, I feel anxious, but I don't want to worry Mum.

'The man who delivered them was a bit odd, he asked for you. And the card is terribly written, I'm not even sure it's proper English. I think it's cute though, you should look.'

The flowers smell sweet. The card reads, 'Say hello to Mother, take care Tommy, love.' I don't like that at all. Nobody knows where Mum lives. I made sure of that.

'Look at this,' I pass the card to Isobel.

'Who do you think it's from?' she says.

'I don't know. Perhaps someone followed us back on the train?'

'Maybe,' she says. 'Do you want me to stay here with her while you sort everything back in Cardiff, just until it's over?'

'I'll have to think about it, but for now, let's enjoy our time here. I'm not letting anyone get the better of me. How about a dip in the sea with Mum?'

'Nope.'

'That's what I was thinking. We can just go down and hold her towel for her.'

I take the card to Mum.

She says, 'See, such jumbled English.'

'It was supposed to say, "Hello, Mother, Take care, love Tommy". I don't know how they messed it up so badly, not that I knew what to write anyway. It wouldn't let me place the order without a message. Silly website. When do you want to swim?'

'Maybe in an hour or so,' she says. 'I might prepare lunch first.'

'Oh, no, Mum, don't worry about that. I'll do lunch.'

'You forget I'm a bit better now, I'll do it. I was thinking of cooking some garlic-butter prawns and spiralled veg, are you two happy with that?' she says.

I say, 'Yea—' Interrupted by the sound of glass smashing. Abrupt. Harsh and piercing. Adrenaline. Heavy heartbeat. Deep breath. Try to play it cool for Mum.

'Stay there, I'll go and find out what that was, it was probably a bird flying into the window or something.'

In the living room, the window is smashed and there's a smooth beach pebble with the words 'Set Terry up' painted on it. The words are red.

I'm enraged. Fucking bastards! I want to kill Arlo. I want to kill them all.

The living room has a dark wood floor. Broken glass glimmers everywhere, some pieces large enough to slit a throat, some small and intricately formed, like diamonds.

'Fucking hell,' I say.

Isobel puts her hand on my back. Her touch is light and lovely.

'Put that in the bin, please,' I say, handing the pebble to Isobel.

Back to Mum, I say, 'It was a bloody bird as well, luckily it was still alive and flying, but it was panicked, I had to catch it and throw it back out. I'll get that window fixed right away, how about getting something painted on the glass, like they do in churches, so it never happens again?'

'Oh, poor creature,' she says.

'You carry on meditating while I sort it out,' I say.

I'm in the living room, sweeping up the glass. Some of the smaller pieces of glass wedge in between the small gaps between boards. I'll have to pick them out.

Isobel returns, she says, 'I buried that rock, in case your

mum found it in the bin, and I had a good look outside, there's nobody around.'

'You're very brave,' I say.

'So are you,' she says.

'I don't think it would be safe here for you and Mum on your own. I'll ask Ryan to come and stay for a week or two. That way, you can come back to Cardiff with me. I can tell Mum he's got an accommodation issue and needs somewhere to stay, something like that. She won't be suspicious.'

'Yeah, that sounds reasonable. So when will you get a chance to talk to Arlo? This all feels a bit wrong.'

'I'm not sure. He's being held, they deemed him too much of a threat to grant bail before his trial. They've linked him to some violent crimes. I think I was involved in some of that. I'm not sure how I'll live with myself when all this sinks in. And I hope he doesn't tell the police I was involved.'

★★★

Isobel and I sit on a pebble ridge while Mum slowly walks into the sea. It's a lovely day with blue sky. The air is mild, and there is no breeze. The tide is high, the water licks the pebbles at the bottom of the ridge when a larger wave comes in. It's a forward, shallow surge of white, brown and silver. As it pulls back, the wet sand is dark brown.

'It's nice here,' Isobel says.

'It is,' I say. The beach is vast, probably a mile long, and beyond the estuary, more beach at Braunton Burrows and Saunton Sands.

'Maybe it wouldn't be so bad to just disappear somewhere nice,' Isobel says.

'I suppose. If it gets to the last day and I can't pay, shall we?'

'Why not,' she says. 'Can your mum fly yet?'

'Probably. Look at her go!' Mum dips under a wave, surfaces fast.

'I'm so happy for her,' Isobel says.

'Me too,' I say.

The waves are about two feet high, and clean. A surfer enters the water. The deeper water beyond the waves is a mix of blue and dark grey. There are shimmery bits reflecting the sunlight.

***

As I'm sitting there on that pebble ridge next to Isobel, I remember the evening I met Terry. I was at my student house, sitting at the desk, trying to do some uni work. It was dark outside, and my room was a little chilly. There was a knock at the door. Someone else answered it.

Emily's voice sounded a bit surprised. 'Hello?' she said.

'Hello, darling,' a man said.

'I'm Tommy's Uncle Terry.'

I knew exactly who he was. There was something so strong and sure about his voice.

'Uncle Terry,' I said, into the hallway.

'Tommy, son, I've got dinner booked for eight, sorry to spring it on you, I couldn't get hold of you.'

His appearance suited his voice, he was dressed in an incredibly sharp suit, his face told a thousand stories, and his eyes were immensely lively.

Emily left us to it.

Terry said, 'Put something smart on and meet me in the car.'

I got into his burgundy Range Rover, intrigued. Nervous. Excited.

He sat with me in the back. He said, 'The famous Leon.'

'Nobody knows about my student house.'

'Don't you worry about that, your little secret is safe with me, son. And I like it. I like it a lot. Two places. Two identities. Simple but lucrative cash businesses to wash the money, brilliant.

'Now you're probably wondering what I'm doing here. Tommy, Leon, whoever you want to be, I'm here to meet the man I've heard so much about. People talk, you know. That's the only thing you can expect people to do, to talk. To talk about others, especially others doing it differently to them. But we'll talk about all that later. For now, Tommy, Leon, whatever you want, come and see my club, enjoy yourself a bit.'

'Leon,' I said.

We pulled up to a property in a terraced row of tall buildings, lights glowing warm at the windows. I wondered what I was getting into. Security opened the door for us, the corridor was narrow but elegant, the paintings, eye-catching. Thick oil strokes fusing reds, whites, and golds to form attractive abstract patterns.

A sharp man behind the desk said, 'Mr Harsham.'

Terry said, 'Hello, Harry, sign Leon here with a complementary membership, and a little gift to cover an evening's entertainment, would you?'

'Certainly,' Harry said. Fair hair, six feet tall, medium build. Thin face. 'And, uh, the amount?'

'Oh, I don't know. How about ten thousand, that will do the trick, I'm sure. Leon, come and find me when you're all set up,' Terry said.

Harry looked a bit surprised about the amount. He asked me to stand in front of a small webcam and give him some details. I gave him the ID I'd bought from the Dark Web and

I said I was Leon Reddick. I gave my Bay House address. He printed a card and swiped it through his machine.

'Full membership, ten thousand pounds, enjoy,' he said, handing the card to me. The card was jet black. I was so numbed to money, a ten grand gift was only mildly pleasing.

I walked into the casino impressed by the size of the room. The reception area was so thin, I didn't expect such a grand space beyond it. To my right was a bar with lots of well-polished glass bottles of spirits arranged in an aesthetically pleasing manner. Along from the bar there was a small stage, with nobody on it.

In front of me, and to my left, casino tables of various sorts. People were drinking and chatting and gambling, all glammed up. This wasn't your standard out-in-town crowd. They were more elegant, more interesting.

There was a guarded door at the far end of the room. I went to it and asked the guard where I could find Terry. He asked my name, checked my ID and membership card, and radioed my request.

A young woman came to escort me to Terry. She was frustrated, but smiling.

We walked through the guarded door, into a thin corridor, to a lift. In the lift, up a few floors, along a corridor, doors both sides. I was nervous, yet curious. Two of the doors were open to rooms with people in them, exclusive social areas of some sort. The other doors were shut tight.

At the end of the corridor was another door, it was made of hardwood, varnished. The woman knocked on it.

Through an intercom, Terry said, 'Leon.'

The woman said, 'Yes.'

Terry opened the door. I entered his office, fascinated by the ordered chaos, the lack of technology. So many books, files, papers.

He closed the heavy door behind me, took a seat behind his desk. He said, 'Tommy, you can be Leon downstairs, and Tommy to me, that alright, son? It wouldn't be right, me, calling you by a false name. Sit down, sit down.'

I examined the scars on his face, and his vigorous eyes.

Terry said, 'Tommy, let's get this clear. Arlo is a fool, Din is a fool, and everyone you've ever heard of in the drugs game is a fool. Except me. And do you know why? Because I haven't had to so much as look at a drug in more than ten years. Are you a fool, Tommy?'

'Under your logic, I suppose I am.'

'You're not a fool Tommy, you're alright. I like you, and it's not often I like what I hear. Carry on like this and you'll be me in fifteen years, maximum. Do you know what it takes to be me, Tommy? You've got to be focussed, and you've got to stay ten steps ahead, sharp, you know what I mean? You've got to be patient, you need to know what's what, and you need to have integrity.'

I found Terry's confidence disconcerting. He was clearly lacking in humility. I didn't like that. I sat still, paying close attention to what Terry was saying.

'When I started out, I was very much like you. I had great ideas, I knew how to minimise risk and about increasing profits, all that. You know what the hardest part was? Putting it into action. Being meticulous all the time, without making a single mistake. That's the trick, Tommy, that's the hard part. You get people like Arlo and Din who do alright for a long time, they do alright because they take the basic precautions, but mark my words, they *always* lose in the end.'

I thought about the Whitehouse. Since Arlo had taken over, it had deteriorated. I felt uneasy. I wondered where the King was. I wondered if the King had ever met Terry.

'Now, this game, this game requires more than just a perfect strategy, there's always a little luck too. It's like chess, but you've got to rely on others taking your moves once in a while. Arlo takes your moves because you can't move your pawn until he's moved his. When you play chess with two people on one team like that, there's a lot more room for error. You know what I did when I moved up the ladder? I got rid of as many people as I could, people who couldn't play a good game, who were on my side, but who might jeopardise my game. Even if they were above me. I wasn't as fortunate as you to sell to students, no, no, I had to sell to young guys and girls on the streets and trust me, that was no walk in the park.

'You're a smart man, Tommy, and I know you know where I'm going with this.'

I did.

'To get to where I am – and trust me, Tommy, trust me, where I am is so beautiful, I have the world in my palm, everything anyone could ever dream of – you've got to be impeccable. You know what the next impeccable move is, don't you, Tommy?'

'It depends on which way you look at it.'

'No. You're absolutely wrong. You've got to get rid of Arlo. You know that so badly it hurts for you to think about it. I know how it is and I know what's what, I've been there. And I'm going to make it damn easy for you. Work for me. Arlo won't have a say in the matter, and he'll be downright happy for you, I'll make sure of that.'

'I won't compromise my integrity. I made a deal with Arlo, I'm going stick with him until the year is up.'

'Integrity is important, perhaps the most important trait a man can have, but what are you applying your integrity to? Arlo – a fool. He's drawn you into more trouble than you deserve, and you know it. That scuff down in Splott, you could have done years for what you did to those guys. Count yourself lucky someone went in there and tidied things up. Count yourself lucky I had people watching over you.'

I wasn't sure how to feel about Terry having an eye on me. I shuffled uncomfortably in my seat. I was grateful that they'd cleaned that mess up. I was aggravated that I had been watched without knowing about it.

'What about you, Tommy? Your cause? Your cause is not Arlo, your cause is your mother, now that's integrity. And what's best for her? Reliable work with me, or risky work for Arlo? I don't need to go on about it, you know how it is. Your next move, Tommy, must be impeccable.'

I thought about it. I thought about Arlo dealing in his own home, I thought about his reluctance to be sharp. I thought about Terry's meticulousness, his reputation, his success. I thought about how Arlo and I were friends, how he had never let me down and how we had a deal. Except for that outburst at my event, but there was no harm done. A deal is a deal, isn't it? He never forced me to hit those guys, that was my choice. And I said, 'I won't betray Arlo.'

Terry looked slightly less dissatisfied, I was surprised, I thought he'd be terribly dissatisfied. He said, 'Okay, son. We'll speak another time. Go and enjoy your night. Put a grand on red for me would you. Red always comes in when it's my call. Trust me, I always win. I'll see you later.'

As I reached for the door, Terry said, 'One more thing, before you go.'

'Yes?'

'You broke the golden rule the other day, you sniffed your own stash, the white stuff. If you don't curb that sharpish you'll be as screwed as the rest of them. Game over.'

★★★

The casino was filled with soft, classical music, and chatter. Everything was clean and elegant. There were five roulette tables, green cloth, sparkling varnished wood around the edges. The sound of small metal balls swirling round and rattling over the numbered ridges. Beyond that, some poker tables, some blackjack tables. There were no electronic machines like you get at high-street casinos.

I sat at a roulette table. Three well-groomed gents in fashionable suits were already playing, their chips spread all over the table. The tall, pale croupier, also well dressed, was handing out chips, and arranging them on the table. His hands were impressively fast and relaxed.

I handed the croupier my membership card and asked for a grand. The croupier scanned my card, pressed a few options on the screen so fast he'd clearly done it ten thousand times before, and handed me one blue chip, with white ridges on it.

'Would you like a drink, sir?' A petite foreign woman asked.

'JD Honey, with ice,' I said. 'Please.'

A tanned man sitting opposite me, probably Greek or Turkish, serious face, bet piles of chips on several random numbers, seldom winning, it seemed. He appeared uncomfortable. He certainly wasn't enjoying himself. A woman, less tanned, in a silvery dress, kept looking over at him from a table on the side. She had a cocktail in a tall glass, with blue, white and silver layers, and a long bamboo straw. I wondered how they made the silver layer of drink.

A chubby, middle-aged man erupted, cheering at a roulette table a few tables on from mine. He was wearing charcoal trousers and a white shirt. Everyone at the table murmured. The croupier paid out five tall piles of purple chips.

The whisky was rich, sweet, slightly stern. I imagined Sammy being there with me, he'd have felt like such a baller. I was about to blow ten grand gambling in the private casino of one of the biggest gangsters in Cardiff. Sammy's dream.

I put a thousand on red. The croupier span the wheel and popped the ball into the side. Even though it wasn't my money, I was a little anxious. I was anxious, because if it came in black, Terry was all talk. If it came in red, maybe he was right, maybe he does always win.

Others placed their bets. The tanned man straightened the collar on his light grey shirt. He slipped two purple chips onto number nine. Purples were five hundred pounds each. The chances of it coming in, thirty-six to one. Potential pay out, thirty-five grand, plus his grand back.

'Final bets, please,' the croupier said.

My palms were slightly sweaty. The wheel spun into a blur.

'No more bets, please.'

The spinning slowed, the ball fell from the smooth bit to the ridges, heart racing, ball bouncing, tak tak tak tak tak tak tak tak, tak, tak, tak … tak.

Croupier said, 'Number nine, red.'

The croupier handed the tanned man thirty-six thousand pounds' worth of chips. The tanned man didn't even smile. I was a grand up and I was grinning. Terry was right, a grand on red. Just luck, maybe.

I gave the croupier my card, asked for all of it. Total capital, eleven grand.

I put a grand on the first third, it came in, a two grand win. That got my adrenaline going a little bit, I had thirteen grand.

A grand on black. No win. Back to twelve grand.

I thought about whether roulette was pure luck, or whether you could anticipate it in some way. It seemed as if we were putting complete faith in fate. There was no conscious control at all. Yet we chose to put our money on a certain number. An active choice. A choice that must coincide with the subtle fabric of the universe, as everything does. I wondered whether I could consciously tap into that fabric. I decided this was not the place for that kind of contemplation; I should stop thinking about it and just try to enjoy myself.

An attractive, middle-aged couple joined the table, they sat to my left. They had a large stack of chips. The man proceeded to scatter chips everywhere, covering every number but a few. I didn't understand that. The woman, who was slender and clearly posh, smiled at me. I smiled back.

Shortly after, Olivia sat to my right. I was surprised to see her there. I felt nervous. I wasn't sure what to say.

'Did you feel it, just then?' she said. Her cocktail dress was black, the back and shoulders were of intricate lace creating enticing patterns and exposing some of the smoothness of her skin.

'What do you mean?'

'Never mind,' she said. 'How's it going, Leon?'

'Good,' I said. 'Yeah, all good.' I wondered at what point she'd decided to call me Leon.

She waved a waitress over, ordered two Espresso Martinis.

'How's it going with you?' I said. I wanted to say, How's Flash? Where's Flash? But something stopped me.

'It's going well,' she said.

'Place bets, please,' the croupier said.

'What should we go for?' I said.

She took a grand chip from my stack, slid it with her long, elegant index finger, slowly, onto number twenty-one. 'Don't get me wrong,' she said. 'I don't know if it's going to come in on this spin. But it will come in while we're here, I know that. I can feel it.'

'Fate?' I said.

'Something like that.'

I mused that perhaps metaphysically she was indeed setting her intention to number twenty-one, and perhaps the subtle fabric of the universe would intertwine with that intention. These concepts are nearly impossible to understand, especially through the logic of words.

'Which number are you going to go for?' she said.

I placed a grand chip between seventeen, eighteen, twenty, twenty-one.

'No more bets, please,' the croupier said.

Olivia and I locked eyes. She was as striking as you could possibly imagine. The sound of the little metal ball spinning against the wheel, the ball tapping the ridges, tak, tak, the sound got slower and eventually my heart stopped, deep sigh, an intense moment. Olivia hadn't blinked once. A second of nothingness. The final sharp sound as the ball settled.

'Number seventeen, black,' the croupier said. We won eight thousand pounds.

'Good call,' Olivia said.

'I wouldn't have made that bet if you hadn't gone for twenty-one,' I said.

'Everything's connected,' she said.

The waitress returned with two Espresso Martinis. Each had a dark-roast coffee bean nestled on top of rich, velvety foam.

Olivia took a glass from the tray, placed it next to me. She lifted the other, sipped from the rounded, shallow glass, gently. 'Enjoy,' she said, taking another grand chip, sliding it to number twenty-one. 'Your move.'

I put a hundred on zero. The ball stopped on number three, red.

'It will come,' she said. She placed a grand on twenty-one.

I went for the second dozen, two grand. Number fifteen came up.

'I've never seen you here before,' she said.

'There's a first time for everything,' I said. 'You and Flash come here a lot?'

'I've been here many times. Flash, not so much. Terry's called him in for meetings once or twice, they had one earlier, and we fell out, so I stayed.'

'I'm sorry,' I said.

'I'll live,' she said. 'I'm not the sort to sulk about a man. Do you care what people like Flash think about you, Leon?' She slid another grand onto number twenty-one.

Two more Espresso Martinis.

I put five hundred on number five. 'What do you think?' I said.

'Strong bet,' she said. 'I think you care all too much.'

Number thirty-three came up.

'Better luck next time,' she said. She took a chip, kissed it. Put it on twenty-one, again.

'I'm with you,' I said. I slid my whole stack onto number twenty-one.

Olivia gasped, delighted, flattered.

The croupier piled them neatly. Others on the table nodded with respect. A big bet. The winnings would be massive. The woman of the attractive couple eyed me longer than she should have with her partner there. Her eyes were light green, her hair light brown and slightly wavy down to her shoulders. Her skin was well moisturised, and her make-up, subtle but effective. I gave her a nod.

'If this comes in, donate it to a homeless charity, and take ten per cent for yourself,' I said. The croupier smiled, spun the wheel, dropped the ball into it.

I took Olivia's hand and we left Terry's club. I had forgotten myself, carried away with the money and the power. It had felt like I was in a film, and that everything that was happening was already scripted.

★★★

Isobel and I are sitting on the pebble ridge, my memory of that night fades. There is a large boat in the distance, in line with where the river meets the sea. I assume it has just embarked on a journey, it probably launched when the tide was high. The tide is receding fast, Mum is leaving the water way further from us than where she entered it. The water is no longer licking the rocks we are sitting on. Mum is smiling.

'I really am sorry I didn't tell you about everything. I lost myself,' I say to Isobel.

'I know,' Isobel says. 'Let's sort this mess out so we can move forward. I hope you never lie to me again.'

'I won't, I promise,' I say.

'How do you feel about this boxing match?'

'It's going to be tough,' I say. 'And I don't feel comfortable losing on purpose. But Terry offered me twenty grand. I can't say no to that.'

'That's a lot of money,' Isobel says.

'Yeah, more than some of the professional British title fights,' I say.

'It's funny how people's dreams come true in the weirdest ways,' she says. 'You've always wanted to be known as a great boxer, and now you're going to earn more than a British title fighter, but you have to lose, and you'll get no glory. And yet, you wouldn't have got into this position if you weren't a great boxer in the first place.'

'I'm not sure *funny* is the word,' I say.

'You know what I mean. Anyway, I spoke to Ryan and Sammy, and they can lend you ten grand between them. I can lend you three. Where does that put you in total?'

'That's very kind of you,' I say. 'I have seven grand from the first fight, twenty from the bank, five from punting that stash, nearly two from robbing those dealers, two from collecting debts, five from Anthony, six from the business, and now thirteen from my best friends. That's ...'

'That's sweet, you are my best friend,' Isobel says. 'So that's sixty. If you take that dive you get twenty, which means you have five spare, you've made it!'

'Unless I don't make it to the fourth round.'

'You'll make it,' Isobel says.

I take Mum's towel down to her. She dries herself off. The sand is cold, wet and refreshing. 'How was it?' I say.

'It was perfect,' she says.

★★★

Isobel and I are on the train to London for my boxing match. I'm horrifically nervous. We're both silent, sitting opposite each other on table seats, closest to the window. The carriage is busy, everyone is quiet. The sound and the rhythm of the train going along the track – taka ta tar, taka ta tar, taka ta tar, taka ta tar – is relaxing, soothing. The man next to me has his laptop out, earphones in, typing away.

Isobel is reading a newspaper that was left on the table. The front-page headline says, 'Immigrants steal your weddings.'

Good old tabloids.

'For once, some nice news,' Isobel says. 'I'm surprised a shit paper like this would report it, but someone won hundreds of thousands on the roulette last month and anonymously donated it to a homeless charity. Isn't that nice?

It was in Cardiff as well.'

'That's amazing,' I say. 'I bet that will change some lives.'

'I'm sure it will,' she says.

I wonder if that was my bet, number twenty-one. The Olivia bet. It must have been, it's unlikely to be such a massive coincidence. Funny how everything is so strangely connected, the good and the bad together, all one big picture. I can't help but laugh at the irony. I could have had more than half a million quid if I had waited for that bet to come in.

Not every stroke in a painting is perfect, a single stroke is usually weak, insignificant, and yet thousands of strokes together, beautiful, we don't often scrutinise every stroke of a painting without looking at the whole thing, why do we scrutinise every little move in our lives?

I bring my awareness to my breath, the sensations in my body. I feel relaxed, but my head is trying to fuck with me. You'll get knocked out. You can't take a seasoned champ four rounds, you're so unfit. You went off the rails, you can't win. All that seshing will have made you slow. This is make or break.

I struggle to bring myself back to the moment.

Isobel smiles at me. I smile back.

It is almost over. I'm so glad she's here for me.

Black cab to the Lion's Maiden. Terry's waiting outside the pub, talking to two security blokes. Terry is wearing a greenish-grey suit. Brown shirt. Black shoes.

The pub is a big one, a traditional pub building painted white, with a thatched roof and black, wooden trim on the edges. Large car park outside. Looks familiar. They all look the same really, don't they?

'Tommy. Isobel,' Terry says. They've never met. I've never talked about her.

'Terry,' I say. We head inside.

'Look, crumpet, how about you go kill some time while we weigh in and talk tactics and that,' Terry says.

'Don't talk to her like that. She'll come with us if she likes,' I say.

'I'd like to,' she says. She's wearing a black dress that falls short of her knees. Her make-up is well done, and her hair is crimped nicely. She looks lovely. Don't think about that. Focus.

The ring is small, probably fourteen or sixteen feet. I don't like the look of it at all. Good boxing is done in a proper-sized ring. There are rows of chairs on all four sides of the ring, spotlights above. Screens on all the walls. A big bar to our left. Not many people here yet. Just one or two people standing by the bar, and a few in black polo shirts walking around, setting up.

'Mr Harsham,' one of them says.

'Binks,' Terry says, walking past.

We enter a side-room. It's colder, smells of damp and concrete. A couple of lads are in their boxer shorts, ready to weigh in. A couple of men in suits stand around some weighing scales. Some coaches in tracksuits stand behind them.

A few random guys are chatting in the corner, wearing jeans and shirts, probably friends of the boxers.

'That's your opponent,' Terry mutters in my ear. He's looking at a guy wearing a blue tracksuit. He's tall and athletic, has a bony face, must have a low body-fat percentage. Looks long, strong and fast. The hardest type of boxer to beat.

I shake his hand. It's firm, warm. I say, 'Good luck later, I hope we have a good bout.' I feel people looking at me, they're sniggering. I'm supposed to lose either way. This is a mismatch to them.

'Nice one that you call it a bout, brother, it reminds me of the old days. All the best, yeah?' he says.

He tightens his grip, I tighten mine. Our hands say, 'We mean business.' His eyes are sharply shaped, narrow, intense brown.

We weigh in at seventy kilos each.

'Do you want to go for a walk?' I say to Isobel.

'Sure,' she says.

'What time's boxing?' I ask Terry.

'Starts at seven, you're on ninth. That's two after the interval.'

'I'll be there,' I say.

'Oi, just hold on a minute, son, what do you think this is? You've got to warm up properly, we've got to go over tactics.'

'We've already talked, I know what I'm supposed to do. I've got my warm-up covered, I'll see you in the ring.' I take Isobel's hand and lead her out of that shithole.

The street smells of car fumes and grime. The air is thick, greasy. The pavements are scattered with stamped-in chewing gum. I don't like this part of London, but it seems familiar. Maybe I was here once when I was a kid. We moved around a lot when I was younger. I don't remember much of it.

'You okay?' Isobel says.

'Yeah, struggling to focus,' I say. 'I'm nervous as fuck.'

'You said it's good to be nervous sometimes, didn't you?'

'I have to channel the energy to fire myself up, I can't seem to do it right now.'

'Is there anything I can do to help?'

'How about this?' I kiss her on the cheek. So soft.

'I love you,' she says.

'I love you too,' I say.

The love is calming. For once, I'm not scared of the commitment.

We stroll for a long while, I hope to come across a park or

something, a bench with a reasonable surrounding. There's nothing, just kebab shops, businesses with the shutters down, aimless graffiti on the matt metal.

Cars droning by, but for once the sound is rhythmic, relaxing. I wish I was in a car right now, on the back seat, Isobel driving, going somewhere far. I always sleep best in the back of a car. They say it's because it reminds us of the womb. Dark, muffled noises, protected, encapsulated. Right now, I feel open, exposed. But I feel alive. I can feel my breath, my heart and the fire in my veins. The fire feels like it's been growing since I was born. It's my fire, Tommy's fire, and Tommy's burning like a motherfucker tonight. After tonight, it's all over.

All the shit I've been through, it was for a purpose. Everything happens for a reason, and I certainly had my reasons. Tears threaten me again, but I hold them in. Now is not for crying. Now is for the fire.

'We'd better head back now,' I say. It's almost 7.00 pm.

Moose and Sammy are waiting for us outside the Lion's Maiden. Moose is my corner man today. Sammy is my biggest fan. He's gleaming.

I'm going to do this last thing, give Terry the rest of his money, and then we're done.

Sammy says, 'Mate, I'm buzzing. This is going to be mental.'

'Thanks for coming,' I say.

Sammy pats me on the shoulder. It's heartfelt.

After tonight, it's all over. Just four rounds.

'Yes, Tommy. You ready? Hello, Isobel,' Moose says. Moose's cheeky grin is contagious, as if he knows he's up to no good, and loving it.

'I'm ready,' I say. And I mean it. I'm ready.

'Hello, Moose,' Isobel says.

'Come on then, champ, let's do this,' Moose says.

One of the bouncers stands in front of him, blocking the door. 'I'll need to see your ticket,' he says.

'Not today you fucking won't.' Moose puts his hands on my shoulders. 'Today, I'm cornering the champ, the boss, the one and only Tommy the Tank. Or is it Leon the Lion?'

We chuckle.

'The Tank,' the bouncers say simultaneously, eyeing me up.

'Yeah, the Tank, but it could be Tommy the Fucking Tank Engine for all you care. He's the champ and that's all that matters, now get out of my fucking way, we've got business to do,' Moose says.

The bouncer looks unimpressed.

'I'm Terry Harsham's boxer,' I say. 'I came with him and weighed in earlier. I'll go and get him if you want.'

'No need to bother Mr Harsham,' the other says. They step aside, wave us in.

'I'm fucking buzzing,' Moose says, looking around the place. It's much busier now, many of the seats are taken, punters are chatting, drinking, laughing. The first match is probably starting soon. The MC climbs into the ring. The spotlights shine into the middle.

'We're going to have to go and get in the zone now,' I say.

'I'll see you afterwards,' Isobel says. We hug.

I'm trembling inside.

'Good luck,' Sammy says.

The changing room is just a concrete cell, no windows. The artificial light is meagre. It's just me and Moose. I wonder where Terry is.

'Let's do this, Tommy, just four rounds, nice and relaxed, focus, focus, focus. Just four rounds, that's all, then it's all yours, this is all over. Four sharp rounds. You can do it easy, you know that, you're the fucking champ.'

'I know,' I say. Just four rounds. Let's do this.

My warm-up starts with relaxation and loosening my muscles. I do this by gently rocking from foot to foot on the balls of my feet. I focus on the sensations in my body to stay in the moment. As I do this, I rotate and swing and shake my arms to loosen them.

The crowd roars from the main room. Focus, Tommy. You are not concerned with the crowd.

Moose rubs my shoulders a bit. There's no need for us to talk, we are feeling each other's sentiment. Moose is confident and relaxed. His fingers are firm on the knots in my shoulders.

As Moose releases my shoulders, I start shadow-boxing. My intention is to find a rhythm, to let my body do the talking, not my mind. The mind is too slow for boxing, there is no time to think things through. I must rely on muscle memory and intuition developed through all my boxing experience. I am confident it is enough.

After shadow-boxing it is pad work. I have a light sweat on now. My muscles feel relaxed and ready to go. Moose says, 'Just tap the jab at ten per cent.'

The tap makes firm yet light contact with his pad. You know when you've hit a pad right, there's always a distinct rhythm in the movement of the fist and the sound of the pad.

'Now forty per cent, one-two.'

My left hits well, right hits rhythmically. I feel good.

'Three shots, sixty per cent.'

One, two, three. All rhythmic, accurate, well timed. This is it.

★★★

I'm waiting for my entrance tune to come on, standing by the door, focussed. The bass synths kick in, my heart fires, 'Gammelan', fucking buzzing, flaming, ready to go. I think of Isobel and Mum, take my attention back to my breath. Focus. The sensations on my nostril. Be impeccable. Moose is rubbing my shoulders. The crowd is large, overexcited.

'Let's go, champ, just four rounds,' he says.

I feel good, strong, confident. I'm going to take this guy four rounds. I'm going to pay Terry back. Everything is going to be okay.

We walk to the ring. There are spotlights and strobes and smoke in my path. I can see the glamour on the screens scattered about the room. Focus, Tommy.

Terry is sitting ringside. He has an empty chair next to him each side. Miserable prick. No, scrap those thoughts, no more thoughts about Terry now. Just feel the boxing. Focus. Breath. In-breath, out-breath. I climb to the side of the ring. Slide through the ropes.

Isobel is standing at the barrier that separates the crowd from my corner. She's with Sammy. I smile and wave. They wave back. Sammy's face is just as expected. He's flying, thriving, loving it, a kid at Christmas. Focus.

I am leaning back on the soft padding in my corner. It is slightly moist, and it is warm, from where the previous boxers have leant on it. Moose puts my gloves on. The second corner guy arrives, the bucket man, one of Terry's lot. Moose hands him my water bottle. It's got honey and lemon in it. Moose slips my gum shield over my top teeth. It fits snug, secure. 'Gammelan' stops. Focus.

A hip-hop track comes on. My opponent makes his ring walk. I focus on Moose, shutting out the crowd.

Moose says, 'Ex-ABA champ, he's going to be able to box, just like you can, Tommy. He's going to be strong too, maybe stronger than you, alright? Be smart and relaxed, and when you get the chance, dig like a motherfucker.'

The crowd goes wild as my opponent enters the ring. He's popular here.

'He's going to have everything you've got and more, except one thing, Tommy. You know what that one thing is: you're a fucking genius. Use it. And you're disciplined and focussed, just like him. Take your time, work him out, don't make any mistakes, anticipate him. No fucking mistakes, alright?'

I like having Moose in my corner.

Focus. In-breath, out-breath. Clear head. Relaxed mind and body. Time to go. Ref comes and checks my gloves for any foul play. Glad he's doing his job. He calls us both to the middle. Tells us to touch gloves. There's something humble about my opponent, I like that about him. He nods at me, we touch gloves firmly, go back to our corners.

The bell goes, the ref moves from the centre. Four rounds. Focus. We edge to the centre of the ring, taking our time, finding our range. He has a good stance, hands high, knees slightly bent, balanced, poised. His muscles are defined and bulging all over his body, like something out of a magazine.

I am so out of shape. No. Focus. In-breath, he throws a jab, he's out of range, I barely need to move, he backs off with his hands high. In-breath, out-breath. He's still focussed, I can see it in his eyes. When he jabs like that again I could sidestep forward and overhand a right while he moves in. But if he's doing that to lure me, he might nail me. Wait and see how he boxes. This is chess.

I begin edging my way in. I hear nothing but my breath, see nothing but his face and body. Just his face, his body. His face, his body. As I get within a few inches of his range, I throw a few feints. He doesn't flinch. He knows exactly his range now, knows I'm just an inch too far from him to land a punch. That's great awareness. I close that inch down with fast feet, jab him in the body, move off to the side, hands up. He counters instantly, hits my gloves with thunderous hooks, my guard is high.

We reset, taking a small step back. That's good boxing, instant counters, fast feet, angles. This is going to be a tough match. Stop thinking. Just box.

He jabs; his big, gloved left hand closes in on my face, covers my line of sight, misses. He steps back, I counter with a jab, he slips it, lands an overhand right, clean on my cheek. A small flash of light in my head. Such power and athleticism. Jesus.

Relax, work him out.

I throw a double jab, neither hit. I feint a jab and throw a big right, making sure to be as fast as lightning. It lands clean, he tucks up, returns with two body hooks and a left hook over the top, all three land, wobbling me. I feel sick from the impact.

'Come on, Tommy, sharpen up,' Moose shouts. 'Take your time, box.'

I take some deep breaths, roll my shoulders and shake my feet out to relax them. I need to throw more punches, use my fast hands, have some confidence in myself. Don't let this slip. I can't let him hit me like that, I'll go down.

Moving closer to each other, finding our range. He jabs, I block and counter, then my hands go off like a machine gun, six shots of thunder to his head and body. Crowd cheers. I step out of range. He looks a little flustered. Focus, more of that. That's all you have to do, defend, counter, take it to the fourth. Now we're talking!

The bell goes, I go back to my corner. I'm out of breath and I feel weak. I'm not going to let that stop me from getting the job done.

'Right, good round, not sure whose that was. It doesn't matter anyway, you're boxing well. Get tighter now,' Moose says. He takes out my gum shield and passes it to the bucket man. 'And relax even more, let those shots go, over and over.'

Many things in boxing have contradictive yet complimentary meaning. You should have a tight guard, but you have to have loose muscles. You have to be light and fast, but your shots have to feel heavy to your opponent.

'How you feeling?' he says.

'Good enough to get the job done,' I say. I take deep, aggressive breaths to get my energy back. Usually after the first round I feel doubt, worry that I can't pull it off. Right now, I feel only confidence. It is almost all over. Just three rounds to go.

Moose sprays a mist of cold water over my face. Sharp, icy kick, shocks me, brings me into the moment. Ahhh. I feel alive. Three bangs on the table signify ten seconds before round two. Moose puts my gum shield back in. My gum shield is now refreshing and moist, with cold water all over it.

'Get in there and get the job done,' Moose says, before he climbs out of the ring.

The bell goes. My opponent comes rushing out. Likely to throw some big punches. Stops just before my striking range. Unexpected. Goes to work with jabs and one-twos, in and out. I stay tight, taking them on my gloves. The work rate stops me settling, stops me working out what I need to do next. Head body head, he lands three hard blows. I'm stunned. Shit. Weak at the knees. Adrenaline keeps me going. It won't forever.

Get his respect. I step out, get my balance, come in with a flurry. He takes them on his gloves and arms, has a good guard, good head movement.

I move off at an angle, come back in, land a straight right, a left hook, a right uppercut. Out. In. Straight three, the right-hand and the final jab land.

I can't keep this up all four rounds, I'm not fit enough. I'm so breathless, becoming sloppier. Boxing at this level needs training, not the remnants of going off the rails, you can't just jump into it.

Don't doubt yourself like that. You know you have the resources to make it happen, no matter what state you're in.

I move well out of range so I can take my time. He doesn't follow, he takes his time too. Back to tactics, lure that jab of his. I work my way into his range, within inches. Step into his range, wait for the jab, it comes, I move out and launch a one-two, but his jab was a feint, two body hooks under my one-two, I'm winded. Fuck. I retreat, desperate for air, ready to blast that right-hand at him if he rushes towards me, my whole chest is tense, shocked, gasping, unable to expand.

The bell goes.

'What you thinking?' Moose says.

'I'm fucking knackered.'

Moose slaps me hard in the face. 'Stop thinking like that, not long to go now, and you can do this crap in your sleep, clear those excuses out of your head and go for it, alright? Really fucking go for it, like your Mum's life depends on it. Because it fucking does, alright?'

Now I'm fired. 'Alright,' I say. 'You're right. No more excuses. This is mine.' It's funny how the doubt creeps back no matter how much you fight it.

I take the centre of the ring, fast. Feint my jab, he moves back, I stay in the centre. He comes closer. I let him edge in, thinking he's safe, then I pounce with a flurry, landing a decent punch or two. It's better that way. Flurries, no thinking, just boxing, fast hands. Inject the venom.

I throw another flurry, this time more aware and in control

of the punches. When you throw flurries, it is best to change the speed and power of each punch, in your own rhythm, to break his rhythm. You use the lighter punches to open his guard and the heavier ones to cause damage.

He throws a few jabs to keep me at bay. I slip one of his jabs and flurry again, this time a hard jab to the body, and then a light right uppercut, a hard left hook. It rocks him. I move out of range. That's how it's got to be. Controlled, impeccable.

He smiles at me, nods. I nod back. This is boxing. A respectful contest between two people.

The bell goes. This is it then. The job is practically done.

'Yes, Tommy, that was your round,' Moose says. 'You know what you gotta do now. It's all over.' His smile is endearing.

It's all over.

'Yeah,' I say. 'Almost there.' I'm puffing heavily, that was a tough round. I take my breathing back to controlled, deep breaths.

'Make it convincing, alright? Go on, get out there and get the job done,' Moose says. 'Round four, the big one, it's all over.'

I come out smiling. It's all over. I just need to make it convincing. I wonder if he's been told I'm going down in this one. Probably not, but you never know. I shouldn't worry about it, just box, get the job done. He's taking his time now. I wonder how to do this, I wonder how to finish it.

I take my range, throw a light one-two to his head, move an inch out of range, he comes forward, I throw another sharp, light one-two, get out of range. None of the shots hit but he knows I mean business, knows if he makes a mistake he will pay.

I let him find his range, let him feint the jab. I feint my

own response. He lets go, falls for it, throws a one-two thinking I'll be where I was last time. He's exposed. I throw a hard right, lands clean, tap his hands open with a left uppercut, he brings them down, I drill a straight right into his chin, he wobbles, I throw a thunderous left hook, which rocks him again, the crowd's impossible to ignore, roaring, I step back, step right. He swings for me, dazed. I throw two devastating uppercuts. He's stumbling. I get my range, six hard straight shots like a fucking machine gun. He falls to the canvas.

I go to a neutral corner, look at Terry. He's so dissatisfied, it's priceless. He knows what's going on.

My opponent is on his feet, ready to go. The ref moves out of our way. I come in, light jab opens him up, hard jab lands, light right uppercut, left hook lands hard. He throws a few punches but I'm already out of the way, he's not in a good state. This is it. It's all over. Find my range again, feint the jab, land a solid right hand. Bam.

The fire is unstoppable now. I lose myself. Punches. Good, calculated, practised, precise punches. Impeccable punches. Blow after blow until he hits the floor. Out. Cold.

The ref calls the match off. I've won. I hear no sound, except the voice in my head. I've won. I've fucking won.

I walk back to my corner. Isobel is there already, I hug her through the ropes, and as her hands touch my back I realise how sweaty I am. I say in her ear, 'We bet all we had for me to win in the fourth.'

She holds me tight, she's trying to find the right words but she can't. I don't blame her. What do you say to that? I kiss her on the cheek, let her go so Moose can take my gloves off. Moose's eyes are wide and wild, his grin booming.

Sammy climbs up to the canvas and hugs me. 'That was bloody brilliant, you're such a baller.'

'I thought you'd enjoy it,' I say.

Terry is standing next to the ring. He wants a word. I ignore him, go and shake my dazed opponent's hand, and the hands of his coaches.

Return to Terry. I lean over the ropes, towering over him. He's at floor level. Looking down on him, I say, 'Seventy-five grand, on your desk tomorrow morning. Nobody gets hurt.'

'I am a man of my word,' he says.

Chapter 11

I'm in Terry's office. The curtains are open, it's light, looks neater than last time. I have a maroon rucksack with seventy-five grand in it. The odds on me winning by knockout in the fourth round averaged at fifteen-to-one. I am rich. Damn fucking rich. The types of bookies Moose placed the bets with are the sort who don't regulate with official bodies, they don't pay taxes, and they pay out in cash. Boom.

Terry says, 'I don't like being lied to, Tommy, but a deal is a deal, and you've come through. I always said you were one of a kind, and I was right. You've blown me away. You're probably wondering why I'm so calm about it all. Well, truth is, Tommy—' he says.

'No,' I interrupt him. 'I'm wondering how much shit you're going to talk before I can leave this place. I've got the good life waiting for me out there. You've got nothing but the bitter taste of defeat, and I bet you've forgotten how to handle it.'

Terry looks dissatisfied. 'Oh, don't be like that, Tommy, we both know you need me. You've got yourself a little cash now, so what? It's not enough to last a lifetime, you know that. Don't go throwing your toys out the pram. Look, how's your Mum anyway?'

'She's none of your business.'

'We'll get back to that later, Tommy. I threw so many bones to those little pups around me, your performance the other day upset a lot of people. The instructions were fucking simple, go down in the fourth. Now I've got a bunch of people asking questions about my reliability, and there's little I can do about it. You know what they want to do, Tommy? They want to kill you, simple as that. Nobody likes a man who can't follow instructions for the greater good.'

'Seventy-five grand, on your desk, three weeks. Nobody gets hurt. I can follow instructions just fine. Nobody gets hurt.'

'I'm not the one who wants to hurt you now, Tommy. You'll never get anywhere making enemies like that. All those people who lost money on the boxing, those guys you and Arlo did over in Splott, your little buddy Flash, the spice dealers, those guys you beat up on Park Place … Jesus, Tommy, you've got more enemies than friends.'

'No, I'm out of this game. I did what I had to and I won. And now I'm going back to my real friends.'

'Look, Tommy, let me tell you a story. You'd better listen up, this is a valuable lesson about the world.

'A couple of months ago I got wind of a drug dealer doing things right for once, one that took his time, made precautions, didn't flash the cash, a drug dealer who was impeccable, a good businessman. A man like me.

'I invited this businessman to my place, welcomed him with open arms, even gave him a tidy little sum of money to spend in my club to show my appreciation of him. I gave this man – you, Tommy, in case you hadn't clocked – the opportunity to work with me, earning beyond your wildest dreams, easy work, work you were doing already. And out of loyalty to your clan, you turned me down. I couldn't argue with that, it was the icing on the cake, the final persuading factor. Reliability, integrity, honour, I simply had to have you – Mr Impeccable.

'You know I'm a man who gets what I want. You see, there are only two types of people in this world. There are those who want and dream, and there are those who dream and do. Me and you, Tommy, we dream and do. You've proved that today, you're as doer as they come. What would a doer do in my situation? He'd make it happen.'

I don't like where this is going. I want to say, Fuck you. Take your money, I'm gone. But I can't. I need to hear what he has to say.

'How did I make it happen? There's not a lot your pal Flash wouldn't do for a box of cocaine fresh off the boat, not a lot at all, and especially when you've gone and got all saucy with his missus. Irresistible girl, might I add, nobody blamed you, nobody could have said no.

'So, I asked our little accomplice Flash to arrange a fake deal, a big one with a London boss. Arlo and Din would need to pool their stash to pull it off last minute. Like moths to a flame, they arranged the deal at Arlo's, just as expected. And when the Londoners didn't turn up? They left the stuff there and fell asleep, ready for the dawn raid.'

I'm speechless. Trying to get a word out. Nothing. So much anxiety. So much fire. I want to knock him out.

'Uh,' Terry says, holds his index finger to his lips. 'Don't act like I didn't do you a favour, Tommy. Arlo was an accident waiting to happen. It was better for us to control it than let the police catch wind without our knowing. I made sure you weren't anywhere near Arlo's before the call was made. And I made sure he'd be held without bail, a suspected violent drug trafficker. I did this all for you.'

Terry looks less dissatisfied than usual. 'This was the ultimate test, and you passed on every pointer, you were brilliant, you exceeded expectations. Even when your mum was threatened, you didn't crumble. You pulled it off like a true champ. You know, you could have set me up, setting me up would have been easy with the police's help, I mean, if it wasn't me who was trying to coerce you into setting me up in the first place. And yet you maintained your integrity throughout, a truly brilliant criminal. Mr Impeccable.'

I want to kill him. 'You're a fucking monster. And you know what? I'm not going to give you the satisfaction. I'm not going to sit here and talk to you like you're a man on my level. I'll tell you how it is, Terry. One day, I'm going to be back.' I slide the rucksack full of money across the desk to him, smacking some papers and a few pens out of the way. 'I'm going to come back, and I'm going to slay you, like a beast. I've already cut off your legs, I beat the beast at his own game, and, yes, I did it with integrity. You'll never take that from me. And when I'm back, I'm going to take your fucking head.'

Chapter 12

Isobel and I are walking around the lake. It's a lovely day. The lake is vast and brilliant, as always. Today, it boasts an exceptionally beautiful plethora of colours and textures. It's absorbing and reflecting lots of the blues and greys in the sky, the whips of the clouds, the smooth glassiness where there are no clouds, and all the sunlight; and it's taking the greens and browns from the trees rustling in the breeze at the water's edge, and they're all rough and vivid; the middle of the lake is silvery in patches and brownish in others. There are ducks on the lake and the path beside it. It's nice and quiet, just the whispering of the leaves, and a few distant sounds of cars. The odd bit of indistinct, distant chatter.

It's all over, Terry is paid, nobody gets hurt. I fucking did it, I fucking won. My friends are safe and well, and I am rich and I can't stop smiling and filling up with tears of joy. Joy for this moment walking around the lake with Isobel and her lovely soft hand in mine and that smile of hers. I love her so much. But in the tears, there's also sadness, because it was traumatic. And I still haven't heard from Arlo. I would rather not think about that. I am exhausted. My body aches from the boxing. I think I'm still in shock.

'Tommy,' Isobel says.

'Yes?' I say.

'Well done.'

We smile. The moment is surreal.

At the far end of the lake there are several small islands completely overgrown with trees and shrubbery. I would like to get onto one of those islands one day. You can't take boats there, a barrier blocks the way. You could wade or swim.

Isobel's hand is cold, yet pleasant.

'Is it going to be strange now, living a normal life?' Isobel says.

'It is, but I won't miss the life or the people I'm leaving behind, or the person I almost became. I'm really looking forward to redoing this year, I want to get a good grade, and I want to do good things for people.'

'I'm sure you will,' she says.

'I am the luckiest man alive,' I say. 'I can't wait to take you and Mum on holiday.'

'That'll be lovely,' she says, squeezing my hand tighter. Still gentle and lovely.

There's a family on a bench in front of us. Two little children, and their parents. The children are wrapped in coats, hoods, scarfs. Both have tablets in their hands, engrossed in whatever they're watching on the screens. Standing tall at the foot of the bench, there are plastic Starbucks cups with what looks like milkshakes in them. Lots of strawberry syrup in one, chocolate in the other.

The sound of someone running fast in the distance behind us. Deep breaths, fast footsteps, thud, thud, thud.

A tree with long, dangling, deep-green leaves dips its fingers in the water. Around it, the water's surface is silver, and brown, and all this is textured with the green reflections of the leaves. It looks magnificent.

I look back, the runner is near. I sidestep one way, Isobel

parts the other way, he's got a clear path between us. I'm flicking my eyes between the weird family with the iPads, and the wonderful tree. Who the fuck brings an iPad to a place like this?

Isobel shrieks.

I'm hit in the back, a hard, clean punch, two more punches. My heartbeat fires up. Ugh, my body isn't up for being punched today, not in the back. I turn, a bit confused, the runner is sprinting away fast. He's got a flick knife in his hand. My breath disappears, I start to throb, feel warmth in my back and something's not right. I feel sick and strange.

Isobel grabs me and I pull her to the floor on my way down. Why am I on the floor? I've only been punched in the back. I attempt to get up, to say something, but my throat won't move like it should and I'm shaking. I'm in shock. Everything's a bit numb and woozy. Fuck. I can't breathe properly.

There's blood on Isobel's hands, on the ground and on our clothes. Rich, dark red blood. Glossy, thick blood.

Isobel is crying, 'I love you, you'll be okay, you'll be okay.'

My vision blurs. Yeah, I'll be okay. But I don't feel okay. Struggling to breathe. Need some damn air. I use all my might to pull myself closer to Isobel. I collapse, with a lovely blurry view of the lake and the sky. It's all pulsing and full of life, throbbing with the rhythm of my heart, almost glistening.

Bloody hell. I've fucked it. Should've seen it coming. I bet when Barbs hears about this she'll say, It's a shame, but it was bound to happen. If he wanted money, he should have got a normal job, just like the rest of us. The thought makes me smile.

'I'll be okay,' I say. There's no sound but Isobel nods and smiles so maybe my lips moved, I don't know, I'm numb and woozy. I say, 'Tell Mum I've had a spot of bother, but I'll be alright.'

'You'll be okay, Tommy, please. You'll be okay. Open your eyes. Look at me. Look at me, please … And when you're better, your mum will come and visit us in Cardiff.'

If you enjoyed Impeccable, please support me by telling people about it; joining my mailing list and following me on social media. The more support I get, the more I can write for you.

jameelsandham.com

@jameelsandham

Jameel Sandham

Jameel was born in 1991 in South Africa, and raised in England. Prior to writing fiction, he spent several years copywriting for businesses and creative marketing agencies. In 2015, Jameel graduated from Cardiff University with a bachelor's degree in English literature and philosophy. He was awarded Cardiff University's Master's Excellence Scholarship in 2016 to study MA Creative Writing, from which he graduated in 2017. After his studies, Jameel became lead boxing coach at Cardiff University, and also founded ethical fashion brand, Rhetorik. Jameel is passionate about using his writing not only to thoroughly entertain, but to provoke thought on everyday sociopolitical issues, especially those that concern underrepresented and underprivileged peoples.

Printed in Poland
by Amazon Fulfillment
Poland Sp. z o.o., Wrocław

49871044R00167